Dangerous Davies
The Last Detective

Leslie Thomas was born in South Wales in 1931 and, when his parents died, he and his younger brother were brought up in an orphanage. His first book, *This Time Next Week*, is the autobiography of a happy orphan. At sixteen he became a reporter on a weekly newspaper in Essex and then did his National Service in Malaya during the Communist bandit war. *The Virgin Soldiers* tells of these days ; it was an immediate bestseller and has been made into a film with Lynn Redgrave and Hywel Bennett.

Returning to civilian life, Leslie Thomas joined the staff of the *Evening News*, becoming a top feature writer and travelling a great deal. His second novel, *Orange Wednesday*, was published in 1967. For nine months during 1967 he travelled around ten islands off the coast of Britain, the result of which was a lyrical travelogue, *Some Lovely Islands*, from which the BBC did a television series. He has continued to travel a great deal and has also written several television plays. He is a director of a London publishing house. His hobbies include golf, antiques and Queen's Park Rangers Football Club.

His other books include *Come to the War, His Lordship, Onward Virgin Soldiers, Arthur McCann and All his Women, The Man with the Power, Tropic of Ruislip* and *Stand Up Virgin Soldiers*, all of which are also published in Pan.

**Also by
Leslie Thomas in Pan Books**

Fiction
The Virgin Soldiers
Orange Wednesday
The Love Beach
Come to the War
His Lordship
Onward Virgin Soldiers
Arthur McCann and All His Women
The Man with the Power
Tropic of Ruislip
Stand Up Virgin Soldiers

Non-fiction
This Time Next Week
Some Lovely Islands

Leslie Thomas

Dangerous Davies

The Last Detective

Pan Books London and Sydney

First published 1976 by Eyre Methuen Ltd
This edition published 1977 by Pan Books Ltd,
Cavaye Place, London SW10 9PG
2nd printing 1980
© Leslie Thomas 1976
ISBN 0 330 25173 2
Printed and bound in Great Britain by
Richard Clay (The Chaucer Press) Ltd, Bungay, Suffolk

CELIA
Well, the beginning,
that is dead and buried.

As You Like It

one

This is the story of a man who became deeply concerned with the unsolved murder of a young girl, committed twenty-five years before.

He was a drunk, lost, laughed at and frequently baffled, poor attributes for a detective. But he was patient too, and dogged. He was called Dangerous Davies (because he was said to be harmless) and was known in the London police as 'The Last Detective' since he was never dispatched on any assignment unless it was very risky or there was no one else to send.

two

Daybreak (they did not have dawns in those parts) arrived over the cemetery to a show of widespread indifference. A laburnum dripped unerringly, cats went home, and the man lying on the tombstone of Basil Henry Weggs ('He Loved All Other Men'), late of that parish, stretched with aching limbs and desolate heart. A wasted night. No one had attempted to blow up the graveyard.

It was not something he had reasonably expected to occur for it would not only have been pointless but so difficult as to verge on the impossible. Nevertheless the scratchy note delivered at the police station had to be treated with some demonstration of seriousness and, naturally, they had sent him. It had proved an uncomfortable but not particularly haunting night. Wrapped in his enormous brown overcoat and spreadeagled on the unyielding stone, Davies had wondered, in a loose sort of way, what the odds were on the morning heralding The Day of The Resurrection. He imagined the stones creaking open and everybody climbing out, rubbing their eyes. But nothing had happened and he was not surprised. It was not his fate to be present on great occasions.

With the day, and its banishment of even the remote chances of both saboteurs and spectres, he dozed briefly and awoke when the cemetery caretaker gave him a vicious push just after eight o'clock.

Davies opened gritty eyes. 'Shouldn't sleep on the slabs,' said the man. 'How can you expect anybody else to respect the fucking place if the law don't?'

Creakily Davies stood up. His overcoat was spongy with dew. The caretaker brushed the tombstone clean as though it were a settee. 'Is that your load of junk outside the gate?' he inquired.

'My car? Yes.'

'What's that in the back seat?'

'It's a dog. He lives there.'

The man appeared to accept this with reluctance. But he did not pursue it. Instead he said: 'You shouldn't park it here. Not in front of the gates.'

'I didn't think anyone would be going out,' remarked Davies. 'I'm surprised you bother to lock the gates.'

'That's to stop people getting *in*,' argued the caretaker. 'Vagabonds and the like.' He regarded Davies with suspicion. 'Are you sure you're the law?' he said suspiciously. 'In that coat?'

Davies looked down the long, wet, sagging length of his coat. His shoes poked beneath its hem as if peeping out from below a blanket. 'Very good for tomb-watching, this coat,' he said gravely. 'Very warm, down to the ankles. I got this at a police sale of unclaimed property.'

'I'm not surprised it was unclaimed,' said the caretaker. He sniffed around in the cold air. 'Anyway, are you going? I've a lot to do.'

'I expect you have,' said Davies. 'Tidying up and that.'

'That's right. You're off then?'

'Yes, I'm off. No bombs, nothing went bump in the night.'

The man could scarcely withhold his disgust. 'I should

think not,' he said. 'You must be mad. Who'd want to blow up this place?'

'Search me,' shrugged Davies. He began to shuffle down the path. 'Good morning.'

He made towards the gate. The caretaker wiped his nose with his fingers and watched the long, retreating, brown overcoat. 'And good riddance,' he said just loud enough for Davies to hear.

Davies was almost out of the gate when he paused by a massive, flat tombstone which had sunk spectacularly at one corner. 'Hoi,' he shouted out at the caretaker. 'Here's one that needs straightening!'

'Up yours too,' said the man unkindly.

At 10 o'clock, notwithstanding his uncomfortable night-duty, Davies was due to give evidence in court. (The Queen versus Joseph Beech. Attempted felony, viz a pigeon loft.) Because he disliked testifying in court, he often wished the pubs opened at breakfast time. Too frequently he found his sympathies on the side of the accused.

First he took the Lagonda and its torpid dog to the tin garage where he kept them. Kitty growled ungratefully when roused from beneath its tarpaulin for breakfast. The dog was a heavy animal with a rattling chest, a cross between a St Bernard and a Yak. Its chest vibrated nastily and it cleared its throat. While it ate he tried to pull a few bits of debris from its matted and tangled coat, but the animal rolled a threat from its throat. Davies desisted. 'Sod you,' he said in disappointment. 'You'll just have to miss Crufts.'

A few hundred yards short of the court was a café painted the appropriate hue of HP Sauce. It was called The Copper Kettle, although the original kettle had been stolen long ago. It was that sort of neighbourhood. The establishment was owned by a villainous couple, Mr and Mrs Villiers, who nevertheless made a sensible cup of tea and attracted a clientele of constant interest to the police. Davies had once good-naturedly bought a tea and a round of bread and dripping for a man in there who appeared to be in some need. He was, in truth, impoverished, mainly because he had failed in an attempted armed robbery on a post office only the day before. Davies's kindly and typical indiscretion might have gone unnoticed but for the fact that the man, when arrested and charged in court, made public thanks to his benefactor from the criminal dock.

Davies drank his tea from a large stony cup and winced as the proprietor, behind the sodden counter, took an investigative bite of the five-pence piece he proffered in payment. He did that every time and, for Davies anyway, the joke had grown cold.

Neverthelsss he was greeted with friendship at the court. As he went through the outer hall minor malefactors of all persuasions, drunks, shoplifters, threatening-words-and-behaviourists, wilful damagers and obscene exposures, bade him a familiar good day.

' 'Morning, Dangerous.'

'God bless you, Dangerous.'

'They nabbed me at last, Dangerous.'

He walked, smiling and nodding to each side like the popular manager of a happy factory. Jealously other officers frowned.

The magistrates' courtroom seemed to him, at times, like a small amateur theatre, with the public spectators, the police, the press reporters and the witnesses playing their clumsy parts, eager for every trivial, shocking exposure, always nodding knowingly as evidence accumulated, always laughing at some dry joke of a magistrate. At times even the accused would join in the laughter and then Davies was tempted to warn him it would not ingratiate him with the trio of looming justices on the bench above.

After the drunks had been processed the courtroom was redolent with the odour of morning-after. A lady magistrate held her handkerchief to her imperious nose. The warrant officer made a disgusted face but, pulling himself together, called: 'Case of Joseph Beech, sir, Number 23.' Davies sighed, pulled off his overcoat as though he were reluctantly stripping to fight and shambled, in his large old blue suit, across the courtroom to the witness box. He stood, Bible poised, ready to make the oath, the suit hanging forward like a threatening avalanche. The magistrate eyed him with a disapproval not far elevated from his examination of the prisoner Joseph Beech who, having ascended the stairs from the cells, now rose as if by some magic in the dock. He shouted 'Guilty!' before anyone had asked him.

Davies took the oath. Then recited: 'Acting on information received, your honour, I went to 23, Whitley Crescent, and there found the accused apprehended by the householder, a Mr Wallace, who said to me: "I have just caught this bastard trying to nick my pigeon loft." '

'Tell them *who* you received the information from then, Dangerous,' prompted the man from the dock eagerly.

'In good time, Mr Beech,' replied Davies, embarrassed.

'Tell them. Go on,' said the insistent accused.

Davies glanced at the magistrate for help. 'Tell us, for goodness sake. Mr Davies,' said the Chairman impatiently. Each time Davies gave evidence in his court it seemed to develop into some kind of farce.

'I'm sorry, sir,' said Davies politely. 'In fact I received the information from the accused himself. I would have included that in my evidence, of course, if he had given me time.'

'From the accused? He *told* you he was going to steal this pigeon loft?'

'Yes, sir. I told him some years ago, sir, that if he ever felt the urge to commit a felony then he could telephone me first so that I could dissuade him, sir. I saw it as a method of keeping him out of prison.'

'It did too,' confirmed Beech smugly. 'I used to ring him up and he'd come and stop me. But this time he was too slow and the other bloke copped me first.'

'I was in the bath,' Davies said apologetically.

'All right, all right,' said the magistrate impatiently. 'Let's not turn it into a performance.' He glanced at Davies and then turned to Joseph Beech. 'You stand a good chance of going to prison for three months,' he said.

Joseph Beech sighed happily. 'I'd like a bit of stir,' he

nodded. 'Last time in the Scrubs I made a model of Bucking-ham Palace out of bits of wood. A working model. It was ever so good, wasn't it, Dangerous?'

At the police station he went into the airless CID room to write his report on the night in the cemetery and to do his football pools. Hardly had he sat down when the telephone rang. He picked it up.

'Dangerous,' said the duty sergeant. 'There's a West Indian run amuck, or whatever it is they do, in Kilburn. He's in his lodgings and threatening to burn the dump down. The squad car's just leaving – they want you along too.'

'Who else?' sighed Davies. He rebuttoned his overcoat and went out to join the two policemen in the squad car. They took only three minutes to the address in a street of downcast lodging houses. Four policemen from another station were already grouped at the door. There was a scattering of ex-pectant watchers in the street. Davies trudged up the broken outside stairs. 'What's this?' he said approaching the police-men. 'A procession of coppers? What are you waiting for – the band?'

'Assessing the situation, Dangerous,' sniffed the sergeant.

'Waiting for me to get my head caved in again, more like it,' said Davies. 'Where is he?'

'Top room. Right at the head of the stairs. He's a tough bugger by all accounts.'

'How about arms?'

'He's got arms and fists at the end of them.' The laden voice was of the wild man's landlady, a sniffling Irishwoman with a malevolent wall-eye. 'He's twice as big as you,' she continued reassuringly. 'And black. They're stronger when they're black.'

Davies eyed her unenthusiastically. 'Why won't he come out? What's he doing up there in the first place?'

'Drunk,' she said solidly. 'Drains a bottle of whisky and a bottle of rum every day. I've told him he'll end up like an alcoholic.'

'Very likely,' agreed Davies. 'Have you got a bucket, missus?'

'I have,' she said. 'Would you be wanting a mop as well? Is it for the blood?'

'Just the bucket,' sighed Davies.

She dragged herself into the dark house and returned to the front with a bucket.

'What's his name?' Davies asked the sergeant.

'Bright,' answered the sergeant looking at his notebook. 'Pomeroy Bright.'

'Pomeroy?' said Davies wearily. 'There's never a Bill or a Ben among them, is there? Okay. Give me the pail, missus.'

The Irishwoman handed it to him. First he leaned up the stairs and shouted, 'Pomeroy, it's the police. Will you come down, please.'

This reasonable request was greeted by the most colourful cascade of Caribbean abuse. Davies felt his eyebrows go up. 'I don't think he's coming down,' he confided to the sergeant.

'Pomeroy,' he called again. 'You can't win, son. Come on down and let's sort it out down here. Why don't you be reasonable?'

'Because I ain't fuckin' reasonable, man,' came the response. 'I'se waiting for you to come and get me. Come right up, man. Come right up.'

'Shit,' said Davies quietly. He turned to the sergeant. 'I'm going up,' he said. 'Will you make sure your storm-troopers are just behind me and not a tenpenny bus-ride away?'

'We'll be there to catch you,' said the sergeant unpromisingly. 'What's the bucket for?'

'What d'you think it's for? I'm not going milking. It's to take the brunt of whatever this nut's going to sling. It's what they call bitter experience. You're sure he's not got a gun?'

'I'm not sure, but I don't think so,' said the sergeant comfortlessly.

Davies groaned, held the bucket in front of his face like a visor and said, 'Right, come on then.'

He charged up the stairs like a buffalo, yelling into the echoing bucket, his overcoat flapping about his ankles. The Irishwoman fell back and crossed herself hurriedly, the police squad, taken aback by the abrupt frenzy, hesitated and then went gingerly up the stairs after Davies.

He threw himself against the door which to his astonishment gave easily. It had not been locked. Pomeroy Bright was waiting for him two paces into the room. He was a huge man and he held a full-length framed wall-mirror like a bat. He was entirely amazed at Davies's entry behind the bucket and stood immobile for a moment.

Davies stopped inside the door and, not being attacked, lowered the bucket. It was then that Pomeroy swung the long mirror. He batted it horizontally at Davies's head. Davies, his protecting armour lowered, had the unique vision of his own consternation reflected in the glass the moment before the mirror hit him. He fell to the dusty floor and was trampled under the boots of his fellow officers rushing in to overpower the West Indian.

When it was over and they had stopped his forehead bleeding he was helped out by two immensely cheerful ambulancemen to desultory applause from the grown and appreciative audience in the street.

Davies let them take him to hospital in the ambulance. He was conscious of his right eye swelling.

'Never mind,' sympathized the ambulanceman as they travelled. 'The mirror didn't break so there's no need to worry about the bad luck.'

It had been a difficult summer for Davies. Not only had the London months been untypically hot and arid but, by the autumn (or The Fall as he, a natural pessimist, preferred to call it) his personal and professional life had deteriorated even further than he, one of the world's born stumblers, could have reasonably expected.

His comfortable and long-standing affair with a Tory widow in Cricklewood had been terminated upon his mistakenly climbing into her teenage daughter's bed, while drunk, and finding himself surprisingly welcome, but later discovered by the Tory widow herself.

Life in 'Bali Hi', Furtman Gardens, London NW, a shadow-ridden boarding house overseen by a Mrs Fulljames, was far from serene. His wife Doris also lived there, but separate from him, occupying her own quarters and glaring at him over the communal table. Other lodgers included a Mr Harold Smeeton (The Complete Home Entertainer), who sometimes sat at dinner dressed as a clown or a maharajah; Mod Lewis, an unemployed Welsh philosopher; Minnie Banks, an outstandingly thin infants' school teacher, and a passing parade of occasional lodgers of all manner of creeds and greeds.

Professionally, it was no use denying it, his activities had been less than glamorous. The arson of the confessional box at St Fridewide's Catholic Church, the theft of a pigeon loft, and even less glorious cases descending almost to instances of knocking-on-doors-and-running-away, was scarcely big crime. It might be asked, indeed he frequently wondered himself, for he was an honest man, why he was retained in the Criminal Investigation Department of the Metropolitan Police, except for the necessity for having someone available in his division to lead the police charge on hazardous occasions. Davies had been thrown down more flights of stairs than any man in London.

He was also utilized for routine checking tasks involving endless plodding of the streets and the asking of repetitious and usually fruitless questions. Through these urban journeys he had become known to a great many people and he himself knew some of them. His nature was such that suspicion only dawned on him by degrees, his view of the stony world he walked was brightened by a decent innocence. He was kind even when drunk.

He was, however, drinking too much, even by his standards, and he had twice been the victim of ferocious attacks by his own dog, Kitty.

Davies, a long man, thirty-three years old, inhabited his tall brown overcoat for the entire London winter and well into the spring. By the first frosts he was resident again.

He was to be seen at the wheel of his 1937 Lagonda Tourer, forever open and exposed to the weather, the hood having been jammed like a fixed backward grin since 1940. It was a car which prompted envy in many enthusiasts, almost as much as it evoked their disgust that such a rare prize should be kept in so disgraceful a condition. It was rusty and ragged. Its fine great brass lamps wobbled like the heads of twin ventriloquists' dummies. Its metal was tarnished to brown, its elegant seats torn and defiled with rubbish. In the back lived the huge and unkempt dog, as foul and matted as the rest of the interior.

His area of operation, if it could be termed that – his 'manor' in police parlance – spread out in a ragged hand from London to the north-west. Fortunately his efforts there were reinforced by many other policemen.

It was a choked place, a great suburb of grit and industrial debasement. Streets spilled into factories and factories leaned over railway yards. A power station, its cooling towers suggesting a touch of Ali Baba, squatted heavily amid the mess like a fat man unable to walk a step further. In winter the air was wet and in summer the sun's brightest and best was rarely more than bronze. Spring might bring an inexperienced cuckoo in from the country but he soon fled for there was nowhere for him. Trees and flowers were born to fight and lose.

There were factories for the making or assembling of soup, dynamos, home electric organs, rat poison, bicycles and boot polish, conglomerated in all their various grimes. Smoke hung about and the dust had no time to settle on Sunday before it was stirred again on early Monday. In the old days the district had been quite famous for its watercress.

Lying amid it all, like an old man's outstretched arm, was the Grand Union Canal, grand in no way now. Its greened unmoving water divided the whole region, its modest but still ornate bridges pinned the banks together. Almost parallel with the canal there were several main, mean, shopping streets, jointing in the way a drainpipe joints at a change of direction. The people of the place were Irish, Indians, Pakistanis, West Indians, Africans and some of the original British. Few of them liked it. It was somewhere to be, to work.

It was evening by the time Davies left the Casualty Department of the hospital with his stitches, his black eye and his aching head. He reported to the police station, where his injuries hardly raised a glance, and then walked to a public house called The Babe in Arms where it was his homegoing habit to drink as much as possible with his fellow lodger and friend Mod Lewis, a Welshman named Modest after Tchaikovsky's brother. Mod was happy to be known as a philosopher. His great talent was loyalty (he had been faithful to the same Labour Exchange for twelve years) and he knew many unusual and useless things, for he had read half the books in the public library.

Mod viewed his smoked eye with resigned sympathy. 'Been leading the charge again, have we,' he sighed.

'Once more into the breach,' agreed Davies heavily. He examined his eye and plastered forehead in the mirror across the bar. 'The eye is nothing,' he said. 'You ought to see my body. Covered in coppers' boot-marks. I'm a sort of human drawbridge. They have me knocked down and then they all run over me.'

Although it was not dole-day Mod bought him a beer and he drank it gratefully but not without some pain.

The public bar was as tight as a ravine, only narrowly escaping being a corridor. Along the windows on to the street was frosted glass, curled with Victorian designs. At that time of the evening, with the lights still on in the fronts of the shops across the road, the homeward figures of the workers passed like a shadowgraph. A rough woman came in and put a coin in the juke box. She played the same tune all the time, 'Viva España', and when she had taken a few drinks she would sing and dance to it as well. She winked at Davies as though they shared some private love, joy or secret. The sound of the record overcame the cries of Job who dolefully sold his evening papers at the corner crying: 'Tragedy tonight! Tragedy tonight!' It was a statement never challenged and indeed frequently true.

'You know,' said Mod the philosopher, pulling his pint glass from his face with a slow strength that suggested it might have been glued there. 'Injured as you are, you're a lovely drinker. Dangerous. Lovely.'

Davies thanked him seriously.

'No, but you are,' pursued Mod. 'I've been watching you lifting that pint. It's like a bird in flight.'

Davies was accustomed to the poet's fancies. He acknowledged it with an encore of the drinking movement which Mod duly stood back to admire further. The demonstration drained the glass and Davies ordered refills.

'It's a pity to see you in such a poor way, especially since your jug-lip has finally healed,' remarked Mod, accepting the beer gratefully as though it were an unexpected pleasure. 'It looked very nasty. Just like a spout. It was painful to sit at the table and observe you attempting to drink soup.'

'It's the first time you've mentioned it,' said Davies, pulling down his lip and examining it in the mirror across the bar.

'Well, I didn't like to before, boy,' said Mod. 'And neither did our fellow lodgers. Indeed it's nothing very new to see you come injured to the dinner table. Tonight they will have a new array to intrigue them.'

'Part of the job I suppose,' shrugged Davies. 'I seem to have spent half my police life looking up from the floor into the face of somebody intent on murder.'

Mod sniffed over the rim of his beer. 'If you ask me that's why they keep you. You're no detective, I can tell that.'

'You've mentioned it before.'

'No offence, Dangerous. But even you must realize that. When did they last give you a decent, wholesome crime of your own to solve? They either have you trekking around knocking on doors or leading the charge up the stairs to some madman's door. For example, where, may I ask, did you come by the jug-lip?'

'A disturbance of the peace,' said Davies. 'A fracas. The sort of thing you're bound to get in this sort of place. Have you ever thought how many people around here are actually at war with each other? We've got two religious lots of Irish, hostile African tribes, Indians and Pakistanis, Jews and Arabs. That's how I got the lip, the Jews and the Arabs. Some fool at St Saviour's Hall got the bookings mixed up and let the place to the local branch of El Fatah and the Jewish Lads' Brigade on the same night. And I got in the middle of it.'

He pulled down the lip again and peered over to the mirror. 'It's gone back all right, though,' he said. He began to think of dinner. 'What time is it?'

'The clock just above your head says six-thirty,' observed Mod.

'Oh, yes, the clock. I forgot that was there.'

The rough woman had drunk enough to inspire a trembling of her heels and heavy calves. She began to emit small Iberian cries. The record of 'Viva España', which she had already played twice, swooped again on to the turntable at her touch of the selector button.

'Let's go before Flamenco Fanny starts splintering the floor,' suggested Davies.

'Indeed,' agreed Mod. 'My stomach, if no other part of me, draws me to Mrs Fulljames.'

People were gratefully going home from work, tramping in tired quiet lines along the dusty fronts of the small shops. It had been a warm autumn day and the industrial sky was gritty, glowing red over the cooling towers of the power stations as the sun quit. The roofs of the terraced houses hung like parched tongues, smutty privet hedges enclosed tight little gardens, dull windows sat on low windowsills. Many of the people who passed were West Indians, Indians or Irish. The lights of the Bingo Hall began to glimmer promptly at seven.

'Bali Hi', Furtman Gardens, was a larger house, ponderous Victorian with a monkey tree in the front garden. Mod used his key to open the door and they walked in on the rest of the residents already sitting with gloomy expectancy at the evening table. Doris, Davies's wife, was staring at her bread-and-butter plate in the manner of one expecting invisible writing to materialize; Minnie Banks, the thin schoolmistress, sat head down like a safety pin, while Mr Smeeton, The Complete Home Entertainer, was dressed in the leather trousers and braces of a Bavarian smack-dancer, in readiness for a later engagement. It was rarely a festive board but tonight seemed even more subdued than usual. To Davies it appeared that they had been awaiting him. He and Mod muttered general greetings and sat down into the silence. Then Mrs Fulljames came powerfully from the adjoining kitchen. She regarded Davies with controlled contempt.

'I thought you're supposed to be a detective,' she began truculently, thrusting her jaw at him. 'That's what I thought.'

'It's a general misapprehension,' said Davies, removing his face.

'Don't be rude,' Doris said to him from the opposite side of the table.

'I take it from whence it comes, Mrs Davies,' sniffed Mrs Fulljames. She revolved heavily towards Davies again. 'A *detective*,' she repeated.

'What seems to be the complaint?' asked Davies.

'*Complaint? Complaint?* Crime, more like it! And right under your nose. Detective indeed.' Her bosom soared as though steam was being pumped into her.

'I've rung the police station and they said to tell you when you got in,' the landlady continued tartly. 'I could hear the idiots laughing like girls. They said no point in sending a copper around if there's one in the house already.'

With deliberation Davies took out his notebook and licked the end of his police pencil. 'You can put that rubbish away,' rasped Mrs Fulljames. 'There's no time for writing things down. There's a suet pudding done in the kitchen.' She glanced suspiciously over her shoulder. A skein of steam was coming from the open door like a ghostly hand trying to attract her attention. She wavered between polemic and pans and decided the pans could not wait. She revolved rather than turned and pounded into the cooking regions. Davies put his notebook away. He glanced earnestly around the table. 'What seems to be the trouble?' he inquired.

Doris, as though doing a reluctant wife's duty, said: 'There's been a theft in the house, that's what. A theft.'

'Good God, I didn't think there was anything worth nicking here,' replied Davies honestly.

'The brass bedstead,' said Doris, trumping the remark. 'The antique brass bedstead in Mr Sahidar's room. It's gone. Antique.' She was someone who always needs to add an extra word.

Davies checked around the table. 'And I perceive that Mr Sahidar is also no longer with us. Am I right in deducing that he and the bedstead went together?'

'Both gone,' sniffed Doris. 'And right in the room next to yours. I wouldn't mind, but it's *right next door*. It makes me feel small, I can tell you.'

'Mrs Davies,' said Davies. 'You can hardly expect me to keep vigil through the night in case a fellow guest makes off with his bed. It's not something that you cater for. In any event I spent last night in the comfort of the cemetery.'

'All we know is it's gone,' sniffed Doris. 'Mrs Fulljames went in there this morning and all she found was a pile of bedclothes and the smell of incense. That bedstead was worth a hundred pounds. It used to be Mr Fulljames's bed.' She performed her customary pause, then added: 'When he was alive.'

'A relic, indeed,' muttered Davies.

'Antique,' put in Mrs Fulljames, arriving from the kitchen with a frightening cannonball of suet on a steaming plate. It looked so heavy that she gave the impression of pushing it rather than carrying it. 'Antique, Mr Policeman.'

Mrs Fulljames attacked the suet pudding with a murderous knife. Davies edged away, half expecting it to scream. She served everyone else first and smashed the final lump on his plate. She went to the kitchen and returned with boiled potatoes, carrots and a jug of Oxo. 'Priceless,' she muttered. 'That bed.'

No one answered. Minnie Banks looked frightened, Mod knocked the suet pudding around his plate and the leather-costumed Mr Smeeton stared upwards as if in dreams he saw the Bavarian mountains. Suddenly Mrs Fulljames dropped her face into the steam of her dinner and sobbed among the vapour. 'It belonged to Mr Fulljames!' she cried. 'The late Mr Fulljames.' Doris leaned across to pat her hand but the sentimental moment soon flew. 'How?' she barked at Davies. 'How?'

Davies fought to dispose of a hot mouthful of suet and meat. He felt it drop burning into his inside. 'I don't know,' he said bitterly. 'How do I know? Mr Sahidar was a Persian. Maybe he *flew* it out of the window!'

Mrs Fulljames regarded him fiercely, an expression helped by half a carrot protruding from her lips like the tongue of a dragon. 'I take it,' she said, taking the carrot out with her spoon and laying it among its friends on her plate, 'I take it you will carry out a serious investigation. Tonight.'

'In one hour,' he promised. 'I'll have this place swarming with police.'

three

Inspector Vernon Yardbird looked sourly across the threadbare rooftops from his office on the fourth floor of the police station. In thirty years in the force, and in that same division, he had viewed the same area, although he had during that time ascended from the Police Constables' room in the basement, next to the cells, to his own elevated office.

He considered he should have gone much further. Not upwards but sideways, in the direction of Scotland Yard. He had always considered that he had a Scotland Yard name. After all, top policemen always had Scotland Yard names. Hatstick of the Yard, Harborough of the Yard, Todhunter of the Yard. What better than Yardbird of the Yard? It had a *sound* to it.

Unfortunately others had seen his prospects differently. He had always been a painstaking policeman, even pedantic, but generally thought to be lacking in imagination. Today he was awaiting a visit from a man from the Special Branch. He did not approve of the Special Branch.

During the summer it had not been unentertaining to look from his window for there was a students' hostel across the first bank of roofs and the girls used to lie out sunbathing on the hot, gritty days. He did not approve of students, but he did not mind having them under surveillance and to this end he had brought a pair of racing binoculars to the office. But now their disporting was done. They had retreated with the sun and even a brief burst of Indian summer had not brought them out again. Now, after a few fine days, dank autumn was spread over the roofs. He did not approve of autumn.

Downstairs the desk sergeant was attempting to placate an old but vibrant widow who had come with a complaint that her neighbours were terrorizing her with almost incessant use of their lavatory chain. He saw the Special Branch man walk in and politely interrupted the catalogue of flushings to speak to Inspector Yardbird upstairs. He told the Special Branch man to go up.

Yardbird did not know him. Detective Sergeant Herbert Green. What a *name* for the Special Branch. It was packed with upstarts, anyway, and this upstart had the name *Green*. He had no time for them these days. Some of them even came from Universities. He did not approve of Universities.

Green turned out to be a pale and diffident young man, almost apologetically placing a file on Yardbird's desk as soon as he came in. 'Ramscar,' he said. 'Cecil Victor Ramscar. Aged forty-five.'

'I know him, I know him,' sniffed Yardbird impatiently. 'He was born around here, baptized, went to school, joined the scouts, and did his first bank robbery all within a couple of square miles.'

'Good,' said the Sergeant easily. 'Then you'll know who to look for.'

'He's back, is he? The bastard. I thought we'd got shot of him for ever. He slung his hook a few years ago.'

'Right. He's been in Australia and in America. Getting his fingers dirty with various things, but he's come back. He didn't come in through any normal channels or we would have spotted him quicker. But we think he's back on your manor, Inspector. He's gone to ground around here.'

'What do you want him for?'

'We don't know.'

Yardbird looked up petulantly. 'That's a bloody good start, I must say.'

Green shrugged. 'It's no start at all,' he agreed. 'But we've got nothing on him. Nothing. We might get him for illegal entry, if we could find him, but we might have trouble in sticking that on him.'

'In that case, what d'you want?'

'We just want him located. And tagged.'

'For nothing?'

'It's nothing at the moment. We think it will be something.'

A thick banging came at the door, no sharp knock with a hand, but a dull contact with the wood. Yardbird called and in came a canteen woman with two cups, thick as chamber pots, sitting on equally substantial saucers. Green saw the mildly red mark on her forehead and knew that she had banged the door with her forehead. They took the tea and the woman shuffled out.

'What's Ramscar up to then?'

'We think he may be going fashionable and doing a little bit of abduction, hi-jacking, hostaging or something like that. He's been involved in some fairly major league things in Australia and in California and he hasn't come back to London for nothing. We think he's lined up in partnership with a dissident group. For money, of course, not ideology. We think he could be the heavy man in a political kidnapping.'

Yardbird sniffed. 'You don't know very much, do you? There's a hell of a lot of ifs and buts and maybes.'

'That's all we have,' shrugged Green. It was not all they had but he was not telling Yardbird any more. 'What we're asking,' he said, 'is that Ramscar is located.'

'Why don't you do it yourself?' asked Yardbird. 'You've got enough people in your office, surely.'

'We could have a couple of men going around this district,' agreed Green. 'But it was thought better that somebody local should do it. Somebody who knows his way around.'

'It was thought better?' inquired Yardbird. 'Who thought it better?'

'The Commissioner,' smiled Green, laying down a good card.

'Oh, I see. Well in that case he's probably right.'

Green drank his tea at one attempt and replaced the heavy cup and saucer on Yardbird's desk. 'Christ,' said Green. 'They need to have thick cups to keep that stuff in.' He smiled in a confiding way at Yardbird. 'It won't matter if absolute secrecy is not possible in this,' he said. 'In fact I think that in a way the clumsier the inquiries, the better. If they can be conducted in such a way as to stir up Mr Ramscar, worry him, make him break cover or play his hand hurriedly, then that might be what we want.'

'One man will be enough?' said Yardbird.

'Have you got somebody like that, somebody who will set up the ripples? Somebody really clumsy?'

Yardbird nodded. He picked up the phone. 'Get hold of Detective Constable Davies,' he said.

The everyday working smoke had sauntered away across the industrial horizon, leaving the sky with a mildly puzzled expression. Davies walked towards the police station. It was not often he was called in to see the Inspector. He did not hurry although they had apparently been attempting to contact him since late afternoon. He had been feeding the ducks by the canal. There were not many people in the streets at that evening time, they had mostly returned from their employments and had not yet gone out to their enjoyments. Even the main road was subdued, giving Davies the feeling that he might be walking in the country. The cemetery which he skirted seemed almost busy by comparison.

They had secured the formidable gates for the night causing him to wonder once again on the reason for this moribund security. Few would want to go in after dark and certainly nobody was getting out. He paused at the big gates and peered in at the dusty greenery strangling the incisive sentiments of stonemasons. He touched his forehead in salute, said a private 'Good-night, all' and continued his course to the police station.

He toyed with the fantasy that Inspector Yardbird was calling him in to investigate something spectacular, a murder perhaps. Davies had frequently thought how he would handle such a matter. Not that they *would* ask him – not unless the remainder of the Metropolitan Police Force had been wiped out by typhoid fever. Even then they would bring someone in from, say, Devon County rather than entrust it to him. Anyway there had been no homicide in the area that day or for some preceding weeks; not, in fact, since a belligerent Pakistani had struck a quiet Irishman dead in front of the Labour Exchange using a tell-tale Eastern dagger to accomplish the felony. Davies had not been required to take any great or glamorous part in that investigation. In fact the brief inquiry he was instructed to make at the Labour Exchange he conducted with such diffidence that he was mistaken in his intention and, after an hour's wait, was offered a job in a laundry. Not for the first time he had determined to put more authority in his approach. He had even been loudly reprimanded by the Labour Exchange manager in front of its doleful customers, for failing to call it the Social Security Department. He had tried to convince himself that he was meticulous in his inquiries but even he had to admit that, for all the time he took, he left a good many buttons undone.

At the next corner to the police station he saw the early prostitute standing against the laurel bush that she always hoped and imagined would frame and enhance her dubious appeal. She was faithfully there at that hour. Her name was Beryl Suggs but he always called her Venus because, he said, she was like the evening star.

'Hello, love. Done it yet?' he inquired solicitously.

'Nothing moving yet, Dangerous.' She returned the smile, drawing back vermilion lips, the bed for a row of ragged teeth. She sniffed the dubious evening air as though it might give her a clue. 'Somebody'll be along in a minute,' she forecast. She looked at him curiously. 'You're out a bit late. I always see you in the afternoons. You're down there feeding the ducks.'

'I'm allowed out until it gets dark,' confided Davies.

Venus laughed and he walked towards the despondent laurels at the police station steps. Somebody, he saw, had written 'Clean up the Police!' with an aerosol spray right across the front of the notice board outside the main door. He ran his finger along the dust of the laurel leaves and thought that the cleaning might well start there. At the base of the steps he paused and felt for his notebook and pencil. He was not going to be caught waiting for them. On one occasion, in the grim presence of a superior officer, he had found it necessary to ask several passers-by for the loan of a pencil and any spare scrap of paper they happened to have

26

on their person. When this proved fruitless he had turned desperately first to the frosty Inspector and, when no help was forthcoming there, to the accused man who had obligingly held out both pencil and paper.

Davies steadied himself at the police station door, in the manner of a wanted man going to give himself up, then entered with what he hoped was a show of confidence. The duty sergeant was at the counter reading out a list of road accidents for the local newspaper reporter who was writing them without excitement in his notebook. 'Anthea Mary Draycott, double tee,' recited the sergeant. 'Minor injuries . . . 'evening, Dangerous . . . St Mary's Hospital. Not detained.'

There were two elderly people sitting on the hard bench of the front office, crouched and anxious as people are in police stations even if they have nothing to fear, and a further set of trapped eyes looked over the top of the frosted glass in the charge room. There was some fresh blood on the wood-block floor of the corridor but Davies deduced, correctly for once, that PC Westerman's nose had been bleeding again.

Davies followed the trail of red into the CID room where the haemorrhaging constable was hung over the washbasin. His eyes swivelled. 'Get the keys, will you, Dangerous,' he pleaded.

The cell keys were hanging on their accustomed hook and Davies, knowing what was required, took them and dropped them obligingly down Westerman's heavy back. The constable gave a small start at the touch of the cold metal, but it stopped the nosebleed.

'Thanks, Dangerous,' he said. He looked up. He appeared to have been eating strawberry jam. 'Funny how the keys always stop it.'

'Just don't ask me to get them out,' said Davies. 'Better wash your face off. It'll look as though we're torturing the staff as well.'

Westerman bent and washed his face in the basin. 'I'm glad it was you and not old Yardbird. I couldn't have asked him. Not again. He's such a bloody misery.'

'Is he upstairs?' asked Davies. 'I've been sent for.'

'That's right, I was forgetting. No, he's gone home. He

wouldn't wait past six, you know that. But I think the sarge has got some message for you.' He looked up and regarded his pink lower face in the mirror. 'Thanks for the keys, anyway, Dangerous. I'd better go in the bog and fish them out.'

Davies went to the police station counter. The local reporter had gone. The sergeant had put a solid folio on the desk before him. 'This is for you, Dangerous,' he said. 'Came up this afternoon from Criminal Records. Ramscar. Cecil Victor. Heard of him?'

'Vaguely. What's he done?'

'Two years, three years and five years,' answered the sergeant. 'Anyway this lot is for you. Yardbird says you're to read through it, peruse it, he says, and go up to see him in the morning. He was a bit grumpy that he couldn't get hold of you this afternoon, but there, that bugger's always grumpy.'

'What's it for? Any idea?' asked Davies.

'Ramscar used to be a bad boy around here years ago. Nasty lad. Then he went off somewhere to the big times. It looks like he's back and they want you to find him.'

Davies brightened. 'Well, well,' he said. 'That's a change anyway. Looking for a real villain. Better than larceny of a pigeon loft.'

The sergeant laughed, picking up a mug of tea and allowed the laugh to serve as a blowing action to cool it. 'What did he get, the bloke that nicked the pigeon loft? What's his name?'

'Beech, Joe Beech,' said Davies, 'fifty-five, plumber. Got the three months he wanted. He's going to make another working model of Buckingham Palace.' He picked up the file from the desk and frowned at its bulk. Then he walked towards the CID room.

The sergeant called after him: 'How in Christ's name can you have a *working* model of Buckingham Palace?'

'Don't ask me,' returned Davies. 'I'm just a simple copper.'

The staff of the Criminal Investigation Department who operated from the station often complained that their communal room was the worst in the entire building, not excluding the cells. It was cold, green-painted and windowless,

28

a high and dusty fanlight excepted. Shut in there a man could lose track of the tread of time. The seasons were only marked by the death-drop of flies from the ceiling in winter and the buzz of their descendants in the spring.

Spread around were some necessary but basic tables and chairs, a couple of disgruntled desks, and some scratched personal lockers. There was a consumptive gas heater and next to it a gas ring with a kettle and a collection of tea mugs. There were three wall adornments: a dartboard, a United Dairies calendar showing a milkmaid and a stupefied cow, and a framed representation of 'The Martyrdom of St Peter'. The saint hung uncomfortably upside down on his cross. His face was not always the most morose nor the most puzzled in that office. There was nobody there now except Davies.

The canteen was still open and he had provisioned himself with a mug of coffee and three flecked pastries. Sitting down he struck his head against the hanging ceiling light. He let it swing balefully and silently like some untolled bell. When it had stopped he opened the file on Cecil Victor Ramscar.

He began at the back. Everything that was known about Ramscar was there, every conviction, every suspicion, every inquiry. There were the criminal blotches of his fingerprints and the photographs taken in prison, getting progressively younger until the final one showed him as a hard-looking lad in the Borstal hockey team. The first entry (theft of clothing coupons) was in 1945 and the last (suspected armed robbery, not proven) in 1968. After that there was nothing but a note: 'Believed to be resident in Oakland, California. FBI information (Ref: FBI 384A) January 1972.'

Twenty-five years back in the folder there appeared a single typewritten sheet of paper. Davies leaned forward in the poor light. Across the top was a penned note: 'Statement by Cecil Victor Ramscar. Reference Missing (believed dead) Celia Norris.' It was dated August 15th, 1951.

Davies read it studiously. It was, as were most of Ramscar's statements in the file, a complete denial. It gave his movements for the evening of July 23rd, 1951 and for several subsequent days. Ramscar, so he said, had been at the races and spent the night of July 23rd at a hotel in Newmarket with two strippers. Davies raised his eyebrows. Ramscar admitted to knowing Celia Norris because her father was a business associate, but denied he had spoken to her or seen her for the week preceding July 23rd or even after that date.

The statement had been accepted by the police after checking. It was stamped and acknowledged at the bottom by a Detective Inspector whose signature Davies failed to decipher. He remained blinking at it. He had never heard of the case of Celia Norris. He rose slowly in the drab room and walked out to the desk sergeant at the front counter.

The sergeant was a shiny sort of man with no hair. Davies knew he would be retiring within a few months. 'Ben,' he asked. 'You've been around here since the Flood. Ever hear of the case of Celia Norris? Vanished in July 1951?'

Ben had a habit of smoothing down a non-existent fringe. He did so now and said: 'Oh yes, I know that one, Dangerous. Young girl, sixteen or seventeen, going home from a youth club, on a bike, I think. Just disappeared. Thin air case.'

'Never found?'

'No, not a trace. Not a sausage. I can't remember it all now but I think her clothes turned up somewhere.'

'Did we treat it as murder?'

'No. Not at first, only after, everybody thought she'd just gone off like young girls do go off. With some bloke or other. She'd done it before and her home was nothing to shout about. In fact, now I come to think of it, Dangerous, her old man was a bit of a villain around here, into all sorts of petty larceny and fiddling. That sort of stuff. I haven't heard of him for a few years. He's probably inside.'

'And it never got off the deck?'

'No, God, they couldn't even find a proper suspect, if I remember rightly. Pulled all the usuals in, but nothing. There was a lot of fuss, in the papers and all that rubbish. The CID here couldn't have solved a bloody crossword puzzle in those days and after they'd hooked in one or two obvious prize choices and let them go, the thing just fizzled out. It's still on the file. I'm surprised you've never heard anyone talk about it. Why did you want to know, anyway?'

Davies had no time to reply. The swing door whirled and in fell a weeping woman holding her head with one hand and a large saucepan with the other.

'That fucker's done it again!' she howled at Ben. 'Bashed me on the head with this! Right on the bleeding head!' Davies backed away. The woman took her hand away to reveal a spectacular bump. The sergeant opened the ledger on his desk with a long sigh which seemed to be repeated by the pages of the book itself. 'Mrs Goodly,' he recited aloud. He wrote it down. 'Vera. Which number Hawthorn Street?'

'Twenty-seven,' she said, obviously thoroughly familiar with the ritual. 'The fucker. I'll swing for him yet.'

Davies padded heavily away. He helped himself to a key from the board behind the counter and went down the corridor to a dark door marked 'Local Records'.

Even then, at that initial moment, he was aware of something germinating inside him. Something moving with caution, but nevertheless moving. He switched on the light and went along the tin-boxed files. It had an entire file to itself: 'Norris. Celia. 1951–'

With his unknown thrill growing, he took the box down and put it on the central table. It creaked open. He pulled out the contents, hundreds of sheets, statements, browning newspaper cuttings and photographs. In a separate envelope was an enlarged picture of a pixie-faced girl licking an ice-cream. A dab of vanilla had got on to her chin and she knew it was there and was laughing about it. On the back was a caption. It said: 'Celia Mary Norris. 5 ft 1 inch. 7 stone 10 lbs. Aged 17'.

For the next two hours he sat hunched in the enclosed room and read through the file. Down the corridor he could occasionally hear the evening life of the police station going on, the drunks, the threats, the weeping, and twice the echoing clang of the doors to the cells. By the time he had reached the last inconclusive page – the whole thing, left, abandoned, run out, exhausted but unfinished – it was ten o'clock by the station clock which he could see at the distant end of the corridor. He folded the documents and replaced them in their tin box. He went out, returning the key to the desk sergeant who had just taken over from Ben.

Outside it was raining. He pulled the huge overcoat closer about him and trotted clumsily to The Babe in Arms. The rough woman was lying on the bar floor having just cracked an ankle during her flamenco. Mod was trying to lift her but when he saw Davies he let her drop to the floor again. 'For Jesus' sake, where have you been?' he demanded. 'I've been stuck here buying my own beer.'

Davies asked for two pints but Mod still regarded him accusingly. 'Fine bloody evening, I've had,' he complained. He nodded towards the rough woman who was now being lifted, howling, towards the door by three strong men. 'Spent all night trying to explain about Spain to that lunatic female. She's never heard of Franco or Don Juan Carlos. All she knows is that "Viva España" thing. She thinks Granada is a fucking television station.' He pulled up and began to look steadily at Davies who was smiling. 'Something's been and happened,' Mod said carefully. 'You've been up to something, Dangerous. What is it?'

Davies let his smile travel over the surface of his beer. 'A murder,' he said quietly. 'I've got myself a murder.'

Mod looked with amazement. 'Your own murder!' he breathed. 'They've given *you* a murder?'

'No,' corrected Davies firmly. 'They didn't *give* it to me. I ... I sort of appropriated it.'

'You ... what?'

Davies grinned: 'I'm not going to tell them about it.'

four

Breakfast at 'Bali Hi', Furtman Gardens, was a fragmented affair. Thin Minnie Banks, the schoolteacher, attempted to correct some abysmal exercise books for the day's lessons, while drinking her weak tea. Mod, undoing *The Guardian*,

32

sat down to his toast, glanced over her shoulder and remarked: 'Training the future unemployed, I see.'

'You can talk!' Her voice was as piping as her frame. 'Since when, Mr Lewis, have you done a day's work?'

Mod sniffed like a managing director and spread his paper. 'It takes a great deal of skill and technique to remain unemployed,' he observed. 'I doubt if your pupils would ever reach the required standard.'

Davies came downstairs and Mrs Fulljames heard him from her kitchen where she ate her breakfast not so much in privacy as secrecy. 'Any sign of my bed yet, Sherlock Holmes?' she called.

'Inquiries are proceeding,' Davies shouted back woodenly. 'You will be informed of any progress.'

'I'll be bloody lucky,' she retorted. 'Who tried to blow up the cemetery then?'

'Nobody,' sighed Davies. He poured himself some tea and splashed jam on a round of stony toast. Mrs Fulljames, cup in one hand, the *Daily Mirror* in the other, appeared at the door of her citadel. '*Anybody* could have told you that,' she jeered. 'How could anyone blow up a cemetery? How?'

Davies lowered his toast. 'It was the misreading of a handwritten message,' he said wearily. 'We had received a warning but it was incorrectly written down, scribbled, in fact. I thought it said something was going to happen in the graveyard with a bomb. But 'bomb' was badly written and I didn't correctly read it. It should have been 'tomb'. But nothing happened to any tombs either. I just got double pneumonia.'

'Police!' jeered Mrs Fulljames, returning to the kitchen. 'You'd make better girl guides. God knows what would happen if there was ever a murder around here.'

Davies caught Mod's eye and set his teeth to fight the toast. He hoped the grinding and the grunts would reach Mrs Fulljames. If they did she took no heed.

Later he fed Kitty, who was prostrate, as usual, in the back seat of the Lagonda, but he left the car and the wheezing dog in the tin garage at the foot of the street and walked, his thoughts full, to the police station.

It was a wan morning with most people by now behind the gates at their work, stragglers at the bus stops, steam curtaining the window of the Copper Kettle Café, and shopkeepers yawning behind their counters. He heard compressed coughing from the waiting room of the doctor's surgery, a milkman on a float clanked with his hazardous load, and two boys, playing truant, squirmed their way through the fence by the railway embankment. For a large place it was often as empty as a village.

At the police station some midnight miscreants were being taken from the overnight cells to the court. There were some familiar faces among the drunks, the drunks and indecents, the drunk and disorderlies and the drunks and incapables, and they saw Davies as a friend.

'Morning, all,' he said as he went through to the CID room. They rumbled their own greetings and stumbled frowstily forward. After they had gone out, shivering in the early air, to walk to the courthouse around the corner, the desk sergeant took out an aerosol spray and played it around extravagantly. 'Yardbird wants to see you at ten, Dangerous,' he called down the corridor. 'He was shitty because he couldn't get hold of you yesterday. Wanted to know what you were up to.'

'Inquiries,' Davies called back down the corridor. He had half an hour so he went to the canteen and bought a cup of solid coffee and two cakes. Then he returned to the CID room and took the file of Cecil Victor Ramscar from his locker. He had intended to go through it again but he turned instead to the one statement concerning the disappearance of Celia Norris. He read it, with an odd guilt, as though he were looking through something forbidden. Then, just as guiltily, he purloined the key of the 'Local Records' room and took down the Celia Norris file. He felt a sharp unreasonable thrill as he opened it again. There she was, laughing up from her photograph, the ice-cream dab on her chin. He ran his fingers thickly down the edges of the documents and statements. All this, and nobody ever found.

Clipped to the front of the wad was a summary of the case and an index of statements. Davies took an absent-minded bite of one cake, and began to read again. He did not like the cake. It stuck to the roof of his mouth. He put the rest in a random file he took from the shelf. One day someone would find a cake in a file. He read through the summary.

Celia Norris had spent what was, almost without doubt, the final afternoon of her life planning her future. At 4 o'clock on 23 July 1951, she had gone to the youth employment office in the town to inquire about the possibilities of becoming a nurse. She had gone afterwards to her home at Hunter Street, almost under the rims of the Ali Baba jars of the power station, had a meal and then left for the youth club at St Fridewide's Catholic Church. At ten o'clock, or shortly after, she had left there on her bicycle. Her boyfriend, William Lind, had remained behind for a sports meeting and anyway his bicycle had a puncture and he had to walk home. So he did not accompany her. To reach her home she would have cycled along the main road to its junction with Hunter Street and turned there, or perhaps taken the short cut, which she had been known to do, being a girl of no nervous disposition, along the towpath of the canal, later joining the main road and completing her journey as before.

After that night nobody reported seeing her. The bicycle was never discovered. Her clothes were found, except her pants. A lipstick she was known to have carried in the pocket of her dress was misssng. A youth called Andrew Parsons, a known underwear thief, was arrested on a call from the attendant of a twenty-four-hour public convenience in the High Street who had seen him handling some girl's clothing in the establishment. The clothes, a green gingham dress, white bra, white socks and brown Louis-heeled shoes, were identified as those worn by Celia Norris on the night she disappeared and presumably died. Parsons, a nocturnal moocher, told the police he had originally taken the garments from the public lavatory where he found them stuffed behind a cistern at one o'clock one morning in July. The shoes were inside the cistern. He believed it was July 24th. When three weeks later he saw in the newspapers that the clothes were the same as were described as belonging to the missing girl, he panicked and decided to return them to the place where he had found them. The police had questioned him for two days and then let him go. He was kept under surveillance but nothing more came from this.

The finding of the girl's garments, and the fact of the missing knickers which Parsons (who was found to have a collection of 234 pairs of assorted women's pants in a cupboard at his lodgings) swore he had never taken or even seen, had turned a desultory search for a wayward teenager who had previously strayed, into a hunt for a body and a murderer. Neither were ever found. Nor was Celia's bicycle.

And it had happened, by all the evidence, at ten o'clock on a summer evening – a warm summer evening too – and yet no one had come forward to say they had seen a girl in a gingham dress on a bicycle. In that anonymously crowded but somehow vacant place, when it was just growing dark, as it would have been, it was not so strange as it might at first seem. People did not stroll in those streets for there was nowhere to go and it was too early for the exodus from the pubs or the cinemas. Television was still a compelling novelty. There was a regular police van patrol taking in the High Street and the canal towpath (policemen on foot beat had recently been replaced) but neither Police Constable Frederick Fennell nor his colleague, PC James Dudley, who were driving their small vehicle in the area until midnight, saw the girl or reported anything unusual. Celia Norris had mounted her bicycle at the Catholic youth club and ridden away into nothing.

Davies remembered Yardbird and opened the door to look at the clock down the corridor. He still had seven minutes. His coffee was looking even more muddy and was now cold. He attempted a drink and screwed up his face. He took a football pools envelope from his pocket (he had resolved to seek his fortune that season) and noted on its back the names of those who had made statements in the case of Celia Norris:

Elizabeth Norris, mother; Albert Norris, father; William Lind, boyfriend; Ena Brown, a friend, Roxanne Potts, another friend; all members of the youth club. David Boot, youth club leader; Andrew Parsons, underwear thief; and the name that had begun it all for Davies: Cecil Victor Ramscar, described as a friend of the girl's family. There were other names, statements made by people who thought they might be able to assist, but mostly nebulous, and, lastly, the negative report of PC Fennell and PC Dudley, who had been on duty in the police van that night.

The clock along the corridor said three minutes to ten. He still had time. From the file he took the envelope containing the various photographs collected during the investigation. They were pathetic little snapshots, sepia now, moments in a life that had not long to run. Celia with her mother, Celia with her dog, Celia at the seaside with a chisel-faced youth wearing a paper hat, possibly William Lind, and, finally, one that must have lodged in the envelope when he had first opened it the previous night. It showed Celia and another girl at what appeared to be a fairground or fête. Both wore summer dresses and were laughing. Standing between them, ten inches taller than either in an open-necked shirt and badged blazer was a bronzed man, grinning. A first glance it seemed he had his arms about their young waists. But Davies hurried into the desk sergeant and borrowed the magnifying glass the station clerk used for reading small print.

'Don't forget Yardbird, Dangerous,' the sergeant reminded him.

'No. No. Just going up,' answered Davies, hurrying back down the corridor. He put the magnifying glass on the photograph. He saw that although the man's hold on the girls seemed conventionally friendly, his fingers, in fact, were curved higher and touched the undersides of their breasts. He pursed his lips. That, he decided, might be David Boot, youth club leader.

Inspector Yardbird was grouped at his window, hands clasped Napoleonically behind his back, legs astride, shoulders square, a growl on his face. He was gazing over the creased and crowded roofs as though he was considering conquering them. He had called aloofly to answer Davies's knock but he remained with his back to the room for two minutes until a subdued cough caused him to turn to see the Detective Constable.

37

'Glad you could make it,' remarked Yardbird caustically. 'Searched everywhere for you yesterday. Where were you? At the pictures?'

'Inquiries, sir,' said Davies.

Yardbird sniffed. 'Well, I've got some further inquiries for you. And this is bigger stuff than you've been asked to handle before. Much bigger. It seems to me you've been rather falling behind in the general run of things, Davies.'

There was nothing but for him to agree. 'Yes, sir,' he answered. 'I've had that feeling myself. I thought I was being, sort of, overlooked.'

Yardbird sat on the edge of his desk. His left foot just reached the floor. He thought he caught a movement from the window of the girl students' hostel and he tried to get a firmer look without Davies noticing.

'Hah,' smiled Davies amiably. 'Do those girls still live across there, sir?'

Yardbird spun so quickly he all but spilled from the desk. 'Girls? For Christ's sake, which girls?' He turned and sat down behind the desk, and, without being asked, Davies sat pensively in the visitor's chair. The Inspector rubbed his face in his hands. 'I don't know, Davies,' he grumbled. 'I really don't know. I consider you for a big job, but I honestly can't tell whether I'm doing either of us a favour. I still can't get the police garden party out of my mind. Those fucking raffle tickets blowing all over the show. And when you'd got back from collecting them somebody had nicked the raffle money.'

'I was a poor choice for the raffle, the wrong man,' admitted Davies. 'It seemed to go from bad to worse, didn't it.'

'The Commissioner thought you were some kind of clown we had hired. I might as well tell you that here and now, Davies. It made me feel pretty stupid I can tell you.' He sighed and thrust his broad chin into his broader tunic. 'On the other hand I was always one for giving somebody another chance. And that's what I'm offering you. Another chance. Did you look through the Ramscar file last night when you came in?'

'Yes, I did, sir.'

'Nasty bugger that,' muttered Yardbird. 'He's been around

ever since I was a young constable in this division. A finger in every criminal pie, a real villain. Larceny, grievous bodily harm, vice, protection rackets, all sorts of things. And very active in the old London gang wars. Mr Ramscar's put bullets through a few kneecaps I can tell you.'

'He's got a big file, sir,' agreed Davies. 'What's he done this time?'

'Nothing,' replied Yardbird. 'Nothing that our splendid Special Branch can prove. And it's them that wants him. They just know he's back in London from abroad, where he's been involved in some big villainy and they think he's come back for a good reason. They think he might be up to political crime now. He likes to keep in the trend. Anyway they want him found but they don't want to set an army looking for him. They just want somebody to track him down. And you're the somebody. Because they think he's come home. He's in this area. You find him.'

'I see. Find him.'

'That's it. Get around his old haunts and his old friends. Ask a lot of questions. We don't mind too much if he starts flapping his wings. I'm going to detach you from other duties. Just see I get regular reports. It shouldn't take you long, a couple of weeks at the most.'

'Yes,' said Davies. 'I see.'

Yardbird looked up. It was time for Davies to go. 'Anything else?' asked the Inspector. 'You've got the whole picture, now.'

'No ... No, nothing else, sir. Just one thing. Can I use my own transport? My car?'

Yardbird, who had never seen Davies's Lagonda or the dog, nodded brusquely. 'If it's decent. If it doesn't let down the force. And ... Davies.'

'Yes sir.'

'Keep the expenses down. If you have to go to the West End go by bus. And not too much boozing in those clubs. Remember, you're not in the Flying Squad.'

Davies thanked him and went out, down the stairs and into the CID room. A detective sergeant called Myer was going through three hundred pornographic pictures. Two other

CID men, looking over his shoulder, examined them for clues. Davies got the Ramscar file and sat down to go through it again. He came to the Celia Norris statement and read it minutely. He took a deep breath and plunged into the rest of the history. But in his mind he could see only a girl with a blob of ice-cream on her chin.

Davies had few notions about locating Ramscar. It appeared obvious that if he were in hiding he would hardly visit his once habitual haunts, although he would undoubtedly contact old associates. Davies thought if he walked about loudly enough and asked a great many random questions then Ramscar might come to him.

In the afternoon he went to Park Royal greyhound races and backed four spectacularly losing dogs, one at evens. He made conversations with a number of shifty men, mentioning Ramscar and showing his picture but it appeared to mean nothing. In the toilet he approached a fellow urinator and waved the photograph but the man, white-faced, retreated, still making water, and with a quaint leapfrogging motion along the troughs. As soon as he reached the door he ran and reported Davies to a policeman.

It was not at all a promising first day. At five o'clock he returned to the police station and, unable to help himself, almost mesmerized, he again took down the file on Celia Norris. He kept looking over his shoulder experiencing the same sensations as when he had, as a boy, secretly examined the illustrations in 'First Aid To The Injured', fearful that his mother would catch him enslaved by a drawing of a woman receiving artificial respiration. He felt contracted inside reading through the unfinished story again, looking at the photographs. He found himself making a stupid little movement with his hand trying to brush that nib of ice-cream from the laughing girl's chin. He reacted with horror when he realized what he was doing. Eventually, unable to help himself, he returned the file and very secretly went out and began to walk the 25-year-old trail of Celia Norris.

Although there had been demolitions and developments on the London fringe of the district, the area of the High Street and the canal were all but unchanged. The cemetery occupied a good many acres at the base of this region and that was as immovable as cemeteries generally are. The canal formed a wedge through the centre and provided another hard argument against change. On the far side the small workshops and bigger factories had been so busy making goods and money during the nineteen-fifties and sixties that few thought of making any improvements. Now they had slowed with the recession, those who operated them were unwilling to finance re-planning or expansion. The High Street, grey and crowded, ran roughly on the same line as the canal, although it curved quickly to cross the waterway at its uppermost end before the power station. It was locked between the immovable and the immutable. To the south the cemetery, to the north the power station, to the west the canal and to the east the solid, three- and four-storey houses of the original Victorian town, including 'Bali Hi', Furtman Gardens (formerly called 'Cranbrook Villa' but renamed after Mrs Fulljames had fallen in love with Rossano Brazzi in the film version of *South Pacific*). It would be half-a-century before anyone thought of pulling those down.

And so the stage remained largely as it was that close night in July, 1951, when Celia Norris began her cycle journey home from the youth club. It was now a gritty October evening. Davies left the police station and after courteously declining the offer of a free intercourse from Venus, the evening star, he set off on foot for St Fridewide's Catholic Church.

The youth club had been in the grounds of the church, indeed it still was, and the girl would have cycled from the main gate. He walked thoughtfully from there to the junction with the southern end of the High Street. The cemetery occupied about ten acres, fronting on the main road, at that point, all dead land. He went at a steady pace (he would cycle it, he decided, at some later time) but increased his step past the graveyard gates because he did not want to be forced into making an explanation to the miserable keeper about the misreading of the word 'tomb' for 'bomb'. The man was bound to be uncharitable. He should introduce him to Mrs Fulljames one day.

At the conclusion of the cemetery there was the customary stonemason's yard with a nice display of crosses and weepy angels, to catch the passing trade, and from this the haphazard High Street began its course. The smart, big, bright stores that grew up in the years of plenty, in the sixties, had found their home in other easier thoroughfares in Kilburn, Paddington and Cricklewood, leaving this street to the small grocers, the tobacconists, the fish-and-chip merchants, the humid cafés, the bright, cheap clothes shops, the betting shops, of course, and several long stretches occupied by the showrooms of second-hand car dealers, the vehicles and the salesmen smiling identical smiles from the open fronts of the premises.

The local newspaper, the *Citizen*, was uncomfortably accommodated in a house, once the residence of the neighbourhood's only famous son, Miles Shaltoe, a writer of somewhat dubious novels who enjoyed a vogue in the early nineteen hundreds. There was a plaque commemorating his occupation under the fascia which proclaimed 'North West London Citizen' and in smaller letters 'Every Friday'. There were also several ladies' hairdressers, one boasting the title 'Antoinette of Paris, Switzerland and Hemel Hempstead'. There were numerous public houses interpolated along the street, with the The Babe in Arms occupying a favoured position adjacent to the public conveniences, two cinemas, the more palatial of which now only featured Indian films, a West Indian Bongo Club and an English Bingo Club, a pawnshop, its avuncular balls first hung in 1896, and 'The Healing Hands' massage parlour, an establishment of more recent roots.

Despite attempts with paint and plastic to brighten it, the street was decayed and tired, sighing for the euthanasia of the demolition man's flying ball. Davies walked along it, as he had many times in his past five years in that town, but now examining the upper windows and wondering if any eyes had looked down from their vantage on the final journey of Celia Norris.

The upper floors, while mostly curtained and closed, with lights behind them at this time of evening, had the occasionally noteworthy difference. There were the premises of Madame Tarantella Phelps-Smith, High Class Fortunes Told, the Winged Victory Ex-Servicemen's Club, the ubiquitous snooker hall and the Quaker Meeting Room, undoubtedly reeking with the rising odours of the Take-away-Curry shop underneath.

The husky evening itself was layered with odours -- Guinness, chips, work and dirt. There was a municipal tree at the junction with Jubilee Road, one of the Victorian offshoots. It was donated by the Rotary Club -- and had a plaque to prove it -- to commemorate the Coronation of Queen Elizabeth II and, despite being protectively caged in an iron waistcoat, it was stricken as though by some long-term lightning.

Davies walked the length of the High Street twice in forty minutes. It was busy with buses and homeward cars now, and with people scurrying from their work, thinking of freedom, food, television or possibly love. He ended his thoughtful patrol at The Babe in Arms and went into the elongated bar. Mod was predictably peering into a half pint, which he had purchased with his own money. He was glad to see Davies for he was anxious to know further about his private murder case and his glass was running low.

'I've started,' said Davies when they were drinking. 'I've started on the case.'

'How far have you got.'

'Nowhere.'

Mod nodded at his beer and at the logic of the reply. 'Will you keep me informed, Dangerous?' he asked. 'I have a lot of time to think, you know. I may just come up with something.'

'I'll tell you,' promised Davies. He glanced up and down the bar. 'She's not in then? Flamenco Fanny.'

'No,' confirmed Mod. 'I think she must have broken her ankle last night when she fell down. With any luck.'

The door opened on cue and the rough woman, her untidy leg in a hammerhead of plaster-of-paris, stumped in supported by a massive walking stick. 'Olé!' she cried.

'Oshit,' said Davies.

*

Even with the annoyance of the rough woman stumping around all night in the bar on her enormous plaster cast it was only with some difficulty that Davies managed to entice Mod to leave and to walk with him to the canal bank.

'If I am to be your Dr Watson, I wish you could arrange for our investigations to be outside drinking hours,' complained Mod. 'If you don't mind me saying so, I can't see how any clues to this conundrum – there, I said it too, beered as I am – are going to be lying around by the canal twenty-five years after the event.'

A man loitering in a shop doorway opposite saw them leave the bar and, after allowing them fifty yards' clearance, walked in the shadows behind. He watched them make for the entrance to the alley between the pawnbroker's, and the massage parlour, then hurried down a service road alongside some neighbouring shops and climbed a fence to reach the canal bank. He ran through the towpath mud, passed a man fishing in the dead of night, and turned up the alley from the canal end. Davies and Mod were wandering towards him.

'It's not clues, it's geography I want to be sure about,' Davies was saying patiently. 'On her way home she might have cycled down this cut and gone along the towpath to the road bridge. I just want to cover the ground, that's all.'

The man who had followed them now approached from the foot of the alley. They looked up from their talk and saw him come, coat-collared, towards them. Davies felt an instinctive touch of nervousness as the silhouette came nearer, as though his new role had given a sharper edge. They had almost to touch to pass each other and, as people do in such awkward circumstances they muttered almost into each other's faces as they passed.

'Good-night,' said Davies.

'Nighty-night,' added Mod.

'Night,' responded the man, a short blast of beer emitting with the word. Davies saw nothing more of him than a pale triangle of face jutting from the collar and pinpoint eyes squinting through rudimentary spectacles. The man had gone to the upper end of the alley before Davies realized that there were no lenses in those glasses.

The alley performed a mile curve and beyond the angle the limp lamplit water of the canal came into their view. The damp, rotten smell was at once heavier. They stood and took in the confined scene. If the girl had gone that way she would have had that same view in the same light as she rode carefully on her bicycle. The helmeted lamp had hovered above the bridge for many years. It was as if it had lost something in the water and was taking a long time to find it.

Davies and Mod were contemplating the chill view, hearing the bored glugging of the water against its old banks when, dramatically, a figure ascended from behind the elevated hedge on their right. They jumped like a pair of ponies. The figure squeaked nervously. 'Oh ... oh ... ever so sorry, mates...' he said eventually. He stood upright against the hedge, five feet above them because of the variant in the ground levels. Davies and Mod regarded him as they would have regarded the appearance of Satan. Davies contained his voice. 'Don't worry,' he laughed hollowly. 'Didn't see you there, that's all. Made us jump.'

'No, you wouldn't, not from down there,' acknowledged the man. 'Completely hidden from down there I am, I bet.' He performed a brief demonstration crouching behind the hedge and calling to them. 'There, can you see me now?'

'No, not a thing. Can't see you at all,' obliged Davies.

'What you doing anyway?' inquired Mod, more to the point.

'The allotment,' said the man, rising and nodding over his shoulder into the vacant darkness. 'Only chance I've got of getting down here. By the time I get home from work and that. I'm just getting a few veg.'

'Good job you know where everything is,' observed Davies.

'All in nice straight lines,' said the man. 'I've got a torch but the batteries went. I've done now, anyway. Finished.'

They continued looking up at him. He was like a politician with a small audience. 'Any good, these allotments?' asked Davies.

'Not bad. Not as good as the power station plots, but not bad either. Here it's always dampish, see. Because of the canal. But the power station stuff gets the spray from the cooling towers. But you get good stuff in both.' He began to heave a sack over the hedge. Davies and then Mod moved forward and helped him to bring it to the ground. He thanked them, wished them a cheerful good-night, then shouldered the sack and went towards the top of the alley. 'He must have a lot of mouths to feed,' observed Mod.

They continued to the end of the cut, the air closing damper with each step. The canal water, near black by day, was in its night-time guise, appearing in the streaky light of the lamp as limpid as a tropical pool. Sitting on the bank, quite close to the bridge, was Father Harvey, the priest of St Fridewide's. He was fishing.

'Now I've seen the lot,' Davies said to him. 'Up there was a chap digging his allotment in the dark, and now you fishing. Caught anything?'

'If I do I'll have you as witness to a holy miracle,' murmured the priest. 'I am only seeking peace. Unfortunately canal banks have become areas of suspicion and a bachelor priest might find it embarrassing to merely walk or stand along here at night. So I fish.'

Davies grinned in the dark. 'I was thinking of nicking you for poaching, Father,' he said.

'Chessus, now, I never thought of that,' replied the priest. 'I suppose I could always plead that I was fishing for souls.'

'You'd need communion bread for bait,' suggested Mod. Davies told Father Harvey who Mod was and the Father nodded up and Mod nodded down.

'We passed a man up there in the alley who was wearing glasses with no lenses in them,' said Davies.

He heard the priest sniff. 'There's a lot of poverty about,' he observed.

'Or maybe it was a disguise.'

'It could have been that,' agreed Father Harvey. 'There's that place of degradation the council have allowed them to open at the top of the alley – the so-called "massage parlour". Hell masquerading as hygiene. He might have been going there and not wanting anyone to recognize him. The pawnshop and the massage parlour are both full of the unredeemed.'

'Good point. You should be in the force.'

'Thank you, my son,' said the priest laconically. They were silent for a while watching the deadpan water as though expecting a pike to bite at any moment. Then the priest said: 'I take it you haven't found out who burned down my confessional box?'

'No,' admitted Davies. 'We haven't got very far on that one. But I don't see it as an act of desecration.' He could see the priest's nose profiled like a triangle.

'I might have told my flock it was a sign from Heaven, or Hell,' said the priest. 'But experience tells me it was boys smoking in there.'

'It won't be easy to find out,' interpolated Mod. 'You won't get it out of them at Confession because you haven't got a confessional box. It's like the chicken and the egg.'

The priest showed no outward reaction. He appeared to be trying to analyse something in the water. 'You know, Dangerous,' he said coming to a conclusion, not turning his head. 'I can't help thinking that you're not really cut out for being a detective. If you could cut your drinking by half, I'd suggest the priesthood.'

'That's a pretty general opinion,' agreed Davies, with doleful sportsmanship. 'But, it happens, I am on an important inquiry at present.'

'Oh, and what would that be? Or can you tell?'

'I think I can. After all you're a man of secrets.'

'It goes with the job,' agreed the priest.

Davies crouched on the dank bank. Mod remained standing as though keeping watch. Davies asked: 'Father, do you remember Celia Norris?'

'Celia Norris,' nodded the priest. 'The girl was apparently murdered. A long time ago.'

'Twenty-five years,' said Davies. 'I've reopened the case.'

'Chessus,' said Father Harvey. 'It was when I first came here. In fact I only knew the girl a few weeks. I can't even remember her face.'

Davies could. 'It was never cleared up,' he said. 'It was just left.'

'You didn't come down here looking for footprints, by any chance, did you?' asked the priest.

'Not quite. But I thought I would just wander along and see if I could get any ideas.'

'She was at the youth club. And they never found anything,' said the priest.

'Her clothes,' said Davies. 'They found those. Except her ... underpants.'

'Ah, her knickers,' agreed Father Harvey. 'Yes, I recall that fact.' He gave the fishing line a few ruminative jerks. 'Perhaps, now, she wasn't wearing any.'

'Father!' Davies said it. Mod began to whistle in the night.

'Well, like I said just now, there's a lot of poverty about. Twenty-five years ago it was no better.'

Davies considered again the priest's nose. In silhouette it appeared a lot longer than in daylight. 'Do you know where Mrs Norris, her mother, lives these days?' he asked.

'Yes, yes. Let me see. Hunter Street, by the power station. She still comes to church, sometimes.'

'Dave Boot,' said Davies. 'Remember Dave Boot, the youth club man, Father? What was he like?'

'Muscles,' said Father Harvey decisively. 'All muscles. He did all this training nonsense. Chessus, he used to make me feel envious. I had a few muscles myself in those days, but I was required to hide them under my cassock. One of the sacrifices of spiritual life, you see. But there were times, I must confess when I would have swopped all the vestments of a bishop for a string vest.'

Davies laughed sombrely in the dark. Mod, who did not have a top coat, shuffled in the cold. Davies took the hint.

'We'll be going then, Father,' said Davies.

'Right you are,' sniffed the priest. 'I wish you well with your mouldy old murder. This one's not only dead, it's been dead a long time. Cold ashes, Dangerous, cold ashes. You might find it's better left like that.'

'It's not an official investigation,' said Davies. 'I am doing it myself. In my own time.'

'Like a hobby?' said the priest, still watching the water.

'Yes, you could say that. Like a hobby.'

five

He began to rake the cold ashes by going to Hunter Street. It was one of the streets grouped around the cooling towers of the power station, midgets crowding giants. The stream and vapour from the towers kept it a perpetual rainy day. But it had compensations, for when the sun came out it filled the damp, melancholy streets with rainbows.

Davies stood at the front of the terraced house, the same as all the others but more in need of a paint. The door hung like a jaw. Months before someone had planted a Christmas tree in the patch of front garden hoping to defy God and make it grow. God had won. It stood brittle, brown, shivering at the first fingering of another autumn. Davies knocked at the door and several pieces of paint fell off. It appeared that a whole system of locks was undone before the thin woman's face appeared.

'What d'you want?'

'Mrs Norris?'

'That's right. What d'you want?'

'I've ... I've come to have a talk with you, if I can. About your daughter.'

'Josie. What's Josie done?'

'No. Not Josie. Celia.'

The eyes seemed to sprout quickly from the face. 'Celia?' she whispered. 'Who are you then?'

'I'm a policeman.'

'You've ... have you ... found our Celia?'

'No. No we haven't.'

'Well go and have another look,' she said suddenly and bitterly. 'Bugger off.'

The door slammed resoundingly in his face and several more pieces of paint fell off. He backed away because he was unsure what to do next. If a door were shut during an official investigation there were methods of opening it again, even if it meant asking politely. But when it was just a hobby it was more difficult.

He went out of the gate and began to walk thoughtfully along the street. Approaching him from the power station end appeared a wobbling motor scooter. It skidded noisily, slid by him and then was backed up. It was ridden by a girl, small and dark. She pulled her head out of her yellow crash helmet which had 'Stop Development in Buenos Aires' written on it, and shook her hair. She only needed the ice-cream blob on her chin.

'Josie,' said Davies. 'You're Josie Norris.'

'You scored,' she said. 'Who are you? I saw you coming from our gate.'

'I'm a policeman,' he said apologetically. 'Detective Constable Davies. Your mum just threw me out.'

'She would do,' nodded the girl confidently. 'Are you going to nick the old man? He said he was considering going straight.'

'No. It's nothing to do with your father. It's Celia.'

'Christ,' she breathed. 'You haven't found something?'

'No. But I'm hoping to.'

'Hoping? Hoping?' she sounded incredulous. 'And I'm hoping to do a straight swop with this scooter for a new Rolls Royce. When I'm eighteen.'

'How long is that?'

'Eight months and three days. I'm free then. You're free when you're eighteen now.'

'So I'm told. I seemed to have missed it.'

'You want to chat to my mum, do you?'

'Yes. Will you fix it?'

'You're serious about it,' she said thoughtfully. 'I mean you're not going to bugger her about and then just drop it again. She's had enough already.'

'I'm serious,' nodded Davies. He hesitated and then said: 'I don't think it was ever properly investigated.'

'Why is it being investigated now?'

He decided to lie. 'New information. A man in prison has talked.'

'What did he say?'

'I can't tell you that.'

She looked at him on the angle. 'All right,' she said. 'I'll get her to meet you. There's a Lyons Caff in the High Street, just by the florists.'

'I know it.'

'Make it three o'clock in there. She shut the door on you because my dad's at home, I expect. But she'll be there.' She regarded him squarely, a small, confident face protruding from a yellow oilskin jacket. 'But, mister ... promise you won't screw her up.'

'Promise,' said Davies.

The afternoon closed early as though it were anxious to be quit for the day. Drizzle. the real thing from the sky, not from the cooling towers, licked the shop windows in the High Street and buses shushed by on their way to Cricklewood. Davies loitered across the road from the café, imagining that he merged with the background shadow, his face almost buried by the bowsprit of his overcoat. He felt quaintly confident in his obscurity and was shaken when the three apparent strangers wished him good-afternoon, by name. Mrs Norris approached, unseen and, unerringly picking him out, announced: 'I'm here.'

Davies, disgruntled, followed her across the rainy road, and into the café. She indicated that she was running the situation by nodding him towards a corner table. Obediently he shuffled off to the marble slab while she joined the self-service line. He watched her from his distance. She had been tall but, although she was only in her fifties, her back was beginning to bend. The face was fatigued and fixed, looking straight at the neck of the woman before her in the queue, her eyes flicking around occasionally but only briefly before returning to the stare. Davies sat and opened the buttons of his coat. An Indian at the next table ate Heinz spaghetti and double chips and was anointing it with whorls of brown sauce. He sang quietly to himself, some song doubtless born in cool faraway hills, interrupting the plaint to slurp loudly from his cup.

Mrs Norris arrived with the tea, her eyes sharp. 'All right, then,' she sighed tiredly when she had seated herself opposite him. 'What's going on about our Celia?'

'New information has come to light, Mrs Norris,' he said in the policeman's manner he sometimes practised before his bedroom mirror. 'A man has talked. I can't tell you what he has said but he has talked.'

'Why can't you?'

'These things have to be proved,' he replied uncomfortably. 'Without preconceived ideas.'

'Preconceived ideas,' she snorted into her tea. 'They was talking about them twenty-five years ago. Is it the same lot of ideas or a new lot?'

He nodded sympathetically. 'Yes, yes,' he said, 'I can guess what it's been like for you.'

'No, you can't,' she whispered, her eyes and nose almost in her cup. 'Nobody can. She was a good girl, Mr Davies. Very good. She used to bring me flowers and not many kids do that. And they tried to make out she was some kind of prostitute just because they never found her drawers.' She sniffed and when she raised her eyes, Davies saw they were smudgy.

'Don't cry, Mrs Norris,' he said with hurried helplessness. 'Not in Lyons.'

'I won't,' she promised. 'It's not so easy as you think to cry. Not after all this time.' She paused then looked at him with sad hope. 'How far have you got?'

'I've only just started. But I believe that after all this time, people will say things they only *thought* twenty-five years ago, or things they didn't even *realize* they knew.'

She nodded. 'People do change their tune,' she agreed. 'I know that. Too well.'

'How?' he said. 'In what way?'

'Well, you know. They're all sympathy and that at the time, then they avoid you and the whispers start going around. About my girl ... And they're still at it. I mean, you know she went off once before. She was headstrong like that. One of the bloody Sunday papers brought the whole thing up again a couple of years ago, "What Happened to Happy Celia?" That was the headline. They sent some bloke to see me. I chucked a bucket of soapsuds over him.'

'You do want the answer, don't you?' he said.

'Yes I do, but not that way. Not all over the bleeding newspapers. Muckraking, that's all that was. It's got to be done a bit on the quiet. That's the only way you or anybody else is going to find out anything.'

'When she went off before,' said Davies, 'was that with a man?'

'I don't know,' she replied almost sulkily. 'When she came back she didn't say. She said she had been away for a change. I never asked her after that.'

The café was almost empty for it was mid-afternoon. Steam rose from the dishes at the counter which had not been in favour at lunchtime. Odours wandered from the back regions. A tramp came in and, after politely taking off his hat and giving his ragged hair a pat with his hand, sat down at a table near to the counter. At that distance he examined the brightly illuminated food like a patron at an art gallery. He knew his timing.

'Shepherd's pie for ten pence? That's less than half price,' suggested the woman across the counter. The tramp shook his head. 'I only got six,' he answered. 'All right, six,' sighed the woman. 'No wonder they reckon you're a millionaire.'

Davies said: 'They ought to do a tramp's pie and sell it to shepherds.'

Mrs Norris did not smile. 'There's some good-hearted people around,' was her only comment. She returned her face to Davies.

Eventually he said: 'Mrs Norris, do you think you could bear to go through it again? To tell me about that one day. I've seen the statements, but I want to hear it from you.'

'All right,' she said wearily. 'Can I have another cup?'

He rose. 'I could do with one myself.'

'I expect it'll go on expenses, won't it?' she asked genuinely.

'I'll fiddle it and make a profit,' he said. He went to the counter and got the teas. The tramp said: 'Hello, Dangerous.'

Unprompted, she began when he had returned to the table. 'It was the 23rd of July. She was at home in the morning, helping me. She was very good like that. It was a very hot day. There'd been about a week of hot weather. In the afternoon

53

she went to the Employment place. It was only a little office in those days, not that great big place they've got now.'

'Times change,' he nodded. 'She was interested in nursing, wasn't she?'

Mrs Norris nodded. 'She'd have been a credit. She was a very kind-natured girl.' Her voice was without inflection, as though she were merely reciting something she had said many times before. 'They had a talk to her about nursing but she came to have her tea and went straight out to that bleeding youth club. She said she'd tell me all about it when she got back that night. And, she never did get back.'

'You didn't like the youth club?' he said.

'I don't know,' she shook her head. 'Nothing was ever said, but there was something *rotten* about it. Father Harvey never watched it like he ought to have done. But he was new here then. But I think he feels guilty about it. I think he knows how I feel about that.'

'You didn't care for Mr Boot?' suggested Davies.

Her eyes came to life, as though in a moment some faith in him had been kindled. Then she subsided again. 'No, I didn't like that one,' she admitted. 'I expect you've seen the pictures.'

'Yes, the one of Mr Boot, Celia and another girl at some sort of garden fête.'

'Ena Brown,' said Mrs Norris. 'As was then. She's Ena Lind now.'

'Lind? Lind? Who else was called Lind?' he said, trying to remember the names on the statements.

'Bill Lind,' she filled in flatly. 'He was our Celia's boyfriend. Just a friend. Like they are at that age. Not really a boyfriend.'

'And he married Ena, Celia's friend?'

'Yes. About three years after. They told the newspaper in that article ... they said they had been "drawn together by the tragedy" or some bleeding muck like that. Drawn together! She was pregnant more like it. They've got one of those council maisonettes now. She looks like a tart and when I see him in the street he turns the other way. Makes out he don't know me.'

'And you didn't like Mr Boot?'

'No. I didn't care for him, neither.'

'Any idea where he is these days?'

'He's at Finchley or Mill Hill or somewhere like that. I saw in the paper he used to run a sort of disco place. And now, I saw an advert the other week, he's got one of these sex shops. Suit him, it should.'

'Still in youth work, eh?' sniffed Davies. He paused. The tea in his cup was beginning to congeal. He drank it quickly and made a face. 'Did they er ... give you her clothes back ... eventually?'

'The police? Yet, I got them back. I've still got them. It wasn't much because it was hot weather, like I said. It was a green gingham dress, a bra and her white socks and shoes. Like everybody knows, her lipstick, just a little Woolworth's lipstick, and her drawers were missing. Everybody.' Her voice was dead.

'You've still got the clothes, Mrs Norris?'

'Yes, but they're hidden away. I'm not showing them to you or nobody else.'

'I see. I understand. Er ... the youth that found the clothes in the toilet and took them home. Did you know him?'

'Poor little devil,' she said unexpectedly. 'That boy Parsons. The police gave him a hard time. They had to get their hooks into somebody, I s'pose. But he didn't do it, Mr Davies. I didn't know him before that time but I've seen him around since. He plays in the Salvation Army band now. I've seen him in the market. He always nods to me.'

'What did Mr Norris think about it all?' he asked.

'What d'you mean – what did he *think* about it?'

'How did he react?'

She considered the question again. 'He was like he always is when there's aggravation, shouting his mouth off, charging around, screaming for the police to do something.' She laughed bitterly. 'Come to think of it that's the only time I can ever remember him *wanting* the police to do something. He was upset, 'course he was, but he shows it different. I woke up in the night and heard him crying downstairs. He felt it all right, same as I did.'

'What's he *like*, your husband?'

'Bert Norris is all right, at times,' she said. He could see her selecting the words with care. 'He's a layabout, that's all. Work-bloody-shy. He's done time, like I expect you know. Silly things. He likes to think he's big. He was like it when I married him but I thought he'd grow out of it. He used to nick ration books then. Now it's car log books.'

'A man who moves with the times,' observed Davies. 'Do you love him?'

She seemed incredulous at the question. 'Love ... him? Love him? Christ, that's a funny thing for a copper to ask. I don't know ... I live in the same house with him if that's what it means. He's not somebody you can love. You don't sort of connect the word with Bert ... not with my husband.'

'He's a friend of Cecil Ramscar, isn't he?'

The remnants of her stare from her surprise at the last question were still on her face. They solidified.

'Ramscar? He went off years ago. Never heard of him since.'

'He's back,' said Davies, deciding to take the chance.

'Back is he?' she muttered. 'I thought there was something going on.'

'With your husband?'

She backed away from the question by returning to the original. 'Ramscar – he used to come around and muck about when Celia was there. He always had his hands around her bottom and that sort of thing, but there, he would have a try with any female between eight and eighty. He reckoned he was big. He tried it on me once or twice...' She glanced at Davies uncomfortably. 'I ... I was younger then, of course, I didn't look quite such an old ratbag...'

Davies protested with his hands, but she stilled him with hers. He felt they were as hard as dried figs. She went on. 'He used to tell Bert that he'd like to 'ave me and our Celia in the same bed at the same time. That's how he was. All mouth and bloody trousers.'

'Do you think he could have caused Celia's death?' asked Davies quietly.

'God knows.'

'He was checked out by the police,' Davies pointed out.

'So was Jack the Ripper, I expect,' she muttered without humour.

She looked up from the depths of her teacup. 'I'll have to go,' she said. 'The shops will be closing. If you want to ask me any more, tell Josie. She works in Antoinette's, that hairdresser by the clock in the High Street.'

'Right,' he said. 'I will. I'm sorry it's been so painful for you. I hope I can do something.' He thought for a moment. She was gathering up her handbag and her coat. 'One thing,' he finished. 'People don't seem to move from this district very much. Most of those who were here then are still here or roundabout.'

She smiled more softly. 'No, people don't seem to move away very much from here,' she said. 'It's very homely and friendly, really.'

six

That night Dangerous went out with Mod and got seriously drunk at The Babe in Arms. Mod was at his most loquacious and informative, extemporizing on the poisoned arrows used, he said, by certain tribes in Upper India, the sexual taboos of the first period Incas and the history of tramcars in Liverpool. On their stumbling way home to Mrs Fulljames's house they found a horse walking morosely along the street. They recognized it as belonging to a local scrap merchant. Mod said they ought to inform the police so he reported it to Dangerous, who took brief notes. They eventually tied the horse to the doorknocker of a neighbouring house and went home to bed.

The following day Davies went to seek out Dave Boot. The sex emporium was not difficult to locate. It was called 'The Garden of Ooo-la-la'. There was a large sticker across the window announcing: 'Sale'. Davies, who had never visited such an establishment, inspected it with ever-ascending eye-brows. A willowy youth was swaying behind the counter, moving to muted music. Davies approached him. 'What's in the sale?' he inquired.

'Everything, love,' replied the youth. 'Absolutely everything. Depends what your requirements are really, don't it.'

'I'm not sure what they are,' said Davies.

'Ooooo, you lads do get yourself in a state, don't you,' marvelled the assistant. 'How about a Japanese tickler, slightly shop soiled.'

'Are the rubber women in the sale?' inquired Davies.

'Some of the older models are,' shrugged the boy. 'They perish.'

'Where's Dave Boot?' asked Davies.

The youth's aloof expression sharpened with the hardness in Davies' voice. 'Dave Boot ... oh, Mr Boot. He's doing something at the disco.'

'Detective Constable Davies,' said Dangerous, showing his card. 'Get him, eh?'

The young man brushed his hair away from his fair eyes and dithered with the telephone. Davies wandered to the back of the shop and, on impulse, slid through a curtain into the back room. He was intrigued to find a partly inflated rubber woman with an attached foot-pump, lolling against a desk. Unable to resist it he depressed the pump and then let it go, then depressed it, and continued with the sequence, watching to his fascination as the woman inflated to life before his eyes. She grew to full size, then to outsize and then to enormous proportions. Mesmerized, Davies could not stop. He went on pumping. The woman grew fatter and fatter. Her eyes, her cheeks and her breasts all bulged hugely. He could hear the rubber creaking. He went on pumping. Her expanding backside knocked a chair over.

'Stop!' The cry came through the door. A tall, thick man in a tight denim suit rushed forward and pulled out a valve in the buttocks. The woman shrivelled horrifyingly.

'If she'd have exploded you'd have killed yourself,' said the man. 'Stupid bloody thing to do.'

Davies was gazing sadly at the collapsing rubber figure.

'Now I know what God feels like,' he said. He turned and smiled without warmth. 'Nice place you've got here.'

'We fill a need,' sniffed the man. 'What did you want?'

'I'm Detective Constable Davies.'

'Yes, Tarquin said. I'm Dave Boot. What was it?'

'Can I sit down? I'm puffed out after that pumping.'

Boot picked up the chair which the woman had knocked down. Davies sat on it gratefully and Boot sat behind the desk. The youth Tarquin came through the curtain and asked if they would require coffee. Boot was going to send him away but Davies said he would like some and smiled his advanced thanks.

'Right, two,' said Boot at the head issuing through the curtain.

'But don't stir it with your finger,' Davies called after him.

Boot grimaced. 'I'm pretty busy,' he said. 'What did you want?'

'Me too,' said Davies amiably. 'Ever so busy. I wanted you to tell me about Celia Norris.'

White astonishment flew into Boot's face. 'Celia ... Celia Norris?' He got it out eventually. 'Christ, that was years ago.'

'You still remember, don't you?'

'Yes, yes. But why ... why now?'

'There's never any particular season.'

'Yes, but ... aw come on. What is all this? The police went through it all at the time. Christ, hours of it. They cleared me. They had nothing...'

'I didn't say you *did* anything,' Davies pointed out quietly. 'I only asked you if you remembered. Nobody's come to arrest you.'

'I shouldn't bloody well think so, either,' said Boot, his skin hardening. 'I think I want my solicitor along here. I can't afford trouble. I'm a businessman.'

'So I see,' said Davies looking down at the deflated rubber woman.

'And there's nothing you can touch me for here, either,' said Boot, following his glance. 'Nothing. It's all legal. Anyway, I'll call my solicitor.'

'Call him if you like,' offered Davies with more confidence than he felt. 'But you'll be wasting your money. Nobody's putting any pressure on you, Mr Boot. We've reopened the case of Celia Norris and I've got the job of checking on people who made statements at the time. That's all there is to it.'

Boot subsided. 'All right then, if that's all it is. But what difference it makes, Christ knows. I told them everything at the time.'

Tarquin came through the curtain, curiously knocking on it as though it were a door. He was carrying a cardboard tray with two plastic beakers of coffee. He smiled wanly at Davies. 'There, Inspector, that's yours.' Davies and Boot took the beakers. The youth backed out. 'I didn't stir it,' he smiled. 'Not with my finger, anyway.'

Davies stared into the swirling coffee and wondered what he had stirred it with. He put it untouched on the table.

'You remember the night when it happened, I take it,' he said, leaning towards Boot. 'When she went off and vanished.'

'Well, of course I remember it. It was bloody years ago though ... how long?'

'Twenty-five,' Davies told him.

'Yes, well, I mean. Twenty-five. It's not like it was yesterday. But I remember it all right. I'm not likely to forget it, am I?'

'I'm hoping you might remember bits now that didn't seem important at the time, now you've had a while to turn it over in your mind.'

Boot glanced at him under his puffy lids. 'All I knew I told then,' he grunted. 'Every single thing. God, I went over it enough with them.'

Davies nodded. 'I've seen your statement,' he said. 'You saw her at the youth club, she went off on her bike and that was that. You didn't even know she was missing until one of her friends told you some days later.'

'That's how it was. Exactly. I said it then and I say it again now.'

Davies mused. He picked up the coffee absent-mindedly and took a sip. Horror rolled across his face as he realized what he had done. Boot laughed sarcastically. 'Don't worry about the coffee. He probably just stirred it with a Japanese tickler.'

Davies grimaced. He pushed the beaker out of reach across the table so that he would not be moved to pick it up again. Then he leaned again towards Boot, confidingly. 'Statements are just sort of catalogues of fact, see. I did this at such and such a time, and then I did that. They're not very filling, if you know what I mean, Mr Boot. A lot of bones and not much meat. They never tell you how people *feel*. I want to find out that. How they *felt* about Celia Norris. How did you feel about her?'

'Feel?' Boot shrugged and spread his hands. 'Nothing. Nothing at all. She was just a kid at the youth club.'

'You didn't fancy her then?'

Boot glared. 'Sod off, I'm going to get my solicitor. Like I said. I should have before.'

'Don't bother,' reassured Davies. 'I'm going now. I only wanted to have a look at you. Just let me ask you one more thing before I'm off.'

Boot sulked and said nothing but Davies pretended not to notice.

'How would you have described her behaviour, Celia's, sexually? She was seventeen. Do you think she was a virgin?'

Surprisingly, Boot thought about it. 'I don't know about her virginity, I'm sure. They used to keep it longer in those days, didn't they.'

'So I understand.'

'Yes, so do I. But they were all full of it. You know ... flirty.'

'Flirty,' smiled Davies. 'Ah, Mr Boot, that's a lovely old-fashioned word, I think I'll write that down.' He took out his notebook carefully, while Boot watched impatiently, and wrote down 'FLIRTY' in capital letters and with great care. He stood back and considered it as though it were some prize etching. 'Flirty,' he repeated. 'Lovely.'

'Well, she was,' said Boot, unhappy that he had said anything, but somehow drawn to continue. 'We used to say they were PTs didn't we, Mr Davies? Prick teasers.'

'Did we!' exploded Davies. 'Did *we* now? And why should we say that? Prick teasers. Just a minute, I want to write that down too.' Boot swallowed heavily as Davies wrote the words painstakingly beneath the word 'FLIRTY'. He regarded the phrase as he had regarded the single word. 'My goodness,' he said mildly. 'That takes you back, doesn't it, Mr Boot? It really takes you back.'

'Not me, personally,' muttered Boot. 'It was just a saying at the time. You must know that.'

'Flirty prick teasers,' mused Davies rubbing his chin. 'Celia Norris.'

'Yes,' said Boot stubbornly. 'Celia Norris.'

'And why would you say that about her?'

'Because I've got eyes,' said Boot desperately. 'I could *see* what she was like, couldn't I? She had a boyfriend there...'

'Bill Lind,' prompted Davies. 'Good old Bill Lind.'

Boot stared at him hard. 'That's him. That poor bugger used to go crazy. But they were all the same, those girls. Today at least, they're honest. They *give* something.'

'Do they?' asked Davies, his eyebrows ascending.

'Surely even you know that. The kids now are more straightforward about sex and that. They don't have the frustrations we used to have.'

'Didn't we just, Mr Boot,' said Davies. He looked again at the three words he had written, studying them as though he thought they might be an anagram. 'Flirty old Celia Norris,' he grinned.

'Flirty Celia Norris,' nodded Boot savagely.

'And Ena Brown,' said Davies. 'Flirty Ena Brown?'

There was no vestige of colour in Boot's face now. 'Ena Brown,' he muttered. 'Her as well.'

At The Babe in Arms a representative of the Spanish Tourist Office was making a presentation to the rough woman who had broken her ankle while dancing to 'Viva España'. It was followed by a similar presentation from the juke box company. The ceremony was attended by press representatives and embryo celebrities who had come to try and get their pictures in the newspapers. The landlord beamed on the scene.

Davies and Mod left the bar early and in disgust, for the evening meal at 'Bali Hi', Furtman Gardens. 'I think I would prefer the silence of that lonely room to the false glamour we witnessed back there,' said Mod sorrowfully as they walked down Furtman Gardens. 'Vanity, vanity, all is vanity and publicity.'

'Commerce,' corrected Davies. He had been telling Mod about his visit to Dave Boot. 'Can you imagine a shop like *that*? Floor to ceiling with sexual fantasy.'

'And he probably does very nicely from it too,' nodded Mod. 'They say that in Arabia there are men who sell *shade* to pilgrims walking the hot road to Mecca. They put up an awning or rent a bit of wall and they charge people to stand in the shade for a few minutes. It's supply and demand.'

At 'Bali Hi' they found a new lodger established at the table, an Indian, Mr Patel, who was soon engaged by Mod who asked about tribal customs of the North-West Frontier about which Mr Patel knew nothing since he came from Tottenham. Thin Minnie Banks squeaked girlishly at the error but Mr Smeeton, on this evening disguised as a harlequin, showed renewed interest.

'One of my acts is a sort of conjuring extravaganza,' he said. 'I wouldn't mind a bloke in a turban to be Gilly-Gilly, the funny assistant. Would that interest you?'

Mr Patel politely refused the offer on the grounds that he was busy with his job as a lecturer in Metallurgy and he did not possess a turban anyway. He apologized that he knew nothing of the tribal customs on the North-West Frontier.

This was digested in uncomfortable silence. Doris knocked her fork on to the floor and they all jumped. Davies said diplomatically: 'I think the tribal customs of North-West London are probably a good deal more primitive.'

'He's a detective,' said Mr Smeeton caustically, nodding his harlequin head towards Davies. 'But he's no bloody good. Not from what we hear, anyway.'

Mr Patel smiled agreeably. 'It is very nice to be in a household where everybody speaks so frankly.'

'Detective!' snorted Mrs Fulljames, appearing from her kitchen cavern with a cauldron of stew. 'Detective!' The pot seemed to be pulling her along like a steam engine.

'Don't tell me you've lost another bed,' observed Davies wearily.

'No. But the other one hasn't been found either,' she sniffed. 'Antique. And I suppose you slept all through the racket last night. All the screams and everything. It woke the whole street up but not you.'

'What did I miss *last* night?'

'Somebody tied a horse to Mrs Connelly's door knocker. Somebody's idea of a joke.'

A glance each from Mod and Davies crept across the table.

'A horse?' protested Davies. 'I'm a policeman, not a groom.'

'It was a crime,' said Mrs Fulljames firmly, slopping out the lamb stew. Davies saw Mr Patel looking at it doubtfully. So did Mod. 'It's quite all right, Mr Patel,' said Mod, his voice booming ghostlike through the vapour. 'It's sheep not sacred cow.'

'Thank you, thank you,' muttered Mr Patel.

'The upset!' said Mrs Fulljames, still pursuing the horse. 'It kept banging on Mrs Connelly's door knocker and neighing or whinnying or whatever they do. And that poor woman came down in her nightdress and the animal walked straight into her front hall. Petrified she was, and who can blame her?'

'Who indeed,' said Davies, staring into the volcanic stew.

'Well *you* didn't hear it,' complained Doris. 'People miles away must have heard it, all that screaming and the horse making a terrible noise. But not you.'

'It went right in, right in the hall,' said Mrs Fulljames, sitting down with her plate sending its veil to her face. The meal was beginning to resemble a séance. 'And it trod on Mr Connelly's foot when he came down to see what was going on. He's off work for a month.'

'A month at least, knowing Mr Connelly,' commented Davies. 'What did they do with the horse, shoot it?'

'It belongs to that terrible man down the town, Scribbens isn't it? The rag-and-bone merchant. They got him to come and take it back. Disgusting business altogether. Poor woman.'

They paused to eat and the steam subsided as they emptied their plates. Eventually Mr Patel said: 'A detective, Mr Davies, most interesting, most. And what, if it is possible to divulge, are you investigating at this moment?'

'Apart from my stolen bed,' sniffed Mrs Fulljames.

'Well,' Davies hesitated. 'A sort of missing person.'

It was early closing day but Antoinette (Paris, Switzerland and Hemel Hempstead) Ladies' Hairdressers remained stubbornly open. Davies loitered in the lee of a telephone box across the street until Josie came out for her lunch at two o'clock. He was, as usual, disconcerted when she immediately walked across the road to him.

'How did you spot me?' he inquired unhappily.

'Spot you? Blimey, half the shop saw you,' she laughed. 'You'd be surprised how well-known you are in these parts, Dangerous. Marie – that's my friend in the salon – you nicked her brother for stealing scrap metal a couple of years ago, but he got off because of some technicality. You'd lost your notes or something.'

Davies sighed. 'I seem to remember that,' he admitted.

'They do, too. Marie said they still have a good laugh about it.'

'Thanks.' They had begun to walk apparently aimlessly along the shut street.

'Then the lady whose perm we were doing said you'd found her front door swinging open one night and you walked in and her old man smashed you over the head with a chair, because he thought you was a burglar.'

'Yes, I recall that too. He broke the chair.'

'Bertha – that's Antoinette – and most of the customers and staff knew you in some way or another. Didn't see them crowding to the windows to look at you trying to hide behind that phone box?'

'Well, I did think you had rather a big crowd in there for a small place,' admitted Davies. 'I thought it was your busy morning, that's all.'

'You talked to my mum, didn't you,' she said.

'Yes.'

'She trusts you, she does. Are you still working on the thing about our Celia?'

Davies arched his eyebrows. 'Of course I am. I've only been on it a few days.'

'What's that after twenty five years?' shrugged Josie. 'I've got some sandwiches. I was going to get a bus and sit up by the Welsh Harp. My scooter's got a puncture. I'm going by the reservoir. As it's a decent day.'

It was too. There had been a smattering of October sun through the morning and, miraculously, it now grinned over the entire sky.

'You can come as well if you like, Dangerous,' said Josie. 'I won't eat all my sandwiches myself.'

'All right,' he said. They walked along the closed faces of the shops. The white bodices of the cooling towers looked strangely clean in the sunshine. They were comfortable in each other's company. The bus arrived opportunely and they boarded it, sitting without speaking on the cross-seats on the lower deck. They reached the Welsh Harp, a shapely lake shining benignly beyond the reach of the factory fumes. Three small sailing dinghies, one with red sails, swam across its easy surface. Davies and Josie walked to a seat overlooking the water and sat down. She opened a packet of sandwiches and gave him one. It was cheese and pickle.

'Your mother,' said Davies through his bread. 'She's never got over it, has she?'

'You don't have to be Maigret to see that,' she commented, but not directly at him. 'She'll never get it off her mind. When the anniversary comes round she's almost mental.' She paused as though weighing up whether to add something. She decided she would. 'It sounds a silly thing to say, I know,' she ventured. 'But it's ... it's almost, sort of, given her something to live for.'

Davies glanced sideways at her and whistled softly to himself. 'That's a strange remark,' he said.

'I said it was, didn't I,' she pointed out. 'But it has, Dangerous . . . You don't mind me calling you that, do you? What's your proper first name?'

'Percival,' he lied.

She regarded him seriously. 'Dangerous . . .' she said. She bit fiercely into her sandwich. She had a sharply pretty face and gentle hair. She had opened her coat and her small breasts just touched the surface of her sweater. The sun blew across her colourless urban face.

'Yes, Josie?' he said.

'Dangerous, you really *want* to do this, don't you?'

'Yes, I do.'

'Why? I mean, why all of a sudden? I don't believe all that cobblers about some bloke talking in prison, even if my mum does.'

'I don't like to see something left,' he replied defensively. 'Just abandoned. Don't you think I ought to find out?' He hesitated. 'If I can.'

'Who is it in aid of, Dangerous?' she asked quietly. She opened the top slice of her sandwich and said to herself. 'No pickle in this one.' She returned her small face to him. 'Who is it for?' she repeated. 'Is it for Celia or my mum? Or is it for you?'

He felt a shaft of guilt. 'It's not *for* anybody,' he protested. 'All I know is that somebody is walking about free today – with blood on their hands.'

'Dried blood,' she sniffed. 'He'll hardly remember it now. Have you ever done a murder case before?'

'No.' He did not look at her. 'This is the first.'

'Did your inspector, or whoever it is, tell you to do it? Or are you just doing it off your own bat?'

'On my own,' he mumbled. He examined the sandwich in his hand and, carefully selecting a site, bit into it.

'I thought so,' she said. 'It's like a hobby, then.'

Father Harvey had said that. The repetition of the word stung him.

'It's *not* a hobby!' he said angrily. 'I'm going to find out who killed Celia!'

'Don't get out of your bloody pram,' said Josie. She was looking at him calmly. 'I don't know whether it's going to make anyone better off, that's all. I might as well tell you, I'd have nothing to do with it. But my mum seems to think you can do something.' She looked up and then held his sleeve. 'Christ,' she said. 'That little boat's turned over, Dangerous. The bloke's in the water.'

'They do it all the time,' answered Davies, looking up. 'People ring us and the fire brigade and God knows who else. But we tell them not to worry because it's part of the sport. They enjoy it.'

'You leave *them* be, then,' she said pointedly.

'We do,' he said. 'One day one of them will drown and everybody will moan and say why didn't we do anything.'

She sighed sadly and threw a whole sandwich at a loitering bird. It flew away in fright, but then returned cautiously, hardly able to believe its luck. 'How far have you got?' she said. 'Anywhere?'

'Bits and pieces,' he shrugged. 'It will take a while. Do you want to help me?'

She eased her eyes. 'All right. But don't let it bugger up my mother, will you. She's had twenty-five years of it.' She seemed undecided whether to tell him something. 'Even now, and this sounds mad I know, even now she seems to think that somehow you're going to bring Celia back – alive!'

'Oh Christ, no.'

'Oh Christ, yes,' she said. 'You can see what I'm getting at. I was a sort of replacement for her, you see. I'm a sort of second-hand Celia. They had another baby after she went but it was stillborn. That didn't help.'

'I bet,' nodded Davies. The man had righted his dinghy and was climbing back aboard. He was wearing yellow oilskins and a life-jacket. Davies said, 'You said a funny thing about your mother . . .'

'About Celia giving her something to live for? Yes, it sounds funny, I know, but that's just how it seems sometimes. If it had not happened, her disappearing, Celia would have grown up like anybody else, got married and cleared off. In a way she's been much more of a daughter for my mum, since she's been dead. If she is dead. No matter what I do, Dangerous, I'll never make up for her.'

He patted her hand with his half-eaten sandwich. 'I see,' he nodded. She smiled in her young way. The sun was still on them. 'It's a pity you never knew Celia,' he added.

'Knew her!' Her laugh came out bitterly. 'I've spent my whole life with her, mate.'

'You don't like her very much do you?'

'There's nothing to like or dislike. You can't dislike a ghost. I never saw her, did I, or 'eard her speak. She's just a name to me. But it's a name that keeps coming up if you know what I mean. If my mum could do a swop, me for our Celia, she'd have 'er every time. I'm stuck with that, see.'

Davies nodded. 'I see.' He waited. 'Do you think your mum knows who did it?'

'I think she thinks she does,' said Josie wiping a stray bean from her chin.

'How about Cecil Ramscar, for a start?'

'She's never said as much.'

'What do you think?'

'Christ knows. I wasn't around twenty-five years ago. But he could have. He sent a wreath.'

seven

He went back to the police station thinking about Ramscar. When he reached there he discovered that the Ramscar file had been locked in a cupboard with the divisional sporting trophies, the supply of tea bags and the tear-gas canisters. The keys were with an officer who was attending the magistrates' court so Davies walked around there.

It was a busy day in the court and as was usual a lot of ordinary innocent people had come in to sit and watch for a while. There were loaded shopping baskets and loaded expressions in the public seats. He entered as stealthily as he could, falling over a wheelbarrow which was being used as an exhibit in the case being heard. Everyone turned to see him. The public laughed, the police and the magistrates sighed, the man in the dock pointed a stare at him, a look threaded with uncertainty. Davies nervously recognized him as the man he had helped with the sack of vegetables over the allotment hedge a few nights previously. He sidled out of the accused's sight.

The prisoner was being called from the dock to give evidence on his own behalf in the witness box. He dismounted one stand to mount the other, reading the oath in a suitably earthy voice. Davies looked around for the sergeant who had the key to the police station cupboard.

He saw him squatting at the end of a row of policemen waiting to give evidence in the court's crowd of cases. Davies advanced with dainty clumsiness, hunched low in the way of a soldier moving under fire, until squatting in his piled overcoat by the officer he persuaded him to surrender the key. He was aware of the court proceedings freezing all around him. He looked up to see the Godlike faces of the magistrates high on their dais regarding him sourly. The rest of the people were either standing or leaning, trying to get a view of the dwarf in the voluminous raincoat who had wafted so clumsily across the floor.

'Mr Davies, is it?' asked the chairman of the bench, knowing perfectly well that it was.

'Yes, your honour,' replied Davies still crouching criminally.

'Will you be long?'

'No, sir. Sorry, sir. Just getting the key to the police station cupboard.' He looked up beggingly to the uniformed sergeant, who, red to the cheekbones, searched and eventually found the key and delivered it to him. Davies began to retrace his progress through the court still at his midget's crouch.

'Mr Davies,' called the chairman. 'There's no need for you to continue with this impersonation of the Hunchback of Notre-Dame. You may walk normally.'

There was laughter in court. Davies, hung with embarrassment, rose to his proper height and bowed at the bench. He backed away and was about to collide with the wheelbarrow when he was pulled firmly into a vacant seat by the court warrant officer. 'Sit down for a bit,' said the exasperated official below his breath. 'Just sit down.'

Davies gratefully sat down. The case proceeded. From the witness box the prisoner was making a histrionic plea. 'That allotment, your lordship, has been in our family for years. My father and my grandfather 'ad it. Then me. It was like our heritage. I took it on, carrying on the tradition, but then I was on the sick for months and I couldn't keep it up and the council comes along and takes it off me. After all those years . . .'

Davies found himself nodding sympathetically. 'They gave it to some other bloke,' said the accused brokenly. 'My land.'

The chairman leaned over logically. 'So you think that entitles you to go in the darkness and steal his produce?' he suggested.

'I manured that allotment,' said the man bleakly.

The courtroom door opened to Davies's right as someone came into the chamber. The duty officer nudged Davies and he took his cue and shuffled out. As he did so the garden gangster was returning to his accused place in the dock. Davies did not know why, but he let himself take a final glance.

When Davies returned to the police station his way was barred by a rowdy phalanx of boys, all noisily disputing the ownership of a ravaged-looking tortoise which squatted neutrally before the desk sergeant on the counter. The sergeant silenced the din with a single shout. Davies ducked and felt it go over his head.

'Now – who found this ugly bugger in the first place?' demanded the sergeant. Through the conflict that followed he called to Davies. 'There's another file of Ramscar stuff come from the Yard, Dangerous. The Inspector said to look through it and then go up and see him. It's in your locker.'

Davies fought his way through the squabbling lads. Several of the smaller ones had begun to cry. He shut the door of the

CID room behind him. A policeman who had been concerned with traffic duty for as long as Davies could remember was sitting masticating over the collection of pornographic pictures which Detective Sergeant Myers had been investigating.

'Hello, hello, hello,' said Davies in his deepest police tone. 'Looking for suspected traffic offenders, eh?' The policeman grinned sheepishly but rose and put the pictures back in a cardboard box. 'It's all right for you lot, Dangerous,' he sighed. 'All I see all day is idiot bloody motorists and lollipop women.'

He went out sadly and Davies took the new Ramscar file from his locker and set it out on the table. It contained reports and photographs from Australia and from America. He went through the material conscientiously, sniffing along the lines of the written summaries and examining the photographs, taken over a period of years, with Ramscar getting thicker and more prosperous as time elapsed.

There was a photograph in a separate envelope marked 'Return to Criminal Records Dept, New Scotland Yard, London'. Davies opened it. To his surprise he found himself looking at a wedding-day picture of Ramscar. He attempted a whistle, another accomplishment beyond him. Nothing but hushed air came out. On the back the picture was stamped 'May 14th 1965'. Davies turned it over slowly. It was an immobile wedding group, everything fixed from feet to smiles, with Ramscar, then in his thirties, hugging a big clouded blonde, whose hair, hat and bouquet were being dragged away by what appeared to be a near-gale. The trousers of the men in the group blew out stiffly like flags. Ramscar had a flower in his lapel and another waggishly between his teeth. Grouped around him were a team of London criminals and their loved ones. Mrs Norris was there, clay-faced, and next to her was a furtive man who, he correctly guessed, was Albert Norris. In front of the group was a dainty girl in a bonnet holding a posy and simpering as small girls do at weddings. At first Davies hardly noticed her but then he looked, and put the photograph under the magnifying glass he once more quickly borrowed. The expression was unmistakable. It was Josie.

He eventually folded the file and carried it up four flights of stairs to Yardbird's office. He knocked and waited for the customary two minutes before Yardbird answered. He had been by the window for there was new cigarette ash on the floor and there was a girl standing on the flat roof of the students' hostel looking out over the streets. But now he was back behind his desk and trying to give the impression he had been working heavily there all the time.

'I've been through these, sir,' said Davies putting the file on the edge of the desk. 'Ramscar's new file.'

'Did they tell you anything?' asked Yardbird, without looking up from the report he was ostensibly writing.

'This and that,' shrugged Davies. 'I've got a pretty good picture of him now. All I have to do is find him.'

Yardbird said with off-hand tartness, 'That's all you had to do from the beginning, Davies. We don't want you to write his life story, we want to know where he is.'

'I've been making inquiries, sir, as well. All over the place. It won't be too long before I run into him, I expect.' He paused, then decided to go on even though Yardbird was still writing, his eyes fixed down. 'He's been in bother everywhere, hasn't he,' said Davies.

'We all know that,' sighed Yardbird. 'All sorts of villainy. I told you that at the very start.'

Davies rose and took the file from the desk. 'I'll keep this then,' he said. 'I'll keep it with our own file. There was enough in that to hang him.'

Yardbird eventually looked up. 'What are you going on about, Davies?' he asked wearily. 'Christ, you gabble on like an old woman, sometimes. Can't you see I'm up to my ears in work?'

'Sorry,' said Davies, moving towards the door.

'What was it anyway? You were just saying?'

Davies kicked himself afterwards. but it seemed to come out of its own volition. 'He looked fair game for a murder charge, once,' he said. 'Remember the Norris murder?'

'He's been close to murder ... *which* murder?'

'Norris. Celia Norris. Seventeen. July nineteen fifty-one. Never solved.'

73

Yardbird put his pen down. 'Now listen, Davies,' he said angrily. 'Don't let's have any of your usual frigging things up. I sent you to find a man, not scratch about with bloody history. I had my doubts about your ability to handle this Ramscar thing, and I should have had a few more. I can see that now.'

'No, sir,' protested Davies. 'I'll find Ramscar.'

'Well *find* him then. Get out and find him, man. And stop mucking about with things that don't matter any more.'

Davies went outside. 'Fuck you for a start,' he said below his breath. 'It matters to me.'

It was a chill afternoon for anyone to be stripping. Davies felt a pang of pity for the girl on the apron stage as she went through the traditional ritual of her work. Her face was distant, her movements never quite synchronized with the music that wheezed from somewhere amid the coloured light bulbs that fringed, but hardly illuminated, the performance. There was little style about the audience either.

There were three overcoated businessmen, curled like moles. A fourth snored voluminously. There was a butcher's delivery man, whose pulpitted bicycle Davies had observed parked outside. He sat in his blotched and striped apron, watching the girl almost professionally. There were two lank-haired youths both of whom Davies recognized from their appearances in court. Sitting on one of the unkempt chairs also, occasioning in Davies a certain surprise, was a Red Cross nurse.

'What's she for? In case anybody faints with excitement?' Davies asked the bouncer.

'Nah, she ain't a real proper nurse,' replied the guardian. 'She couldn't stick a plaster on your arse. She's part of the show.'

'What does she do then? The kiss of life?'

'Nah. She takes 'er duds off, don't she. You know, black stockings and that gear. Nurses strippin' is a favourite.' He nodded disparagingly at the tableau of watchers.

A small, featureless man with dangling arms had been dispatched to find Albert Norris. The messenger now returned, ambling across the stage, passing within an inch of the performing girl's ramshackle bottom, and approached them like an obedient chimpanzee. ' 'E's gorn,' he said. 'Just gorn out the back way.'

Davies stepped between the turgid customers, whose trance he failed to disturb, and strode briskly on to the stage, excusing himself with a bow to the occupant, and then went out into the street through an exit situated within inches of the plywood wings. He failed to close the door fully and was followed by a howl from the girl: 'The door! Shut the bleeding door!' He mumbled an apology and turned but she, naked as she was, emerged half way through the opening into the street, made a violent remark, and slammed the door.

He was in a long road, a service access, behind some shops, and he immediately saw Norris, who had reached the end and was turning into the main road. Davies went at a hurried amble after him. Norris, a small man, was, however, wearing a check overcoat and was an easy target. Davies reached the junction with the main road just as Norris turned to see if he was following. Norris paused, then went into a cinema, following a series of pensioners waiting to pay their reduced afternoon prices at the box office. By the time Davies had reached the foyer Norris was inside.

Davies paid for a ticket. He stood and as his eyes came to terms with the surroundings he could see that the place was ranked with empty seats with an island of twenty or so patrons gathered together, as though for mutual protection, in the centre. Davies trod cautiously towards them. When he reached the small colony he saw that it consisted of old age pensioners, softly chewing, faces rapt, spectacles reflecting the spectacle which was now dawning on the screen. The exception was the chequered figure of Albert Norris sitting incongruously among them. There was an empty seat in the row before him.

Davies pushed along the row of sharp knees and hands and sat in the seat. He turned immediately and looked at Albert Norris. 'Can you see all right?' he inquired politely.

'What you following me for?' asked Norris bluntly.

'Shush.' 'Shut up,' chorused the aged people.

'Sorry,' apologized Davies generally. He watched two minutes of the film then returned to Norris, the weasel face set among all the small rabbit faces.

'I wanted to have a chat with you,' he said at just above a whisper.

'Shush.' 'Hush.' 'Shut your mouths,' complained the old folks. The crone next to Davies dug him in the ribs with her spiked elbow. He kept looking at Norris.

'Chat?' asked Norris. 'What we got to chat about?'

'All sorts of things,' answered Davies. 'Ramscar for one.'

He saw the man's face change even in the dimness. But then his shoulder was seized and he turned to see the angry expression of an aged man standing over him. He wore a bowler hat at a threatening angle.

'Why can't you poofters go and sit somewhere else?' demanded the man. 'Comin' in 'ere spoiling the fillum for decent people.' A chorus of threatening support came from all around.

'If you want to hold 'ands or whisper sweet bleedin' nothings go and do it in the park,' the spokesman went on. 'If you don't pack it up we'll set on you.'

'Set on them!' quivered a voice.

'I think we'd better move, angel,' said Davies.

'Funny bugger,' glowered Norris. He got up and pushed his way past the elderly. Davies did likewise. The old people pummelled them and struck them with sticks and umbrellas as they went by.

'Nancies!'

The old fashioned taunts pursued them up the central aisle. Davies put his arm affectionately around Norris's waist. Norris shook him off and they made their exit to a wild chorus of raspberries.

They walked, a yard apart like friends who have recently quarrelled, along the towpath of the canal. The afternoon had become dimmer and on either side the houses and the backs of shops and small factories stood in a cold frieze.

'Where's Ramscar?' asked Davies.

'How in the 'ell do I know?' returned Norris. Davies

decided that all Josie had inherited from her father was her smallness. His eyes were hard-bright.

Davies watched the aimless water of the canal. Norris said, 'If you don't pack up bothering me and my missus and my daughter I'm going to complain. Even a copper can't keep 'arassing you, or didn't they ever tell you?'

'Harassing?' said Davies heavily. 'Harassing? This is the first time I've had the pleasure of your company, Mr Norris.'

'But you been at the wife and Josie,' argued Norris. 'I hear what's going on. And I don't bloody like it. I'm clean. I 'aven't done anything in two years. No, my mistake, four years. So you got no reason.'

'You know why I'm checking, then, I take it?'

'Our Celia, so you reckon,' said Norris. His hard small face turned to Davies. 'She's dead and nobody knows who done it. So don't give *me* all this crap about digging the whole bloody thing up again. It's bleedin' cruel, disgusting, the way you coppers go about things sometimes.'

'Did Ramscar do it?' inquired Davies quietly.

'Oh Christ! No, no, no, he didn't do it.' Norris stopped on the towpath. He caught Davies's sleeve fiercely. 'Listen, mate,' he said firmly. 'Ramscar *didn't* do it. Let me tell you that for gospel. He was at Newmarket. Do you think I would have kept it quiet? She was my girl, you know.'

Davies stared at the bitter face. 'Where's Ramscar now?' he said.

Norris began to walk on angrily. 'I told you, I don't know. He cleared off abroad years ago. I thought even the police knew that.'

'I've heard he is back,' replied Davies. A duck moved unemotionally along the canal and was followed by its mate, cruising under the bridge. Davies wondered if their feet ever got cold.

'Well you know more than I do,' said Norris. 'I ain't seen anything of 'im. You'd better ask somebody else.'

'What happened to his wife?' asked Davies. He could see that Norris was genuinely astounded.

'Wife! Christ almighty, that only lasted a month. Fuck me

– his wife! I'd forgot all about her. God only knows where she's gone. I don't.'

'What was her name?'

Norris stopped and spread his sharp hands. 'I don't know, Mr Davies, I don't know. Straight up. Elsie or Mary or something, I don't know. I hardly knew her. It was bloody years ago.'

'May fourteenth, nineteen sixty-five,' recited Davies. He was disappointed that his incisive knowledge had no effect on Norris. All Norris said was, 'Very likely was.'

'What did she do, this Elsie or Mary? For a living.'

'Oh, Christ. I don't know. If I knew I've forgot.'

'Was she on the game, perhaps?'

Norris considered it. 'No, not that. Cecil was very particular.'

He pulled up short as if he realized he was talking too much. They had reached the part of the towpath where the humped bridge with its lamp intervened across the canal and the tight lane ran up to the pawnshop and the massage parlour in the High Street.

It was a natural place to pause and they stood on the rise of the bridge, looking down at the inclement water.

'Why did Cecil Ramscar send a wreath?' asked Davies.

Norris nodded in a dull movement. 'My missus, I suppose, or Josie. One of them told you.'

'Why did he?'

'You're so fucking clever,' said Norris nastily. 'With your questions and bloody answers. Cecil didn't mean to send a wreath. He's not thick. He asked another bloke, a dopey bugger called Rickett, to send some flowers. Sort of sympathy, just like you'd send flowers to somebody if they wanted cheering up. Cecil reckoned it would be nice and he got stupid bloody Rickett to send them. And Rickett got pissed at the pub and sent a wreath instead. Cecil got narked and had Rickett seen to.'

'Seen to?'

'Sorted out. He don't walk proper now.'

'Mr Norris,' said Davies. 'Could you just run through the events of the day that Celia vanished.'

Norris looked deflated. 'Oh bloody Christ,' he moaned. 'Do I have to? You've heard it all from my missus. I wouldn't mind if it was really Celia you was trying to sort out. But you're just having a sniff around for other things. I know, mate, I know.'

Davies dismissed it. 'I'm investigating the disappearance and presumed death of Celia Norris,' he said formally. 'Will you tell me what the events of that day were.'

Norris leaned on the bridge and gaped at the unremarkable canal.

'What happened that day?'

'It was when I was working for a car firm. In the West End,' said Norris patiently. 'I saw her in the morning just before I went to work and I didn't see her again. That's all. I told the coppers everything at the time. But they've never done nothing, have they?'

His voice had subsided and the final words came out wistfully. Davies said: 'We're still trying. That's why I want to see Ramscar.'

'Back to him,' said Norris, his suspicion returning at once. 'You'd rather see Cecil than anything, wouldn't you? This whole thing wouldn't be some copper's plan to get at Cecil, would it? You wouldn't be using our Celia to try and get him, by any chance?'

To his amazement Davies saw that Norris's small frame was flooding with emotion. His face shook. Suddenly he turned away and leaned on the parapet of the bridge, put his head in his elbows and wept. Embarrassed, Davies stood back. He pushed out a tentative hand and then withdrew it. Norris continued to sob.

A small girl and an older boy appeared on the towpath and began to walk across the bridge. When they saw Norris they stopped and regarded him with huge interest. Davies made ineffectual movements with his hands.

'What's the matter wiv 'im then, mister?' asked the boy. The little girl had curved over and was now arched under Norris's bent body attempting to look up into his face. It was as though she were peering up a chimney.

'He's upset,' mumbled Davies. 'You two run along.'

'What's he upset for?' inquired the girl. She was smaller than the boy, but she had jam on her face and she looked determined.

Davies shrugged. 'He's lost something precious in the canal,' he said unthinkingly.

Norris looked up slowly. His eyes were blood red, his skin puffed and wet. 'I suppose you think that's bloody funny, don't you?' he said. 'Copper.'

eight

Gladstone Heights was a vantage point above a stiff hill at the back of the town. The council flats at its brow had a view and, as though to celebrate their prestige, the housewives had washing hanging like banners and bunting high up there, exalted, where the air was almost clear.

Arrayed below were all the streets, curving like fan vaulting, the dull blade of the canal cut through the hunched houses, the factories making plastics, steels and alloys, paint and fertilizer, cosmetics and baked beans. Each added its own puff of smoke to the congested sky, each ground relentlessly, grafting and grubby. Particles of grit performed a saraband above it all.

The flats – for some environmental reason – could only be reached by a steep footpath, the road terminating far below. Davies left the Lagonda and Kitty on the lower slope and began to walk. He bent like a large sherpa as he tackled the tarmac hill. The view expanded with every pace. It was said that Mr Gladstone, when Prime Minister, used to come to this spot for solace and rural refreshment. Now the fields and country trees did not begin for another ten miles.

Ena and William Lind lived on the crown of Gladstone Heights. It was Davies's second ascent. The first time there had been no one in their flat and he descended disconsolately

on the steep road, thinking that a watchman's hut in telephone communication with the summit might be a reasonable
expense upon the ratepayers.

This time he had, at least, the assurance that there was
someone at home because he had carefully calculated the
location of their flat among the piled windows and he saw
now that, like a welcome lighthouse, there was illumination
in the window. Davies thought how useful the situation
would be for anyone wishing to send signals down into the
town.

As a compensation for the gradient walk, each block of
flats had its lift and Davies waited gratefully on the bottom
landing for it to descend. Also waiting was a man who complained of the wind that rifled through the concrete doors
and corridors.

'Sometimes up here,' moaned the man, 'you can actually
'ear it whining through your trousers. Whistles everywhere.
What a place to put human beings, I ask you.'

'It's a long way,' agreed Davies.

'Stand up on this hill,' the man pursued. 'Face east and the
wind blows straight from Russia and up your legs. There's
not another higher hill between here and the Ural Mountains.
And this is where they put us.'

The lift, like a biscuit tin, came down and opened. A
woman got out with a shopping bag and pulled her collar up
around her face before launching herself outside. She emitted
a muffled reply to the old man's greeting.

'That's not, by any chance, Mrs Lind, is it?' asked Davies
half way in the lift.

'Mrs Lind? No, that's Mrs Cotter. Mrs Lind's better than
that.' The resident eyed him with fractionally more interest.
'Going to call on Mrs Lind, are you?'

'Yes.'

'Fourth floor. Number thirty-six,' he said.

Davies thanked him and got out at the fourth landing. As
he left the lift the man muttered enigmatically: 'Very nice
too.'

Nevertheless Davies was surprised when his doorbell ring
was answered by a woman in a leopard-skin play-suit. Her

81

face was carefully put together and her blonde hair assembled like a creamy confection. She idly held a large glass of crème de menthe in one hand and a copy of *Vogue* was tucked under her opposite arm. From the flat's interior came a full, but not indelicate perfume, and the sound of Elgar. It was eleven o'clock on a Monday morning.

'Oh, hello,' she said. 'Can I help you?' The tone was modulated cockney.

'It is possible you may,' replied Davies, straightening his own voice. 'I am Detective Constable Davies. I wondered if I might take a little of your time.'

'A detective!' She coincided a purr and an exclamation. 'How terrifically thrilling.'

She performed a quick, practised sequence. She let him in, poked her face out of the door, looked once each way and withdrew. She saw that he had seen her.

'Am I being followed?' he inquired to relieve her embarrassment. She laughed throatfully. 'You never know who's poking their nose in your business around here,' she answered. 'Council places.'

She led him into the room. It astonished him. Everywhere was lime green. The walls, the tons of curtains, the undulating three-piece suites, the carpet. On the settee was a green cat. 'We call this the green room,' she explained seriously. 'Would you like a crème de menthe?'

'Er,' Davies hesitated. 'Yes, yes. Thank you. It's a bit early in the week but I will.'

'It's never too early,' she smiled, going to a cocktail cabinet with a maw that lit musically when it was opened. 'I love the Green Goddess.'

'Yes, it's nice,' agreed Davies lamely.

There was a colour television in a green casing in one corner and a stereo deck next to the cocktail cabinet. He looked around for the speakers but they were well concealed. 'I think Elgar's such an enigma,' she said, returning with the drinks and jerking her head in the direction of the music.

'Yes, I suppose he is. Was.'

'Is,' she said. 'I sit here, listening, just listening, wondering what he is trying to say.'

'My whole life's like that,' agreed Davies.

'Ah yes, your police life.' She moved closer and handed him the green glass. He could feel a warmth from her.

'Let me take your coat,' she said. 'I'm afraid I like a bit of fug in here. And you have to turn council heating right up before you can even feel it.' He rolled off his great ungainly overcoat and she almost fell forward with the weight of it. She carried it to a bedroom that glowed pink as she entered it. 'Did anyone see you come up?' she called.

'An old chap and a lady going shopping,' he replied.

She tutted as she re-entered the room. 'They're so nosey, you see,' she said. 'Did they know that you were coming here? Actually here?'

'Well, yes. The old chap. He directed me. Funny old boy. Said the wind comes straight from the Urals.'

'Mr Bentley,' she said confidently. 'Silly old sod. Excuse me, but he is. Goes around talking like a professor but he hasn't a clue really. Straight from the Urals. What's the Urals, anyway?'

'Mountains in Russia, I understand,' said Davies.

'In that case he could be right,' she acknowledged. 'I heard his wife going on about it but she's as ignorant as shit, if you'll excuse me again. She was saying the wind came from the urinals. Anyway he saw you.'

'I'm afraid he did.'

'It'll be all over the flats by tonight,' she said confidently. 'No privacy. Why don't we sit down. Move over, Limey.' She gave the cat a firm push.

'Good name, Limey,' offered Davies. He hesitated. 'I've never seen a green cat before.'

'It's pricey to get him dyed,' she sighed. 'But he's something to talk about when people come to dinner.'

'I imagine,' said Davies. He finished his drink. He was aware of her nearness on the settee. He sat with his hands on his knees, as though he were in a railway carriage. 'Perhaps I'd better tell you why I am here,' he said.

'Ah yes,' she replied as though it were only of minor importance. She smiled fully as he half turned to her. Her teeth were smooth and menacing, white versions of her finger nails. 'I'm not afraid,' she added. 'I know I haven't been wicked. Well, not in a way the police would be interested.' She leaned forward abruptly and the heavy breasts, scarcely contained in the catsuit, bulged as though they wanted to view him also. 'It's nothing my husband has done, is it?'

'No. He's not in trouble.'

'I thought not,' she said with disappointment. 'I don't think he's capable of getting into trouble. What's it about then?'

'Remember Celia Norris?'

There was no quick reaction from her. He watched for it and all that occurred was a slight roll of the breasts. Her face was half away from him, however, staring at the cat which had begun to wash itself hysterically on the green carpet, perhaps in some forlorn foray to rid itself of its hue.

'The police are not still raking around with that?' she commented eventually in the same assumed modulated tone. 'That's all a bit old hat now, isn't it, Celia Norris?'

Davies clasped his hands firmly before him like an insurance salesman trying to make a selling point. 'Oh no, not really,' he said. 'Look at it this way – there's somebody walking around free today who did away with that girl. I'm trying to find out who that person is.'

'But it's years!' It sounded like exasperation. It was in her face, the lines suddenly cracking through the accurately applied make-up. Her arms she folded tightly in front of her in the manner of a washer-woman, pushing her breasts up towards her chin. 'Years,' she repeated, getting up and walking away from him across the room. 'What good can it do now?'

Davies elevated his eyes to see her standing above, confronting him. His steady expression stopped her. She sat down, not lightly, not with studied elegance, as she had done before, but with a heavy middle-aged clump.

'It keeps coming up,' she sighed. 'And I suppose it always will keep bleeding well coming up.'

'Until it's solved,' observed Davies.

'All right, have it your way. Until it's solved.'

'It came up a couple of years ago, didn't it?' he pointed out quietly. 'In the newspaper.'

'That. Yes, that's right.' She hesitated. 'Well they offered me two hundred quid and I jumped at it. *He* went mad of course, my husband. But then he would. He's such a wooden bastard, you know.'

'No I didn't.'

'Oh Christ, *him*. You've never met anybody like him. If he picked his nose it would be on his conscience for life.'

Davies was watching the cat. It had finished its desperate licking and was now running its green tongue around its chops.

'Your husband, Bill, that is...'

'William,' she corrected purposefully. 'He likes to be called William. See what I mean?'

'Yes, I see. Well, William Lind, your husband. When you were all in your teens, those few years ago, he was Celia Norris's boyfriend, wasn't he?'

She nodded. 'For what it was worth.' She laughed sharply. 'She don't know what a lucky escape she had.' Immediately she glanced guiltily at him. 'I didn't mean it like that,' she said.

'Was he always so ... wooden?'

'Yes, always. Even as a kid he was a prissy bugger.'

'But you married him. Didn't you have a baby?'

She smiled a pale smile. 'You've been checking up, haven't you. I lost the baby. I was always a loser.'

'Sorry, I'm stupid,' he said, embarrassed.

'That's all right,' she sighed. 'Anyway, I married him like you say. I knew what he was like but I thought he had a bit up top, you know, as well. Brains. I thought he might get somewhere. Make a life a bit comfortable.'

'And he hasn't?'

'Ha!' The snort was almost masculine. 'If you call a capstan operator "getting somewhere".'

Glancing at his glass Davies was moderately surprised to see that he had finished his crème de menthe. She saw the action but made no offer to refill it. 'I've got a friend coming in a minute,' she said hinting that it was in explanation. 'A girl friend, of course. Clare. We get up the West End three or four times a week. Walk around the shops, go to the pictures and that. It's harmless enough.'

'I would think it is,' agreed Davies blandly, wondering why she had said it. 'I won't keep you long. Really I just wanted to ask you to recall, in just a few words, what happened on that evening. When Celia disappeared. Just as you remember it.'

She sighed. 'Well I've done it all before. Another time won't matter. She was at the youth club playing table tennis with Bill . . .'

'William?'

'I call him Bill behind his back,' she shrugged, '. . . and off she went home on her bike. It was about ten o'clock. Just getting dark. Nobody ever saw her again.'

'Bill, William, stayed behind for a football meeting didn't he?'

Scorn quickly accumulated on her painted face. 'Football! He didn't play football or go to football meetings. Afraid of getting kicked. No, he stayed for something. Probably a netball meeting, that's more like it. He liked to see the girls playing netball.'

'Why was that?'

'Probably liked to see their drawers.'

'Oh, I understand.'

She glanced at him suspiciously. 'Here, don't think *he* did it. I've got no bloody time for him, but he wouldn't do that. Not that sexual sort.'

'The sexual sort?'

'Well you don't have to be a detective to work out that she wasn't done for her money, Celia. But *not* Bill Lind. He was there, in the club, for a good half hour afterwards. Anyway, not him.' She turned to him determinedly. 'You're talking about a man who even now won't have a bath unless he's wearing his swimming trunks!'

'Swimming trunks?'

'His bloody swimming trunks. And I've told that to nobody else. Not even Clare, who's my mate. I'd be too ashamed. He wanted to lock the door at first, but I wouldn't have that. Not in my own home, with just the two of us here, so he put on his swimming trunks. Every time he has a bath he's in there like bleeding Captain Webb.'

Davies wanted to laugh but her face was crammed with unhappiness. 'He comes from that sort of family,' she sighed. 'I've heard his mother talk about a *chest* of chicken.' She rested her face in her hands and Davies sat embarrassed, wanting to touch her sympathetically.

Instead he said. 'What about this man Boot? Dave Boot?'

Her head came up slowly as if it were on a lever. She was about to answer when a melody played at the door. 'Clare,' she forecast. She stood up and composed her face into the smile it had carried when he had first walked in. 'I'll give you a call,' she said. 'At the police station?'

'I'll give you the number,' he said, writing it out for her. 'We'd better fix a time. I don't like being in there longer than I can help. It's miserable.'

She smiled like some genteel hostess. 'All right. Eight to-night. I'll use the phone box on my way home.'

'Eight?' he said. 'You won't be home to get your husband's dinner then?'

'No I won't,' she said. She moved towards the door as the melody again warbled blandly. Davies thought how much the bell suited her.

She paused inside the door before opening it. 'I don't do a lot for him,' she said across her shoulder. 'But then he doesn't do much for me.'

Because the call was promised for eight o'clock he had to miss dinner at Mrs Fulljames's; he sat moodily in the CID room eating a hapless sandwich. He was wondering whether to eat the crust when the phone rang.

Ena was mildly brazen in a giggling sort of way. He thought he could smell the ruby port and lemon drifting over the wires.

'Listen,' she said confidingly. 'I reckoned it would be better on the telephone, but I've thought about it again. What the hell, I don't care. I'll tell you face to face. Can you meet me somewhere?'

'Now?'

'Yes, before I change my mind.'

'All right. Where are you?'

'I'm in a phone box at Willesden Green Station, Clare's gone off home.'

'I could be there in ten minutes,' he said.

'Come to the pub across the road from the station, The Lame Elephant. I don't mind waiting in there. I'm not proud. I'll be in the saloon bar but I won't get a drink. I'll wait for you, then you can buy it.'

'Right. I'll be right along.'

He needed two hands to pick his overcoat up from the adjoining chair. It had been raining and the coat was porous, doubling its already considerable weight and bulk. It was like pulling a wet walrus on to his back. He went out, raising a heavy hand to the sergeant on the desk. His Lagonda stood, as ever, open to the rain but Kitty had crawled below the green tarpaulin. The dog lay in the back seat like an ominously covered cadaver. Davies got in and started the engine and Kitty growled with it. The great headlamps of the car careered grandly through the drizzle and the dreary streets as Davies drove towards The Lame Elephant. He wondered why, if Ena Lind despised her husband so much, she talked about them having people around to dinner.

She was waiting in the saloon bar, enfolded in a coat of dyed rabbit, the space on the knee-high table before her cleared suggestively.

'Double port and single lemon,' she said. 'You're all wet. You look like a sponge.'

'My car leaks,' he explained, going to the bar. He got her double port and single lemon and a scotch for himself and carried it back to the table. 'No crème de menthe?' he said.

'They wouldn't know what that was in here,' she sniffed. 'If the masses don't drink it, they get confused. They're all bloody Irish anyway.'

Davies rolled off his coat again, considered the reliability of a coat-hook on the wall and decided not to burden it. He hung it on the chair next to him. Ena Lind regarded him doubtfully.

'You're a bit of a mess, one way and another,' she sniffed. 'Haven't you got anybody to look after you?'

'Well,' he said drinking his scotch, 'I do have a *sort* of

wife. We live in the same house – it's a kind of boarding house – but we don't live *together*, if you understand what I mean.'

'I understand all right,' she said, 'Very well indeed.' She studied the inside of the saloon bar. It was the period of the evening when it had begun to swell with people and with smoke.

'If people had homes,' she murmured, 'the pubs would be out of business for a start.'

'True, true,' he agreed. 'But if there was a vote on it, homes or pubs, I bet the pubs would win. Will you have another?'

'You've soon swallowed that.'

'Yes, I tend to get through the first one quickly.'

'I can see.' She disposed of her drink. 'Right-o then. But this one's on me. No arguments.' She pressed a pound into his hand and closed his fingers around it. Her hand felt dry on his damp skin.

'All right,' he nodded. 'Thanks very much.'

'Have a double,' she suggested. 'I expect you'd have got a double for yourself, wouldn't you? Might just stop you getting pneumonia.'

He grinned gratefully and ordered the drinks. He returned to the table and raised his glass.

'Cheers, Ena,' he said.

'Here's to Celia Norris,' she replied soberly.

He looked at her on the sharp angle. 'Well,' she said, catching his askew eyes. 'Why not? It's been a long time. She's *still* dead. Maybe, wherever she's got to, she'll like us to drink her health.'

'All right,' he agreed. 'I thought it was a bit late for that, that's all.' He pushed his glass upwards. 'To Celia Norris, then.'

'Yes,' she affirmed. Her glass ascended a few inches. '*Our lovely Celia.*'

'What's that mean?' he inquired quickly. 'Saying it like that?'

'Well she was,' replied Ena Lind with assumed conviction. 'Lovely. Nice little figure, pretty little face, suffered spots, but still pretty. Tiny bottom. The boys used to enjoy to watch her playing table tennis, or better still netball, so they could get a glimpse at her arse.'

'Only the boys?'

'And some men, of course. That's what you meant, isn't it?'

'Yes. Men. Like who?'

'Let's have another drink. If I'm going to tell you I don't want to hold myself responsible for it.'

'That's a good excuse. All right. Same?'

'Same,' she smiled. She looked quite attractive in a full, forty-year-old way. Her teeth were large and splendid and her face rounded and smoothed with the wrinkles well subdued. The stitched and tinted rabbit skins looked plush on her. She sensed his thoughts and opened the fur down to her middle so that her breasts lounged indolently against it. She smiled and he turned and went to get the drinks. He bought himself another double scotch.

'Do you always drink that?' he asked, putting the double port and single lemon on the table before her.

'That and crème de menthe,' she said. 'Mostly when I'm out I drink this. It warms me up. Green's very cold, don't you think?'

He sat down. 'Now tell me,' he said, turning towards her. 'About the men?'

'There was only one really, one who *did* anything,' she said. 'Could you guess who that was? Come on, let's see if you're really a good detective.'

'Ramscar,' he guessed.

Her etched eyebrows jumped with genuine surprise. 'Fancy you saying that,' she said softly. 'Ramscar. Blimey I'd forgotten all about him.' She thought about it. 'Yes . . . I suppose you *could* be right, too. I must say I hadn't thought about it like that. He used to hang around Celia a bit. Flash bugger. Wandering Hands Society, you know what I mean. He was a friend of her father's, and he was a crook you know. Still is, I expect. No, I wasn't thinking of Ramscar.' Her voice trailed as though she had conjured new possibilities from old memories.

'Boot then,' prompted Davies. 'He's runner-up.'

'Right, second time. Dave Boot. He'd had Celia.'

'*Had* her? Sexually?'

'Is there another way? He'd had her and he'd had me and some of the other girls as well. We were all fifteen when we joined there, at the youth club and I reckon he got around us all in a couple of years. We used to think he was terrific. Terrific. I don't mind telling you now. It's all gone a long time ago for me.'

With blunt wistfulness she added: 'I could do with him now, these days. Instead of that dud sod I'm married to. Oh, he was manly, Dave Boot. You know, sports singlet, muscles, fair hair, tanned. He used to go up and lie in the grass by the Welsh Harp every day in the summer because he only worked in the evenings, see. I came across him up there one day when I was mooching along by the water. He had pieces of tin, sort of squares, like the sides of a biscuit tin all around him. He told me it was to catch every bit of sun, reflecting it.

'We used to think he was great. And there wasn't many of us he hadn't fucked by the time he'd finished. He only left the really pimply girls or the fat ones alone. And we all knew who he was having. We used to fight about him.'

'Dave the Rave,' murmured Davies to himself.

'That's what they call him now,' she nodded. 'I've seen his picture in the local papers. He's got this disco at Finchley. I've fancied calling in and surprising him. But he wouldn't know me now. I bet he's still having them as young as ever. Could I have another drink? Here I'll pay for this one. I don't want to cadge. Please.'

He nodded, reluctant to break her story, and took the money to get the drinks. The barman winked at him, looked across at Ena, her prow heaving like an ice-breaker, grinned and gave the thumbs up sign. Davies ignored him.

He had another double for himself and found the short journey back to his seat took slightly longer than before. He would have to watch it. He didn't want to lose her now. For a moment, after regaining his seat, he thought he *had* lost her. She sipped at her drink then leaned back and closed her eyes. Her face was set and passive. He gave her a nudge.

'What's the matter?' she inquired, curiously opening only one eye.

'Oh, sorry, Ena. I thought you'd dozed off.'

'No, no. I was just thinking about it. About Dave.'

'He ... he definitely had sex with Celia then? You're pretty sure of that?'

'Not pretty sure. Very sure. I was there, mate, I was there. He had us both at the same time. The first time, anyway.'

'Oh.'

'Well, we were only kids and we thought he was Mister Wonderful.' She had closed her eyes again as though trying to recapture the immensity of Boot's muscles. 'The two of us, Celia and me, being friends, used to giggle about it and make out what we'd like him to do to us. And then, one day, he did it. Just like that. It was a bit of a shock, but a nice shock, if you see what I mean.' She glanced at him to ascertain if he had seen what she meant. His whiskeyed eyes were attentive. He nodded her on.

'Funny thing was, it was afternoon. It must have been in the holidays because we was at school then. We'd gone around to the church which was where the youth club was, as you know, to do something or other, like help getting things together for a church fête. We helped to put a sort of side-show together and Father Harvey, who'd just got there in those days, was helping us, farting about like he still does, but eventually he went off to pray or something and suddenly, in the vestry Dave put his arms around our waists. Celia had been bending over getting something and he gave her a pat on the bottom, just playing, and I bent over, laughing like, so he could do the same to me. I remember saying something like: "Not one without the other, Dave." So he smacked me too. That seemed to start it. We went out of the vestry and all three of us ran across the grass to the youth club, where he had a key to a storeroom. I remember being so hot and excited. I felt like I was flying. I was scared too, of course, petrified. But I could see Celia was just the same, excited but frightened, and I thought then, "*She's* not having anything *I'm* not having" And that's how it was.'

She had given the appearance of reciting to herself. Now

she waited and looked at Davies. He leaned towards her like a peckish dog. Her returned expression indicated that she required him to say something.

So he said: 'I'm glad he didn't do it in the vestry.'

She shrugged seriously. 'He thought Father Harvey might come back, I suppose. It was nothing religious. He wasn't all that religious, Dave wasn't.'

Davies felt weary because of the drink but he still managed to raise his eyebrows. 'Do you want me to go on?' She inquired mischievously. 'I bet you do.'

'I'd like you to,' he admitted.

'I'll need another drink, I think,' she said apologetically. 'I'm under a bit of a strain.'

Davies got up carefully as though not to disturb her train of thought. He had run out of money but the publican knew him and told the barman to go ahead with the drinks. 'Another copper in his pocket,' said the man caustically as he poured them.

'Piss off,' muttered Davies and returned equally clumsily to Ena.

'Really,' she said. 'It does me good to talk about it. It's years since I was able to talk about it to anyone. In detail.' She smiled expansively. The port on her breath met the whisky on his half way between them in an invisible but potent alchemy. He intended only to nod to her, signalling her to recommence, but his head seemed overweight and it dropped forward and collided with her shoulder and her cheek. She patted him affectionately. 'Now don't you doze off before I've finished. This isn't a bedtime story.'

He forced himself away from the rabbity comfort of her shoulder and cursed the curse of drink. 'I'm listening,' he mumbled. 'Very carefully, I'm listening.'

'You'd better. We're getting to the really wicked bit now. Where he fucked us.' She giggled. 'Not that we would have used a word like that *then*. Not in those days.' She almost bit into the double port and single lemon. Davies had the nous to reflect that it appeared to have a less wearing effect than scotch. 'You want me to go on?' she said.

'I can't wait.'

'So, as I said, we went across to this storeroom and there he undressed both of us. We just stood there like a couple of nits, hands hanging down by our sides, not daring to look at each other or move, and he took our clothes off for us. First he took one thing off Celia, then he turned to me and took something from me. Celia was wearing her first bra, but I was already two cup sizes ahead, I remember feeling quite proud of mine. He took his time over it, that Dave, the devil. I remember the sun coming in the window, watching it, because I was too nervous to even look at his face. Then we stood there, stark naked, Celia and me, sort of shivering like you do. Nervousness. I could feel goose pimples all over me. We both felt a bit stupid just *standing* there with him looking us over. Celia – she couldn't help it – started to giggle and so did I. But he told us to stop laughing and he was serious, very stern, so we did. We would have done anything he wanted. I remember wondering what was going to happen next and whether I could get pregnant. But I didn't think about that for long. He hadn't touched us, not our skin, not sexually, only to get our clothes off, but then he suddenly took down his track suit trousers – he always wore a track suit, sometimes a blue one, sometimes red, and then his support whatsit, his jock strap, and out came this great *thing*. It seemed enormous to us then, and even now, allowing for always remembering the good things, you know, even now I reckon it was something frightening.

'We still didn't know what to do. I could see Celia was scarlet and I could feel my face burning. Then, bold as you like, she reached out and touched it. I was bloody amazed, I can tell you. But she did. She put out her hand and sort of patted it on the end and then she caught hold of it in her fingers, wrapping them right around it. I thought: "Right, you're not being left behind, Ena." So I grabbed hold of his whatsits.'

'Whatsits?' asked the bemused Davies.

'Oh God, you know. Underneath. Testicles. Is that clear enough?'

'Yes, yes. Very clear.'

'Right, well I did. And I grabbed *hard*, all eager not to be outdone, and Christ, he nearly went through the ceiling! I mean, I didn't know, not at that age, that men are tender under there. Poor Dave. He tried to screech, but he had to keep his voice down at the same time in case anybody heard. You should have seen his face. It was like a horror film with no sound. You can imagine. I was really ashamed and embarrassed, especially as Celia was doing so well. But after a bit, he felt better, and water went out of his eyes, and he started playing about with us, and us with him and eventually he got us over to the club trampoline and had us both on that.'

'Trampoline?' uttered Davies from his fog. 'Trampoline?'

'Right. He had a few minutes with Celia first and then a few minutes with me. It didn't half kick up a dust too, on that thing. I remember all the bits of dust floating in the sunshine coming through the window.' She paused as though remembering particularly the sunshine. 'And that was that,' she said. 'The first time. After that it happened on and off. Not regular. Just on and off. And never me and Celia together again.'

'When did it stop?' Davies remembered to ask.

'After Celia. After she'd gone. He never did it with me again after that. I suppose he thought it was unfair, sort of thing. One without the other.'

Their glasses were empty. Davies, confident of the publican's cooperation, rolled to the bar for a last refill. It was a minute to closing time. He returned to her. She had her painted lids closed again and once more he thought she might be asleep. He had some difficulty in focusing her. But the sound of the glasses clunking on the table caused her to open her eyes again.

'Did you think that was interesting?' she inquired in the manner of a popular lecturer.

'Most informative,' he said cautiously. 'And there were others?'

'Lots,' she agreed. 'Celia and me saw him having it with a girl called Potts, Roxanne Potts, one night. He had her across the vaulting horse in the club.'

'He used all the equipment then?'

'Dave was a trained gymnast,' she said seriously. They drank their glasses quickly and went towards the door. Shakily she helped him to get his ponderous overcoat over his arms and shoulders. Then, to his astonishment, she said: 'But you don't suspect him, Dave, of course, do you? Not of murdering her. He wouldn't do a thing like that.'

It had ceased raining, but the night air was smeary and damp. He drove her to the foot of Gladstone Heights and she rolled herself close to him in the front of the Lagonda. 'Doesn't the top go on this thing?' she inquired hazily.

'Not since the war,' he said. 'It's stuck and I haven't had time to fix it.'

'What's that lump under the canvas thing in the back seat. It's not a dead body, is it?'

'Sort of. It's my dog, Kitty. He might as well be dead. He hardly ever stirs. Only his bad chest and jawbone when he's eating.'

'How old are you?' she decided to ask.

'About thirty-three or five,' he said. 'I'm not sure.'

'I'm older than you,' she grumbled as though it were his fault. 'At least three years.'

'It happens to everybody,' he said to comfort her. He stopped the Lagonda at the foot of the mountainous path to the council flats. He did not feel inclined to walk up but he could not let her stagger the gradient alone. They rolled drunkenly out of the car, and like old pals, their arms about each other, they trudged up the climb.

'Is that a light in your window?' inquired Davies, looking up to the rearing buildings against the watery stars.

'He leaves it on,' she sniffed. 'To guide me home. He ought to have been a bloody coastguard.'

Talking was an effort. Their spirited breaths puffed into the night air like the snorts of dragons. They reached the entrance to the flats gratefully. Davies kissed her on the plump cheek. ' 'Night Ena,' he said. 'I'll be trundling down.'

'Wait,' she insisted quietly. 'See me up in the lift. Just to the door. He'll be asleep. He leaves the light on but he goes to sleep.'

He eyed her with what suspicion he could muster, but her face was as roundly innocent as before. He took her elbow and then went to the tin lift. It arrived at a quick rattle and they stepped in. She pressed a button and the door closed but the awaited sensation of ascent did not follow. He looked at her, puzzled, and saw she was opening her coat and quickly her blouse. A protest engulfed his throat but she worked like lighting. Her big pink brassière was hooked in the centre of its cups and she had flicked it open in a moment, her voluminous breasts tumbled out, and without waiting, she caught hold of the back of his head and violently smashed his face into them. His cries were smothered by warm, scented flesh, but he could hear her making short gasping requests. 'I want you. I've got to have a *real* one! A real one!'

'I'm not free! I'm promised!' Davies howled desperately from the clutch. She pulled his head violently away by the hair. His senses were revolving. He knew he had the horn.

'Don't you like them?' she demanded. 'Not good enough for you?'

'Yes, yes,' he pleaded. 'They're nice, Ena. Really super. Big. But Ena ... Put them away!'

Her reply was to smash his face down into her bosom again, grabbing the back of his hair and wiping him up and down as though he were some kind of hand mop. She released one hand and it dived to his trousers. With a cry of triumph she caught his enclosed penis in a fierce grip and, amid it all, he suddenly knew why Dave Boot had screeched out all those years ago. It was an iron grip.

His hands were thrashing about like a penguin off balance. One set of fingers found the control panel of the lift. He pressed everything he could find. Three times the lift went up and three times down while he struggled with her hunger and wrath. They were thrown off balance against the metal sides and then on the floor. From that position like boxers who have delivered simultaneously damaging punches they gazed at each other. Her white balloon breasts were still swinging from her front, their reddened nipples glaring resentfully. It was nothing to the fierce look in her eyes. She came at him with her nails and her handbag. He tried to rise and she flung him against the wall. His panicked fingers found the buttons and the lift dropped spectacularly, throwing them over again as it bounced on the ground floor. This time Davies scrambled up first. He found the 'Door Open' button and pressed it furiously.

The door opened and outside was his dog, Kitty, a great wet-matted mound of hound, howling terribly. With unerring instinct it had sensed the battle and, rousing from its stupor, had lumbered from the car and pounded up the hill. Now, with the same unerring instinct, it fiercely attacked Davies, knocking him to the ground, snarling in his face and finally biting him on the arm. Davies collapsed. The dog saw what it had done and leapt on his prostrate body howling apparently with remorse at its error.

Ena Lind, weeping from every pore, shovelled her breasts back into her garments as she pounded violently up the concrete stairs. Doors were beginning to open and lit squares jerked into windows but it did not stop her sniping from the first landing.

'Serve you bloody right, you sexless berk!' she cried. 'I hope the bloody dog screws you!'

'Please lady,' muttered Davies lying against a cold wall. 'Don't put ideas into his head.'

nine

Among his unnumbered shortcomings as a detective was the fact that he neither harboured suspicion nor cultivated caution in the appropriate proportions at the important moment. He reflected deeply on these absent traits during his vacant days in hospital following the violent attack on him by two men using a dustbin.

The invitation to the attack was lying on the front door mat that night when Davies reached 'Bali Hi' after so narrowly fighting off Ena Lind and his own dog. The dog's teeth, soft and mouldering fortunately, like the remainder of the creature, had impressed his arm but it was the fiery memory of Ena's wanton breasts which clutched his thoughts more deeply on his journey to Mrs Fulljames's front door. He had permitted himself a long medicinal draught of scotch from a bottle which he kept secretly in the Lagonda before garaging the car and Kitty for the night. Then, before his hazy eyes they appeared – those breasts floating like cream, pointed balloons, wobbling just beyond reach, disturbing and hot in the chilly night.

His hands felt pulpy as he reached for his key outside the door as he considered once more what a narrow escape from rape he had experienced. Calamities he knew like old familiars but being raped was something new and hardly the thing for a Metropolitan Police detective constable to have to admit even to himself.

The note on the doormat had to be taken out and read by the street light, for lights-out in Mrs Fulljames's house meant what it said. Under the lamp Davies perceived the pencilled invitation 'For important information be by the canal bridge at 23.45 hours.'

He wondered if the message could have come in some roundabout fashion from Father Harvey. Although that conclusion did not fit the twenty-four hour timing. He did not think the Roman Catholic Church had yet got around to writing '23.45 hours'. 'After Vespers', perhaps.

Nevertheless the note seemed frank enough. Somebody trying to help him. Somebody with information to give or to sell. The thought of a trap or an ambush never occurred to him which, to some considerable extent, was why his professional career was so generally scattered with physical injury. Davies always thought the best of people.

He perceived that the perspex of his watch which that night he had remembered to wear had been dented and starred in his struggle in Ena Lind's lift. He held it under the street lamp and, having distinguished the hands from the cracks, he saw that he had only five minutes to fulfil the rendezvous by the canal. He would need to walk, for, having put the Lagonda away, he knew that neither the car nor the dog liked to be disturbed once they had been stabled for the night. He turned up his deep damp collar once more and strode towards the High Street and the sloping alley that led to the canal.

They saw him coming as soon as he began passing the illuminated shop windows in the main street. They had been arguing in criminal undertones about the wording of the message they had dropped through his door. One thought that it was a mistake to say '23.45 hours', but the other held that because it looked more official it did not engender so much suspicion. No felon, he argued, would be suspected of using twenty-four hour divisions. It was a clever detail.

The thought had come firmly to Davies that it might be some sort of official communication, the time quotation being the basis of this consideration. Perhaps after all, it *was* Father Harvey, using man-made time in his off-duty life. He remained with the notion while he turned between the pawnshop and the massage parlour, both closed and cold, and entered the alley. The ambushers began to move in then, closing behind him, tiptoeing, the dustbin suspended between them as if they were some fairy refuse collectors. Davies heard nothing until the swift swishing sound and a stunning clang as the dustbin was turned over his head and he was engulfed in a dark, closed, curry-smelling world with his head and shoulders jammed firmly and his hands flipping helplessly. They could not have found a better fit if they'd measured him.

He revolved in confusion and alarm, the darkness and the stench revolting and revolving with him. Then they went into the next stage of the attack, producing pick-axe handles from the verge of the allotment fence and belabouring the dustbin with them. Davies had never been so hurt or so frightened. The blows battered and rained on the metal, smashing him from side to side so that his head clanged against the sides like the clapper of a voluminous bell. His attackers, after the first close flurry of blows, and knowing how helpless he was, stood back and took good long swings at him, denting the tin walls with each violent blow. They belaboured his hands too, crushing them to his sides, but not his legs. That was for later.

Davies pirouetted like a large ballet dancer. Separate from all he could feel his ankles turning like cogged wheels. Each man dealt him a final blow. They then caught him by the sides, took the dead weight, and dragged him grunting towards the canal. One of the pair retained his pick-axe handle. They stood Davies on the bank of the canal and while one held his dropping body steady the other took a final cruel swing and brought the wooden weapon violently across the backs of his legs. He toppled forward and went gratefully into the canal. The two men left, collecting the other pick-axe handle on the way. They might need them again.

It was Father Harvey who heard the discordant campanology of the blows upon the dustbin (others did too, but it was not a neighbourhood where people, in general, investigated disturbances the same night). The priest had been sitting late in his study, in thought spiced with modicum of prayer, studying a plan for a do-it-yourself confessional box. The arson of the former box had caught both the insurance company and the ecclesiastical authorities in a niggardly mood and the weeks without a place to unload sins had resulted in an accumulating backlog of guilt throughout his parish. He was thus considering erecting a temporary structure himself and was biting his clerical lip over the plans when he heard the clanging of the smitten dustbin. He went to the door of his house, ascertained the direction of the resounding metal and returned to get his fishing rod. It was truly, an excuse for being abroad late at night, and it could be a handy weapon.

He heard the heavy splash as he reached the canal bank and looked and saw the two hurrying shapes by the humped bridge. He walked quickly and bravely in that direction and reached the bridge in time to see a curved flank of the dustbin, illuminated by the bridge lamp, gradually submerging like some secret submarine. His first thought was merely that some rowdy youths had dropped it into the black water as a joke, but before he turned away he took a final look, and saw a pair of trousers and attached boots break the surface surrounded by glugging bubbles.

Father Harvey had, in his youth in Ireland, been one of the

best swimmers in Dingle, County Kerry (not as distinguished as it might appear since his contemporaries were fishing lads who preferred to keep a hull between themselves and the water and never went into the sea, except by accident). Now he did not hesitate to take off his encumbering black priest's gown and his black patent leather dancing pumps which he wore as slippers. He stood there in his vest and long underpants. Then came the hesitation. He looked over the parapet of the bridge to make absolutely sure that he was not too late, and would be jumping for nothing. He saw the same trousers and bobbing boots, sighed a prayer, crossed himself and then eyes closed, plunged clumsily into the cold canal.

Dropping blindly, he struck the dustbin with a spectacular splash and clang, legs wide like a knight leaping on to the back of a steed. It sank at once with Davies trapped within it and the priest astride. They gurgled down into the cold, dank tunnel of water. The icy blow took Father Harvey's breath away. Then the stench of it surged up his large dilated nostrils. But his flailing arms immediately caught the projecting legs and he hung on to them. He knew that once he let go he would never find them again in that awful place.

The priest burst to the surface. His snatched prayer of gratitude was truncated by a full mouthful of canal, which he spat away before launching himself for the bank mercifully only a yard away, towing the dustbin and its contents behind him. He was a strong priest and – more than that – determined, unwilling, despite his supplications, to wait for Providence to perform miracles on his behalf. He reached the edge and hung on and shouted at the height of his soaked voice. His cry was heard by a man sitting through the night, guarding his allotment (there had been much rustling on the vegetable patches in the area since the rise in shop prices and the publicity given to the court case involving the vegetable robber). The man hurried to the bank. He was, fortuitously, a strong man, used to digging the London clay, and he eventually pulled Father Harvey from the canal. Together they then got hold of Davies's dustbin and brought that to dry land. They pulled it away and Father Harvey emitted a wet gasp when he saw who was inside. 'Dangerous,' he said addressing the unconscious face, running with fresh blood since there was now no water to wash it away. 'Dangerous, what in the name of God are you up to?'

Father Harvey went to visit Davies in Park Royal Hospital, three days later when they had completed pumping him through, stitched his wounds and opened his eyes as far as possible.

'It's no wonder the water went straight through you,' remarked the priest eyeing him. 'You're full of bloody holes.' He glanced guiltily sideways down the ward because of his swear-words.

'I leak all over,' agreed Davies dreamily.

'Ah, you're a strong, tough man, I'll give you that,' said Father Harvey. 'I thought we would be preparing for your wake. Even on the canal bank I got to wondering what religion you pursued. I didn't know, but I gave you the last rites just in case. One thing about us men of God, we know our rites.'

Davies attempted a smile. 'It would have been more to the point if you'd tried the kiss of life,' he remarked.

'Every man to his calling,' replied the priest, unruffled. 'It's fine to see you're still with us on this side, anyway. I wouldn't guarantee you much of a future over there, beyond, you know. Not being a policeman.'

'If it wasn't for you happening to be out swimming at that time of night I would be most certainly beyond,' said Davies. He moved his hand gratefully towards the priest who, glancing privily around the ward first, patted it with his own.

'A very nasty business,' said Father Harvey. 'I suppose the police force must be combing the area, whatever that may mean.'

'They'll hardly think to give it a scratch,' said Davies with certainty. 'An attack on a copper – particularly *this* copper – is nothing special. The Inspector, Yardbird, probably had a good laugh and asked the lads to watch for anything suspicious on their way home from work.'

'Charity rarely begins at home,' agreed the priest. 'Do you know who might have done it?'

'I've got a fair idea,' said Davies, a light coming from his reduced eyes. 'All I have to do is find them ... him.'

'It's a wonder they didn't crack your skull even before drowning you. It must be even thicker than I thought.'

Davies tried a bigger smile but it hurt him all over his face. 'One of my copper colleagues tells me the bin came from the Indian Restaurant,' he said. 'It had a lining of dried curry. Tough stuff that curry, especially from that dump. It saved my life.' He regarded Father Harvey through his bruises and stitches. 'You're a good bloke,' he said genuinely. 'Thanks. When I've got this lot over with I'll find out who burned down your confessional box.'

'I'm thinking of building a temporary structure,' the priest told him. 'There's a nasty backlog of unforgiven sins piling up, and my superiors are not being very sympathetic, nor is the insurance company. If you happen to know of any reasonable wood lying around that I might make some use of perhaps you'll tell me. I saw some very decent planks in the yard of Swindell's the undertakers, but I'm not sure that would morally be quite correct. Sitting there tight surrounded by the best cedar would make me feel uncomfortable. I'll be long enough in my coffin when I truly get there.'

'Better than being scuttled in a refuse bin,' said Davies. 'Did you run up any expenses, by the way? You know, with your clothes being waterlogged and everything?'

The priest shook his head. 'My underwear was dry by the morning. I put it over the church boiler. The only charge will be for the dry cleaning of my clerical gown which I threw off before throwing myself into the canal. Unfortunately I tossed it into a particularly filthy puddle. I'll send you the bill. At the cleaners they always charge it as a maxi-coat.'

Mrs Fulljames and Doris came through the door of the ward and stood there in plastic truculence; one pink and one sky blue crinkly and crackly raincoat with transparent overshoes of the same synthetic material tied about their ankles, imprisoning their feet like specimens. They remained stiffly at the door, the raindrops dripping from their gulleys and gutters like melting ice. They examined Davies at that distance, squinting their eyes and screwing up their faces, backing their heads away, as though trying to get a true perspective of his injuries. He sat taut and propped in bed, wondering why they had come.

'Fine bloody mess you look,' snorted Mrs Fulljames from the door.

'Yes, a fine mess,' confirmed Doris loyally.

Davies believed he heard Mrs Fulljames snap her fingers and the two plastic dragons advanced on him, their scales creaking as they strode. But he was spared. A voice croaked at the distant end of the room and caught his landlady's attention. 'Oh, just look, Doris,' she said in a pleased way. 'There's that polite Mr Wellington, who used to be our milkman.'

'So it is. Mr Wellington,' agreed Doris. When she smiled Davies sometimes thought he caught a distant glimpse of her youth. But it was soon gone. 'Wonder why he's in?'

'Let's go and see the poor soul,' said Mrs Fulljames. She wheeled stiffly, luffing like a sea-soaked sailing barge and made for the extreme end of the ward. Doris, with not so much as a splintered glance at her husband, followed obediently. They waved wet waves to Mr Wellington as they went. Davies astonished himself by experiencing a touch of jealousy. He eased himself up in his bed and saw the milkman sitting up in real excitement and anticipation.

It was almost ten minutes before they returned. 'Such an interesting man, that,' chuffed Mrs Fulljames, as though that was an entire and acceptable excuse for their divergence. 'He's so polite, isn't he, Doris? And he's been everywhere.'

'Milkmen usually have,' observed Davies painfully.

Doris stared at her husband's dented and stitched countenance. 'He's eaten your Smarties,' she said bluntly, as though wanting to get it over with. 'I brought you some Smarties, but Mr Wellington's had them.'

Once more Davies felt illogically hurt. He scowled and the pain told him not to do it again. 'Thanks for bringing them anyway,' he muttered. 'It's the thought, really, I suppose.'

'Of course it is!' interpolated Mrs Fulljames extravagantly.

She hovered across his sheets now as though enjoyably anticipating performing an operation on him.

'And he's *so* interesting,' echoed Doris, still with a hint of guilt. 'He's done *so* many things.'

'He's eaten my fucking Smarties for a start,' grumbled Davies bitterly.

Mrs Fulljames held up a restraining arm like a point-duty policeman. Some rain, as if retained by capillary action in the creases of her pink plastic sleeve, now drizzled on to his sheet. 'We will send some more,' she said in her final way. 'So stop being a misery. You don't look as though you could manage a Smartie anyway.'

'I expect they feed you by tubes, don't they?' agreed Doris. 'You'd never get a Smartie down a tube.'

'Anyway, you know what *you* did, don't you?' asked Mrs Fulljames.

'I gather,' said Davies wearily. 'That I got a dustbin put over my head, was then bashed about something fearful, and finally knocked in the canal.'

'You also left the front door open,' said Doris frostily. 'Your key was in it.'

'Oh?'

'And somebody walked in and stole the hallstand,' Mrs Fulljames finished it for her, perhaps afraid Doris might not achieve the right emphasis. 'My antique hallstand.'

'Antique?' queried Davies. 'That object was antique?'

'It belonged to Mr Fulljames,' muttered Doris, indicating that was a mark of authenticity. 'The late Mr Fulljames.'

'Perhaps that Persian bloke – the one who nicked the bed – has been on the prowl again,' suggested Davies dismally.

'You're being frivolous,' said Mrs Fulljames haughtily. 'I'll bet you're laughing all over your face behind that mess. Anyway we didn't come here to argue. How long will you be in?'

'Christ knows. The embroidery class is coming back tomorrow. I reckon they're going to try and keep me as a demonstration model or something.'

'How long?' insisted Doris. 'Tell Mrs Fulljames.'

'I don't know!' He managed that most difficult of all vocal achievements, a quiet shout.

'Do you want your room kept? That's the point.'

Davies was horrified. 'My room? You *wouldn't* let my room?'

'It's economics, Mr Davies. That's how we have to live. Surely even you know that.'

'Jesus wept. Don't let it. I'll keep paying.'

'In that case, all right,' sniffed Mrs Fulljames indicating a load had been taken off her mind. 'We'll discuss the hallstand at some other time. I don't feel up to it now.'

'Nor me,' muttered Davies trying to slide under the sheet.

She produced a newspaper from her plastic folds. 'I brought you this,' she said as though they had reached a truce. '*Evening News*. Last night's. But in here it makes no difference, I suppose.'

'None at all,' he agreed defeatedly. 'The world hardly exists.'

They backed towards the door. Then Doris, unexpectedly, gave a little birdlike dart forward and kissed him on his sore cheek. A final minor cascade of trapped rain escaped from her hat on to his face. 'Bye, then,' she said, then anxiously: 'You've, you've got your insurances all paid up, haven't you?'

Mod Lewis came through the door like a felon. 'I'm not all that keen on this place,' he explained on tiptoe when he reached to the foot of Davies's bed. 'I was a porter here once, you know, during the crime wave. Someone kept stealing the patients' false teeth. By night, see.'

He rolled his eyes melodramatically. 'Everybody was suspect, boy. Even the consultant surgeons. Everybody got left with a nasty taste in their mouths. Especially the patients.' He advanced around the side of the bed to Davies, as though his experience as a porter had given him some professional knowledge. 'Aye, that's better,' he said, surveying the swollen face approvingly. 'Nice job they've done there, those sutures. It'll all go back in place eventually. It's subsided even now.'

'You've been in to see me before?'

'Oh yes, man. Course I have. The first morning, as soon as I heard. It was a good excuse for not going to the library. But you looked very poorly, Dangerous. Never saw a face like it.'

Your head was all swelled up. Reminded me of the old globe of the world we had at school. That was knocked about too. I sat with you for an hour or more. You were right out and since I had nobody to talk to I amused myself by tracing the major rivers, sea and air routes on your face – and the railways, of course, most interesting.'

'That's one thing about me, I'm never boring,' said Davies. 'Do you think you could get a message to a young woman for me.'

'Josie,' said Mod confidently. 'She's coming in tonight. She read it in the local paper and she came into The Babe in Arms. Nice little girl. Bit skinny. Bit young for you. She wanted to come this morning but I said I'd come first. Just to see you were passable.'

'Am I?'

'Passable,' nodded Mod, but with some doubt. 'You're sort of going down from when I last viewed you. Who did it?'

'Ramscar, his lot. It must have been,' said Davies quietly. 'Out to kill me, I suppose.'

'Davus sum non Oedipus,' quoted Mod, looking at him glumly. 'Publius Terence, Roman poet.'

'What's it mean?' asked Davies.

'I am a simple man, no solver of riddles,' obliged Mod. 'I read it yesterday and I thought how fitting it was.'

He had been standing but now he pulled the small visitor's chair confidently to the bedside. 'But you must be standing on *somebody's* toes, that's for certain,' he said.

'In my blundering sort of way,' agreed Davies.

'Ever thought that's maybe why you were put on to the Ramscar business in the very beginning?' suggested Mod. 'Maybe they didn't want anybody who'd be too ... well ... subtle.'

'Everybody who comes in here is so kind,' sighed Davies. 'Is anybody feeding my dog?'

'Mr Smeeton, The Complete Home Entertainer,' Mod told him. 'I tried to feed the foul thing but it bit me. So I sent Mr Smeeton. He went along in his dog outfit, on the way to one of his performances. He says he is coming to see you.'

'Not in one of his costumes, I hope.'

'Probably,' said Mod. 'He said he'd come by on the way to work. So you know what that means. One of his extravaganzas.'

'I can't wait.'

A silence dropped between them for a moment, as it does at hospital bedsides. Mod wanted to say something. 'You've heard about the hallstand being nicked, I suppose,' he said eventually. Davies sensed that he had intended to say something else.

'They came in, you know,' he replied. 'Mrs Fulljames and Doris. It was terrifying. She even gave my Smarties away.' He looked at Mod through his bruises. 'What else was it you were going to say?'

'Well, nothing really. I was just wondering ... not prying into your business as a police detective or anything. I was just wondering how it was going. The Celia thing.'

Davies had spent his prostrate hours going through it all portion by portion. 'I keep turning up stones, and finding wiggly things underneath. Very odd things some of them too. Very nasty, some. But they don't seem to have any connection. A couple of hours before I was duffed up I thought I'd found a good lead, something that's been reeking for years and, sure enough, out it came.'

Mod continued thoughtfully. 'Perhaps, begging your pardon, Dangerous, perhaps blundering about like you're apt to do, you've stirred up more than one dirty pond.'

'Listen Mod,' Davies said. 'When I feel more up to it, I'll tell you what I've found so far. It's a lot, but it's nothing, if you see what I mean. You might be able to see something that I can't.'

The Welshman nodded. 'That's more than probable,' he accepted. 'In the meantime, I've done something on your behalf. I thought while you was stuck in here I'd take over on the case of Celia Norris for a few days.'

'And what?'

'Oh, I've done nothing really. Nothing at all. And I don't want to interfere, if you understand me, casting aspersions or anything. But I did *notice* something. I'm not going to tell you what it is because it would be putting ideas into your head – and at this stage they might not be the right ideas. They certainly wouldn't be very welcome ideas, take it for gospel. I'll point you in the right direction and then you'll have to make the same conclusions yourself.'

Davies stared at him. 'All right. What is it for God's sake?'

'I've just looked up the account of the Norris murder in the files of the local paper, in the *Citizen*. I take it you've done that?'

'One of the first things,' confirmed Davies. 'The press cuttings are all in the dossier. I read that right through.'

Mod got to his feet. 'Well, when you get out of here go and take another look – in the files. See if you can see what I think I saw. All right?'

'Can't you tell me now? Come on, Mod. You're supposed to be my pal.'

'Thank you, but no. Have a look yourself. I'm not being the cause of any unpleasantness. Goodbye, Dangerous. Hope you're better when I come in next time.'

'Rotten bastard,' muttered Davies. But Mod just laughed and went out.

Mr Smeeton, The Complete Home Entertainer, materialized at the ward door that evening, as Mod had forecast, his feet hoofed, his chest chestnut and a life-sized horse's head tucked beneath his arm.

'I've taken on a partner,' he confidingly said as he came across the floor. Visitors' conversation in the ward stopped. 'I've left him outside. He's the back-end.'

'Where else?' agreed Davies. 'Nice to see you're branching out. Taking on staff. You'll have to be a bit careful, though, won't you, about who you employ for the arse. It seems to me that could be a bit risky.'

'It's a clean show,' said Mr Smeeton primly. 'And I employ only clean people.' He put the horse's head down on its ear on the bed. It grinned at Davies glassily. Mr Smeeton carefully examined him. 'Nasty,' he breathed eventually. 'Very nasty. I knew a bloke in a knife throwing act who went off with his partner's wife. I remember going to the hospital. He looked just like you.'

'I do an act with a dustbin,' said Davies. 'Followed by a spectacular dive into icy water.'

'So I understand,' said the entertainer morosely. 'And you left the front door open and the hallstand was stolen. We've had nothing but moans about that around the table ever since you've been in here. She's a hard woman that Mrs Fulljames. She would never make the grade as a theatrical landlady. No kindness in her. Somehow I can't see her lifting a midget up to the lavatory chain.'

The face ached as Davies grinned. He adjusted it again. 'No, somehow Mrs Fulljames doesn't fit that picture,' he agreed. 'Thank you for feeding Kitty, by the way.'

'Glad to help,' said Mr Smeeton kindly. He stamped his hooves on the floor. They sounded real. People looked up again. 'I'll have to be going. Our show begins at eight. I hope you're out soon.' He picked up his horse's head from the blanket and swivelled one of its eyes. 'See you then. Toodle pip.'

As he reached the door, the head wedged awkwardly under his arm, Josie walked in. Her small face looked very pinched. Her stride was jerky. 'I suppose he'd been to see you,' she guessed. 'Him with the horse's head.'

'Right,' nodded Davies. 'They keep trying to make me laugh.'

She looked at his face. Then she sat down heavily on the little chair, took both his hands in hers and began to cry on them.

ten

As it was Sunday evening it had begun to rain. The Salvation Army band formed their circle, their small Stonehenge of faith, outside their Citadel, and turning their blue backs on the rest of the town and the world, began to play inwardly.

It was the wrong season for it to be anything much more than a private gathering. In the summer they often had people in the dry street, loitering, offering advice or ribaldry, while they sang their songs of love. There was, at that season, a man who contrived to do a cockney soft-shoe shuffle to their tunes. But now, in the dumb autumn dusk, there were only two outside the circle who took any notice of their burly playing or heard the hope in the words they proclaimed.

The first man was always there, at any time or term, an active simpleton who enjoyed conducting the band behind the true conductor's back. He had followed every sweep of the hands and arms for years and, in truth, performed them faithfully and well. This shadow had also acquired a Salvation Army cap from an Army Surplus Store and it gave his corded face a certain peak of religious authority. Sunday night was the gladdest night of the week for him, not because he heard and accepted their salvation, but because it was the only night of the week when he was not alone. The other witness was Dangerous Davies.

They had discharged him from the hospital with the well-meant advice to be more careful in the future. He had walked painfully that evening to the police station to write the required official report on the attack and his comrade officers had gathered around him, inspecting his injuries, poking him as though he were some manner of specimen, and discussing among themselves various wounds suffered by policemen in the past. He was grateful to return to the rain. He had walked under it in the direction of the shuttered High Street and heard, through the veil of the evening, the sounds of the Sabbath band.

Davies had always admired and enjoyed the Salvation Army. Even on this evening, drear and dun, they seemed to puff out warmth, as though the fervent breath emitted through the oompah instruments was pumped from some special Christian boiler. Standing there by the telephone box, on the second day of his two-day convalescence, the street lights through the squared post office panes making a guard across his damaged face, he remembered years ago how his mother had dearly wanted to join the Salvation Army. But

112

his father had disliked the bonnet and had forbidden her to wear it. They were both dead and gone now and he wondered idly whether part of his father's purgatory was to sit and watch his mother wearing an eternal hat of Booth's blue and red.

Davies was observing Andrew Parsons, pumping warm low notes through a tuba. He was a cubed man with a serious and solid face (which anyone who plays a tuba must have since it is an instrument which precludes a smile), level shoulders, legs planted surely astride; a long way travelled from the bag-eyed lad who had stolen ladies' garments from half the washing lines in the neighbourhood. Davies approved.

The commandant of the little band stopped the music for a prayer. Presumably as a privilege of rank he was handed an umbrella, ringed with the army's blue and red, and clutching it between his hands in the manner of some different faith with a crucifix, he said a compendium of prayers. He then commenced a sermon, taking predictably as his text (and not for the first time, Davies imagined) the assurance about where two or three are gathered together in His name, there will He be also. Now that they were not playing their instruments, the band seemed to sink lower in the street almost as though the drizzle was quietly melting them. The sermon was too long for the liking of the pseudo-conductor outside the circle and he began shouting: 'Get on with the hymns!' and 'Stop the bleeding rabbiting!' which finally provoked a bassoonist to turn and threaten, in a thoroughly unchristian fashion, to close him up for good.

Likewise Davies found that wisdom and water were poor mixers, so he slyly slotted himself into the telephone box, pretended to be making a call, and observed Parsons from there. The commandant, he perceived, seemed to shout all the louder for his benefit, or perhaps to cast his words to the windows of the street, alight and uncaring all around. His mouth opened so wide that the rain dropped in. But nobody heeded. He was a wilderness crying in a voice.

Eventually the band played again and, as if God were also relieved that the sermon was ended, the rain eased and the faces of the bandsmen dried out. At the end came a prayer

113

and Davies emerged from the telephone box to meet the demanding eyes of Parsons who was making the collection in his hat.

'Hope you've enjoyed it, sir. Would you like to contribute something?' he asked in a way that indicated that Davies owed an admission fee. Davies looked down at the floor of the hat. The simpleton had placed two milk bottle tops in there and Davies added the twopence which he had held in the cause of realism during his bogus phone call. Parsons, who, from experience, had accepted the milk bottle tops without argument, stared at the two pence and then at Davies, shaming him into putting a further ten pence piece. The coin lay like a silver moon in a black sky.

'Thank you, sir,' said Parsons, looking down into the black-bottomed hat. 'We're saving up for a new concert hall.'

The money was, nevertheless, religiously counted and after another humphing hymn and a prayer, so quiet it was almost an aside, the cordon bleu broke and its members went off through the damp dark, nursing their instruments like infants. The banner was examined and Davies heard the portly woman who had borne it, sigh, 'Sopping wet again. Take all week to dry.' He turned and followed Parsons through the streets.

'Pity there weren't a few more of us there,' he observed chattily, catching up with the square, striding man. Parsons looked round quickly and grinned grimly. 'Can't expect it this weather,' he said philosophically. 'It takes all our faith to keep us out there. Be much easier in a nice warm citadel.'

'Still it was enjoyable even in the rain,' said Davies. 'I couldn't see the Catholics having High Mass in those sort of conditions.'

'No, that's true enough,' agreed Parsons thoughtfully. 'You couldn't burn incense or candles on a night like this, could you.' He walked a few more yards and then asked: 'Are you a Christian?'

'No. I'm a copper.'

Parsons showed no surprise. He continued walking and nodded quietly. 'Yes, I thought so. I've seen you around. Your face seems to have changed, though.'

'It's old age,' answered Davies. They had reached some untidy steps leading up to one of the narrow Victorian houses. There were odd curtains in every window. 'You live here?' he asked.

'Yes. Up the top.'

'Can I come in for a minute? I wanted to ask you something.'

Again, Parsons did not seem to think it was unexpected. Davies thought that perhaps he never thought anything was. 'Yes, if you want,' he said starting up the steps and manoeuvring his tuba to get his key. 'About Christianity, is it?' he asked unconfidently.

'No. I'm afraid it's about crime.'

Parsons opened the front door carefully. 'All right,' he responded, keeping his head to the front where it was almost touching the red and yellow diamond glass. Briefly he appeared to rest his forehead against the pattern. 'But keep the noise down, will you,' he asked over his uniformed shoulder, 'I don't want the landlady to know I've got anybody in. Especially the police. She's not an admirer of the police.'

'Mine's the same,' answered Davies truthfully. He crept through the front door after Parsons. They went up the dim stairs quickly but with stealth, along a corridor hung with cooking smells and shadows, and eventually, when Parsons had unlocked a further door, into a bed-sitting room, tidy but tired.

'Never married then?' inquired Davies sitting in a cold armchair while Parsons bent to light a gas fire.

'Wouldn't be stuck up here if I did,' replied Parsons, again not put out by the question. 'I've lived here thirty years.'

'Man and boy,' added Davies. He leaned back. Sitting on the chair was like sitting on the lap of a large, clammy woman. He drew his wet coat closer to him. 'You must have been here when you had the trouble.'

'The trouble?'

'You know, Andrew. The bother about Celia Norris.'

Parsons stood up slowly, still facing away from him towards the gas fire which was now spluttering around his shins. There was a mirror suspended above the fire and he looked at Davies in that. 'Oh God,' he said resignedly. 'Won't you ever leave me be?'

'I know, mate, I know,' nodded Davies with genuine sympathy. 'These things follow you.'

'Hardly anybody knows now about my stupidness in those days. I keep hoping it's all past and done and over. What's your name anyway?' He turned away from the wall and the mirror.

'Davies. Detective Constable.'

'Ah, you're the one they call Dangerous Davies.'

'Everybody knows,' sighed Davies.

'It can't be very important if they send you,' said Parsons bluntly. 'Not a constable.'

'Routine,' said Davies not allowing his annoyance to appear. 'Purely routine. Something's come up, about the Celia Norris case, that's all. Maybe a new lead.'

'After – what is it – after twenty-odd years? I would have reckoned all the leads were as dead as she is,' muttered Parsons. He sat down in an identically worn armchair opposite Davies so that they flanked the gas burner. Only one element was burning.

'People change their minds, think about things differently, say things they wouldn't have said at the time.' Davies repeated, as much to reassure himself as inform Parsons.

'That is all very well,' said Parsons his tone weary. 'But you look at it from my point of view. I've tried to live it down, forget it. People have just about forgotten it now, around here, and I don't want them remembering.' He looked up with a small fierce desperation at Davies. 'It's taken me two years to learn to play that tuba,' he said.

'I'm really sorry,' answered Davies. 'But there's no need to worry. If we can get through this now it will be all over, done, and nobody will ever know any different.'

'Until the next time.'

'There won't be any next time,' urged Davies, leaning towards him. 'Not if we can clear it up this time, with your help and the help of others, then it will be over for ever. It's going to be painful, for you, I understand that very well, but it needn't take long.'

116

Parsons sighed and clasped his hands before him. Then he rose and put his tuba away in a cupboard as though to keep it from knowing what was going to be said by and about the man who blew into it. Parsons returned to the chair. 'I don't drink,' he said. 'So I can't offer you anything.'

'Forget it,' said Davies. 'I'm thinking of packing it in myself.'

'Does you no good,' said the Salvation Army man firmly. 'No good at all. Rots your inside, strong drink.'

'Agreed. Now, will you just tell me, as you remember it, what happened. I've read the statement that you made at the time, like I've read all the others, but I'm asking people to repeat them because now, after all this time, they may just possibly say something different that will provide a lead.'

'All right, but there's just one thing, Mr Davies. I don't *do* that any more. Understand? You know, the knickers thing. It's all gone and I'm cured. I was only a kid then and I was lonely. You never think of youngsters being lonely, do you? It was the loneliest time of my life. Now, what with the Salvation Army and the tuba and everything, I've got plenty to keep my mind occupied. No more knickers.'

'Just go on,' Davies encouraged. 'I understand all you've said. We all do things we're embarrassed about at some time in our lives. Me, not excepted . . .'

'Oh,' said Parsons interested. 'What have you done?'

Davies knew he was beginning one of his familiar spirals. The suspect was interrogating him. 'Never mind,' he said firmly. 'Just start off *now* and tell me how you remember it.'

It took twenty minutes. How he had found the girl's clothes in the all-night toilet, but minus the knickers. How he had kept them until he realized, from the newspapers, that they were the garments of Celia Norris. How he had taken them to the toilet again and been seen by the attendant. It had not become any the less pathetic over the years, nor diminished because a grown man was talking about the foibles of a boy. The story was retold in a flat voice. Parsons sat, his head almost between his knees, never once looking up. When he did, at the conclusion, raise his head, Davies saw that his eyes were streaming.

'All right,' said Davies getting up and patting him on the level shoulder. 'I'm sorry, Mr Parsons. Thanks for going over it. I just wanted to get the public bog thing straight, that's all.'

'Is that all now? Is that the lot?'

'Well, I hope so. I can't promise I won't be back. There may just be one or two points. You never know. Anyway, thanks.' He felt it would be wrong to offer the man his hand so he turned and went out of the door and along the corridor. He had gone down the first three stairs when Parsons called after him from the door, in a sudden burst of tears. His voice trembled as he tried to cry out and keep it quiet at the same time. 'And good riddance too! To bad rubbish!'

Davies waved his hand sadly in the shadows and continued down. Parsons closed the door and quietly sobbed against its panels. 'Next time put something decent in the collection too,' he sniffled. 'Mean copper.'

He went, almost dragging himself to the bed, and began to take his stiff uniform off. He took off his tunic and trousers and folded them over a chair. He shivered and he saw that the single bar of the gas fire had gone out. It was cold standing there in his brassière and panties.

The police station charwoman was languidly washing down the noticeboard when Davies arrived in the morning. The front steps had also been washed down and the brass handle on the door shone with odd brilliance. It was almost as if they had cleaned up the place to welcome him back.

'Waste of time this is,' said the cleaning woman, eyes drifting aloft as she washed the grime from the glass of the notice board. 'No sooner it's done than it's filthy again. This was always a dirty station, Mr Davies.'

'At least you can see through the glass now,' observed Davies chattily. She made a swift examination of his damaged face but made no comment, apparently concluding, not unreasonably, that it went with the job. He leaned closer, examining the several newly-revealed photographs of Wanted Criminals. 'It's time it had a clean,' he joked. 'According to this we're still looking for Charlie Peace.'

'Good luck to him, I say,' she replied, his observation

foundering. 'It's a wonder you lot catch anybody. Not the way this place is run.'

Inside the station, the duty sergeant patiently tried to assemble the physique of a lost dog. He had taken the chart of known breeds from the wall and was holding it up for a wiry old lady to point out the type most approximately to her missing friend. 'He's got a head like that ... and, let me see ... a body like that and ... oh, yes a nice stubby tail like that ... and long legs – like that one there.'

'That makes him a camel,' murmured the sergeant, writing patiently in his book.

A haunted pair of eyes leaned over the top of the charge room door and two mislaid children awaiting their mother sat on the corridor bench playing 'Find the Lady'.

Police Constable Westerman had been stricken with another nose-bleed and was sprawled in the CID room looking like a riot casualty while someone went to get the cell keys to drop down his back.

'The gov'nor wants to see you, Dangerous,' he said bravely through the blood. 'Are you feeling better?'

Davies was touched that the first inquiry after his health had come from one who was so riven with suffering. 'Much better, thank you,' he smiled painfully. 'You're not too good, I take it.'

Westerman decided not to risk taking away the scarlet handkerchief again, so he merely rolled his eyes tragically. Davies went upstairs, knocked on Superintendent Yardbird's office, and, at the call two minutes later, went in.

Yardbird looked at his scarred face but his expression did not change. There might have been more reaction if Davies had been wearing a different suit.

'We're all very pleased,' said Yardbird.

'Oh, good, I'm glad,' said Davies painfully. Every stitch seemed to hurt.

'Well these things happen when you're a policeman,' said Yardbird. He got up from his desk and went, as though by habit towards the window. The rooftops were like a frozen sea. There was no sign of movement from the Students' Hostel. 'All good experience for you, Davies.'

'Yes sir. Splendid.'

'And it shows that you've stirred him up. Ramscar. It shows he's worried. That's what the Special Braach are pleased about. I bet he's had you followed ever since you started asking questions about him.'

Davies nodded. He remembered the man with no glass in his spectacles. 'I expect they have, sir,' he muttered.

'If you'd kept your eyes open you wouldn't have walked into it. And, for Christ's sake man, fancy just falling in their laps by taking any notice of a note put through your letter box. And going alone. That was the stupid thing. Sometimes I don't think you'll ever make it, Davies.'

'Sometimes I think that myself, sir,' Davies had to admit.

'Well, anyway, all's well that ends well. We know at least that they've risen to the bait.'

'Yes,' nodded Davies. 'Even when I'm the bait.'

'Listen, Davies,' said Yardbird turning from the window. 'You can jack this in, if you wish. I'll get somebody else on it. I was thinking about doing that anyway.'

'No, no, I'll be all right, sir,' protested Davies. 'I've got a little score to pay back to Mr Ramscar now. Nobody puts a dustbin over me and gets away with it.'

'All right,' said Yardbird. 'And I take it you're concentrating on this now and not digging up old murders.'

'Yes, I am.'

'Good, Christ, if every copper in the Metropolitan Police spent his time raking up unsolved crimes the Ramscars of this world would have a bloody marvellous time. It would be mayhem. Get your priorities straight, for God's sake. I hope you won't be wanting sick leave because of this?'

'I'm working now,' said Davies evenly. 'When it's over perhaps I'll take some leave then. Let the stitches heal properly. I think I'd like to go and see my uncle in Stoke-on-Trent.'

'Good,' said Yardbird, returning to his desk. 'Might do you the world of good. Now, go and find Ramscar.'

eleven

That night Dave Boot was wearing his best hair, a reddish confection clouding to orange around his clay face. His suit of lights danced and his body lit up with violent, violet flashes, as the console before him hammered out its songs of popular wisdom and illumination. He was pleased to see a big crowd, but not entirely surprised since Mondays was free entry when he hoped to salvage at the bar what was lost at the turnstiles.

From his rostrum Boot was thinking how tall teenagers grew in these times. He could see them standing silhouetted like trees against the vermilion walls at the back of the room. Then the tallest and widest tree of all swayed forward clumsily through the wobbling dancers and Boot saw that it was Dangerous Davies.

Boot found himself shaking within as well as without. He watched Davies come nearer, trying to dance but all out of beat, treading and kicking the young people around him so that they pushed and elbowed him in retaliation. He was shepherding a small, pinched, dark-haired girl. They neared the flashing hues of the rostrum. The illuminated Boot leaned over angrily. 'What business have you got here?' he demanded.

Davies looked up cheerfully, his grin now, at last, the deepest gash in his face. 'I'm a golden oldie, love,' he answered. 'A rave from the grave.'

Performing an adapted veleta, he jogged Josie away. 'So that's Mr Boot,' said Josie quietly. 'Celia's mate.' Davies did not know how she meant that. He had told her nothing. 'What a bleeding sight,' she added. 'Like a fairground gone mad. I hate all this stuff, Dangerous.'

'I thought all young people liked this. It's pop,' Davies said. 'I wish I could do it. It would be somewhere to go on a Monday night.'

Josie curled up her nose disdainfully in the half-dark. 'I can't stand it,' she repeated. 'I'm folk.'

'Oh, are you,' he said. 'What's that? Folk?'

'Folk,' she repeated carefully. 'Folk music. I've got eighty-three long players. There's a club called "The Truck Drivers" I go to.'

Davies nodded. 'I've seen that. In Kilburn. I always thought it was a transport caff.'

She gave a half-inch grin. '*This* is the transport caff,' she said. 'Bloody orange hair. Look at him up there.'

'I think we'll just quietly hop out now,' murmured Davies. 'The dog has seen the rabbit and the rabbit the dog. That's all I wanted. He'll be worried now. We'll go and have a pint or something and see Mr Boot later. Thank you for the dance, Josie.'

He dispatched Josie home in a taxi before going back to find Boot. He paid the driver in advance and then saw that she was gesticulating behind the window in an impersonal way. She had edged the window down by the time he had fumbled with the door. Her small face had appeared framed in the aperture. 'Now, Dangerous,' she warned seriously. 'Don't – please – get into any more bother. And don't get drunk. And don't stay out late.'

'No,' he replied to all three demands. She pushed her face through the gap and kissed him inaccurately on his top lip. He patted her face clumsily and then waved to her as the taxi went away.

He returned to the club and strolled in, conspicuously incongruous, among the slight teenagers in the shadows. Boot had gone.

'He's off early,' shrugged the lady in charge of the cloakroom. 'He sometimes takes sort of half a night off on Mondays because they don't pay, do they? He's gone. But he's only just. You might catch him in the car park.'

Davies went out hurriedly. The lines of cars at the back lay inert. There was only a motor cyclist, bowed under the egg of his helmet, kicking his machine to a start. Davies walked quickly around the cars to make sure that Boot was not merely lying low. He disturbed three back-seat couples (in one car a recumbent girl had her feet pressed against the ceiling in confined ecstasy), before the motor cyclist droned by and he saw in the car park lights the orange wig curling out of a bag strapped behind the seat.

Boot was beyond the gate before Davies's belated shout escaped. Davies turned and scampered clumsily towards his Lagonda, upsetting his sleeping dog with the urgency of his arrival and the bursting noise of the starting engine. Kitty began to cough irritably. A young voice called out 'Peeping Tom!' as he made for the gate. He saw that Boot was held up at the traffic lights at the foot of the hill.

Boot had now seen him and he drove the motor cycle smartly along the main road hearing the animal roar of the Lagonda emitted behind him. It occurred to Davies that there was a lot of traffic coming in the opposite direction for a night so early in the week. He kept Boot's ruby rear light just in sight and was surprised to see it sag and suddenly wobble as the machine was turned off the road and into the car park at Neasden Underground Station. He became wedged in some traffic at a junction. He noticed it was swelling from the direction of Wembley. The delay was enough time for Boot to leave the motor cycle and walk into the entrance of the tube station.

Hurriedly, if humanely, Davies threw the canvas sheet over Kitty, who snarled, and then went in pursuit of Boot. He ignored the ticket office and clumped in disarray down to the platform where at once he saw Boot, clutching his crash helmet like a trophy beneath his arm, at the far end. A red train was snaking into the station and Boot kept calm. As Davies stumped towards him he stepped aboard. As Davies hurried the length of the train he saw that it was crammed with men. He reached the final door, the one which Boot had entered, and stepped resolutely inside, forcing himself among the tight, overcoated, enscarved, encapped and encapsuled bodies. There were protests over his entry and his bulk, but the doors closed, crushing him into the mass and that was the conclusion of any arguments.

'What you fink of the twin-strikers, then, mate?' asked the man next to him.

'Rubbish,' said Davies, making a guess. 'Powder puffs.' He

could not see Boot in his immediate vicinity. He stood on tiptoe until several of his abutting neighbours told him to stand proper. The man who had asked him about the twin-strikers stared at him, having, in fact, addressed the query to a companion beyond Davies's shoulder, a companion who now emerged and, after joining his questioner in a haughty look at Davies's face, settled into a further discussion of the game.

England, Davies perceived, had been playing, not very competently, at Wembley Stadium. 'I reckon that referee's a wanker,' said the fan closest to Davies's left ear. 'And the linesmen. Both wankers.'

' 'S'no use calling them wankers, mate,' replied the man next to his right ear, having overheard the confidence. 'Not when all the bloody forwards are wankers. And the fucking defence.'

The first man told him to shut his face and there came a verbal altercation followed swiftly by a fist fight, with Davies jammed between the two antagonists. One had, with swift initiative, grabbed the other's England rosette and was trying to ram it into his mouth. A kick landed on Davies's ankle and another apparently found a target somewhere else because cries were followed by a renewed outbreak of fighting. All at once Davies felt like an elephant trapped in a river by crocodiles. He lumbered about trying to keep out of the way while the tight battle jabbed and butted all around him. A scarf was being tightened around a reddening neck. He was trying to avoid revealing he was a policeman but when he was forced to shout this revelation the only reaction was that somebody kneed him in the valley. The entire jammed carriage seemed to be swaying with the battle, arms and fists, heads and oaths, flew about the tubular space. Davies tried to reach for his warrant card but he could not free his hand, trapped beneath an anonymous but hard armpit.

The mêlée was resolved abruptly and simply by the train's arrival at the next station, the doors opening and the bursting battle, or a fair proportion of it, being spilled on to the platform, where it rolled about with increased gusto. When the doors slid to a close again one-third of the original pas-

124

sengers were gone. Such fighting as was left in the train reduced itself to incomplete skirmishes and bitter looks.

A morsel-sized man, almost smothered by his England
muffler and rosette, had been pummelled into one corner by
the fierceness of the engagement, and now squatted on the
floor trying to reassemble his spectacles. 'I wouldn't mind,' he
complained. 'But they're all supposed to be supporting bleeding England.' Standing immediately behind him, watching
Davies, was Dave Boot.

Davies moved close to him. Even the mutterings all around
had now descended to sullenness or attempts at a sane
analysis of the game. Davies said to Boot: 'Do you come
here often?'

'Only when there's a football match at Wembley,' replied
Boot. 'Then the roads get jammed. Now where would you be
going?'

'With you,' said Davies simply.

'Listen, you're not following me to my place. I live with
my mum,' said Boot unexpectedly. 'And I don't want my old
lady upset by the police.'

'Where do you live?' asked Davies.

'You'll have to wait and see where I get off.'

The train arrived at another stop and more men dis-
embarked. Some waved their rattles in melancholy defiance
in the damp lamplit air.

'I don't mind asking you a few questions here,' said
Davies, who did mind. Boot knew it was a bluff. A sharp
expression seeped into his eyes. Both were aware that the
men around them had all produced newspapers from behind
the creases of which they were listening avidly. 'Go on then,'
challenged Boot. 'Ask.'

Indecision swamped Davies. He looked around at the ears
projecting from the papers. 'I can wait,' he said. 'I can wait
until we get off.'

'How's your murder?' asked Boot loudly. The eyes joined
the ears ascending from the edges of the pages. 'Fancy you
being involved in a nasty business like that.'

Davies glared at him. 'Shut up,' he demanded throatily.
'You're showing us up.'

'Grisly thing, murder,' continued Boot unconcerned. 'Especially being involved so deep, like you are.'

'I'll arrest you and drag you out at the next station,' whispered Davies. 'I'm not kidding.'

'What for?' asked Boot more quietly. 'You've got nothing to arrest me for. What's the charge – being cheeky to a copper on the London Underground?'

They were interrupted by the formidable entry of a ticket inspector at the next station. As though he had been purposely briefed he homed straight on Davies. 'Ticket please,' he boomed. Others around began fumbling.

'I haven't got one,' muttered Davies. 'I was ... I would have paid.'

'They *all* say that. They *all* want to pay once they're nabbed,' boomed the Inspector. 'That's why London Transport is losing money. People like you.'

'I didn't know how far I was going,' explained Davies hurriedly. He put his head close, almost affectionately next to the inspector's bristly neck. 'I'm a police officer,' he whispered.

'Oh, are you now? I've heard that one as well,' claimed the inspector with a booming grin. 'Well, sir, can I see your warrant card?'

The entire compartment now stood expectantly grouped to watch Davies produce his warrant card. Those without a good vantage stood on the seats or levered themselves up on the hangers. Boot stood watching Davies and his discomfiture with an adjacent smile.

'Warrant card?' said Davies. 'Oh, all right. This is very inconvenient I can tell you.' Even as his hand went to his pocket he knew it would not be there. He remembered last seeing it on his bedside table back at Mrs Fulljames's. The hand returned empty-handed. The other hand went into the other inside pocket and then to the outside enclosures of his coat. 'I had it,' he protested desperately. 'Somebody must have picked my pocket.'

The inspector laughed knowingly. 'You haven't got a warrant card, you haven't got a ticket, and you don't know where you're going until you get there. Does that sum it up, sir?'

Davies nodded miserably. 'I'm afraid it does. But I am a policeman, honest.'

'He's a friend of mine,' nodded Boot. 'I can vouch for him. And I've got a ticket.'

'Are you a policeman, sir?' inquired the inspector looking at Boot with a respect that he had not wasted on Davies. 'No. But I can identify myself.' He went quickly to his pocket. 'These are my business cards. And here's a letter from the Mayor of Neasden in connection with some charity work I am performing. It has my address on it.'

Davies, on instinct, tried to get a sight of the address but the inspector, giving him a quick, foul look, took it out of his view. 'Mr Boot!' said the inspector. 'Ah yes, I know you! From my boxing days in Willesden. Remember you well, Mr Boot.' He glanced, still disparagingly at Davies. 'Well, if you can vouch for him, that's good enough for me. He'll have to pay his fare though. He won't get away with that.'

'I'll see he pays it to the ticket collector when we get out. We don't know how far we're going yet.'

'Oh, all right. I'll trust him then,' said the inspector. He turned to the white-faced Davies. 'Now I'm putting you in Mr Boot's charge,' he said. He wagged a big, red finger. 'And just remember – you're on your honour.'

Passengers left the train at every station and few boarded to take their places. When the adjoining seats became vacant Boot, enjoying himself, rolled his eyes suggestively and Davies grumpily followed him to them. Eventually there remained only a mothy-looking woman near them and two men, both wearing England rosettes as big as their faces, who sat at the extreme end of the carriage, on opposite seats, contemplating each other in antagonistic silence.

Davies frowned at the passing stations and then at the map. The train was under the Thames and heading for home at the Elephant and Castle. Boot was clamped in silence, taking a newspaper out of his pocket and reading it minutely. Davies sat uncomfortably. The mothy woman stood up and gathered her spreadeagled belongings to her, eventually, and got from the train. Now there only remained the two men and they were at the far end. 'All right,' sighed Boot, folding away his paper. 'What's it all about?'

'I hope you enjoyed your fun,' replied Davies sourly.

'I saved you from being thrown off the train for not paying your fare. You might have even been arrested,' Boot pointed out.

'Yes, very good of you, mate. Now where exactly are we getting off?'

'I'm not getting off,' said Boot firmly. 'You can if you like. But I told you, I don't want any copper following me home and upsetting my mum. It's not as if you've got a warrant or anything. Like I told you before, my solicitor ought to be present.'

'She means a lot to you, your mum,' commented Davies.

'Funnily enough she does,' replied Boot sharply.

'Did you use to go home to your mum in the old days – in the good old days, remember? Did you go home to her after screwing Roxanne Potts on the vaulting horse?'

'Who the hell ...!'

'Roxanne Potts, now there's a name to conjure with.'

Boot looked miserably thoughtful. 'Jesus, you've been busy digging them up, haven't you. Roxanne Potts. She must be forty-odd now.'

'She was fifteen then,' said Davies quietly. 'So was Ena and so was poor dead Celia Norris. Remember the trampoline? Nobody could accuse you of not using the equipment.' He made a bouncing movement with his hands. 'Davy go up, Davy go down. Davy go up ...'

'Pack it in, will you, you bastard,' snorted Boot. He looked along to see if the men at the far end of the carriage were listening. They had stood up to get out. The train was at the end of the line. They looked around curiously at Davies and Boot, then stepped down and hurried away with collars pulled around their ears. As each of them walked past the window their eyes came around the sharp end of their collars to look at the two who remained in the train.

'Elephant and Castle,' said Boot, half getting to his feet. 'It stops here.'

Davies eased him back into the seat. 'But I don't,' he said.

'Now we've travelled so far together I want you to listen for a while and then I want to hear your story too. I suggest you do it now, Booty, because later it could make things much nastier for you.'

Boot sat down. 'We can't sit here,' he argued lamely. 'The train's finished for the night.'

'We'll wait until they throw us off,' said Davies cheerfully. 'It's warm and comfortable and it's quiet. We can talk.'

'Who's been talking to you?' asked Boot. 'Roxanne Potts?'

'No. I haven't had the pleasure of meeting Roxanne. Try again.'

'That Ena.'

'That Ena it was,' approved Davies. 'Ena Brown that was. Ena Lind that is. She married dashing Bill Lind, you know, and now lives in a council penthouse overlooking the entire world. You know, she's even got a green cat.'

'Sometimes,' observed Boot, 'You sound like you're drunk when you're not.'

'You don't believe she's got a green cat? I'll take you along to see it if you like. It's really something to see.'

'No. No thanks. I'll pass on that one.'

'Ena would love to see big muscled Dave again. You could wear a singlet and a jock strap. She'd know you meant business then. Take a trampoline along and – provided you could take it up in the lift – you could have a rare old time together. Just like the old days.'

'You can't touch me for that, Davies. It was years ago.'

'So was the murder. I could touch you for that.'

Boot's face stiffened as though he had suddenly realized the magnitude of the business. 'And murder is a wound that time won't heal,' encouraged Davies close to his ear. 'You'd better tell me all you know, Booty.'

'I told you, I didn't have anything to do with it. Not killing her,' said Boot dragging the words out. 'Straight.'

'All the more important that you should tell me what you did have to do with them,' urged Davies quietly. 'Otherwise I might think you *did* do that bad thing.'

A London Underground man strolled along the platform, a languid West Indian, buried by life below a cold city. He was supposed to check the train but as he passed the carriage where they sat his attention was caught by a new cinema poster. He examined it casually, quietly embroidered the heroine with a curly moustache, and continued his echoing patrol without seeing Boot or Davies. They did not see him either. Boot was whispering to Davies about teenage girls who had seduced him in the days that used to be. Davies was listening. He was waiting. The doors of the train slid together in a sleepy embrace and it moved. Boot looked up, but now he had begun he seemed reluctant to let anything get in the way. For his part Davies would have detained him on the train even if he had known it had just begun a journey to Addis Ababa.

Eventually Boot had told everything he knew or remembered or cared to relate. He had not been looking even occasionally at Davies's face. Few people do when they are telling something difficult from their past. When he thought he had come to the conclusion of the story, he did glance up as if he thought Davies might have dropped off to sleep. But the big, scarred face was still watching him. The brown overcoat had settled around the policeman's shoulders like a mound of damp earth.

'We're moving,' Boot said nodding at the darkness that was stumbling by the window. 'God knows where we're going now.'

'It's no bother,' yawned Davies. 'These things find it difficult to get out of London. You hadn't finished, had you?'

'Yes,' hesitated Boot. 'I think I've told you everything, officer.'

Anger gathered in Davies's face like an extra bruise. 'Don't you fucking "officer" me, Booty,' he threatened. He stood up and grabbed the other man's lapels, lifting him from the seat. 'Tell us about your boxing days then,' he said. Boot's face stretched tight and he began to say something. Davies, however, picked him up and threw him the length of the carriage. He landed, half-sitting in the open area by the doors. 'It's all right, inspector, I can vouch for him. I'll see he pays his fare,' Davies called up after him. Boot, his features drained, looked along the seats from his place on the floor. 'You're out to get your own back for that,' he whispered. 'You're like all of those police buggers. All for yourself in the end. You're going to do me over because I made you look small.'

Davies at once beamed into a real smile. 'No, I wouldn't do that, Booty. Not to *you*. Not while we're having such a useful talk.' He walked over and hauled Boot up from the floor with excess gallantry, brushing him down and replacing him in his seat. 'But,' he said when they were seated again. 'But, I want to tell you something. For your own comfort and convenience. If you don't think of a bit more of that story, the bit you've left out, I'm going to chuck you down to that other gangway next time. That furthest one up there. And then I shall come and stamp on you for taking the piss out of me in front of all the football fans. All right. You've got that clear?'

Boot's head went up and down as though it were on a hinge. 'What *else* then?' he asked.

'The night, Booty,' said Davies, his nose almost in the man's ear. 'The night of July 23rd, 1951.' His face dissolved and he broke into a fragment of song. 'That perfect night, the night you met, there was magic abroad in the air . . .'

'Celia?' said Boot.

'Too bloody right, Celia,' confirmed Davies quietly. A little smoke of excitement began to rise within his heart. Boot watched his fists close. 'That night.'

'We had it,' said Boot. 'Sexual intercourse, that is. She pestered me. They all did. Christ, I was on the point of exhaustion sometimes.'

'Rotten lot,' murmured Davies.

'And she kept on at me. It was her turn, she said. So . . . so . . . that night I told her to come to the store after she had told everybody she was going home. And I saw her there.'

'Why did you kill her, Booty?'

'I DIDN'T KILL HER!'

His shout echoed strangely through the carriage. The train was clattering and curving on its nameless journey. Davies reached for the lapels again, picked up Boot and flung him the distance to the far doorway. He lay on the ribbed wooden floor looking around him, trying to find his breath.

'There, I told you I could do it,' Davies remarked. He walked, swaying with the train towards Boot. Boot sat up and hid his head in his hands like a frightened boy in a school playground. Davies hung above him on the straps. 'Now,' he said. 'Do you want me to throw you back again?'

Boot spoke from his sitting position, his face still enclosed in his hands. 'I had her knickers,' he said. 'I got rid of them after. But I didn't kill her, Davies. Straight I didn't. She was all right when she went from me. She went off on her bike.'

'Leaving you with the prize pants,' said Davies. The smoke within him had become a small fire of triumph. He had *solved* something!

'She ran off without them,' muttered Boot. 'We'd had a row, a dispute...'

'About what, Booty?'

'Oh, for Christ's sake. It's twenty-five years ago...'

'What about?'

'I wanted her to do something, you know what I mean, and she wouldn't. She suddenly turned all Catholic and said it was a sin. And I started to kid her about it, just kidding, and she got wild as hell ... and...'

'I don't know what you mean,' said Davies, 'You said I'd *know*. But I can't even guess. What did you have the fight about?'

'You are a bastard,' muttered Boot. 'You just want to hear me say it, don't you.' He looked up as he felt the damp sole of Davies's shoe pushing him in the shirtfront, an inch below his Adam's apple.

'That's right, I want you to say it,' said Davies. 'My imagination is a bit limited about things like this.'

'I wanted her to ... give me a gobble,' said Boot, his head going back to its hiding place between his hands. He looked up and his expression collided with Davies's look of outraged disbelief. 'You know...' Boot mumbled. 'A gobble. You know what a gobble is.'

'It's a noise a turkey makes,' said Davies.

'Oh, Christ. Stop it. I wanted her to take it in her mouth. But she wouldn't.'

'I don't blame her,' said Davies. He had become outwardly

even more calm. 'I wouldn't like to give you a gobble either.'

Boot's head was trembling in his palms. 'And that was it. She got all ratty and slapped my face and I caught hold of her wrists to stop her. I was only playing, really, but she took it all seriously. Then she kicked me, hard – very nastily too – and rushed out. I saw her get on her bike and she went. That was the last I saw of her.'

'Leaving you with her bloomers. Something to remember her by.'

'That's the lot,' said Boot miserably. 'That's all. Make what you like out of it.'

Davies stepped back and sat on one of the seats. 'All those years ago,' he said shaking his head at the wonder of it. 'And you can still remember how hard she kicked you. And all over a little thing like a gobble...' Boot squealed as the big man jumped at him. Davies picked him up and thrust him back against the swaying curved walls. Three times he banged him against the wall. Then he turned and threw him half the length of the carriage again. Boot lay on the floor, moaning. He got up as far as his elbow. 'You ... you fucking hypocrite,' he howled. 'You only do this because you've never had a gobble in your bloody life!'

He was saved from almost certain death by the lurch of the train. Davies stumbled and stopped. He sat down heavily on the cross seats not doing anything. Suddenly he felt very cold. He could see fingers of rain hitting the windows and extending down. 'Look at that,' he called to Boot at the far end. 'It's pouring. We've been nice and dry in here, anyway.'

One of the doors communicating with the next carriage opened noisily and an overalled and undersized man poked his head through. He took in the scene as though it were not entirely unfamiliar. ' 'Ere,' he inquired. 'What you doin' still on the bleeding train? This train is in the washing shed.'

He made a short bow, like a man having delivered a brief but important oration, and vanished behind the closing door. He returned in five minutes with two other longer men. 'There,' he said. 'That's them. Look, that one's got blood all down him. They been having a fight.'

Davies had, by then, fixed Boot in the seat beside him and

had put his arm affectionately about his shoulder. 'L'il dis-agreement,' he informed the trio. 'Few drinks then the argy-bargy. But we're all right now. Mates again, ain't we, Booty?' The head in the arm nodded as it was powerfully squeezed. 'And we'll go orf 'ome quiet. Thank you, gentlemen.'

'This way then,' said one of the men ungraciously. 'You got to go right through the train to the end. You can get out there. And don't be sick, somebody's got to clean this train. You're trespassing anyway, you know that?'

'I know it, but I can't say it,' grinned Davies stupidly. 'Come on, old mate. Let's get going. We'll wish these kind gentlemen a fond goodnight.' He lifted Boot out of the seat with his one enclosing arm and then staggered with him along the central aisle and into the next carriage. The London Transport men followed them at a carriage-length. Davies and then Boot, in response to another squeeze of the arm, began to sing drunkenly. 'Dear old pals, jolly old pals ... Give me the friendship of dear old pals.'

twelve

He and Mod had a profound drinking session in The Babe in Arms the next evening. Mod held forth vigorously and variously on the flaws in Darwin's Theory of Origins, pro-duced a logical explanation of the miracle of Moses striking the rock to bring forth water, and related how, in Edwardian times, it was a common embellishment to have goldfish swimming in the plate glass lavatory cisterns of great houses. It was not until they had been deposited, like two clumsy sacks, on the wet midnight pavement by the Irish publican and two eager barmen that the matter of the murder was mentioned.

'Is this an opportune moment to inquire as to whether you pursued my investigation into the local newspaper coverage of the late melancholy event?' Mod asked in the posed manner he often affected when drunk. He struggled up from the pavement, confident he could stand and at once toppled again. Davies was leaning against the wall of the public house spread across the bricks as if he feared it was about to fall. He looked at the horizontal Mod. He seemed a long way down.

'You get yourself in a bloody deplorable state, Mod Lewis,' Davies reprimanded. 'Why are you wallowing on the pavement?'

'Because I can't get up, Dangerous,' replied Mod practically. 'I do believe my legs have finally gone. After all these years. Oh, I shall miss them a terrible lot. They've been good pals, these legs have.' He looked at Davies and measured the distance between them. 'Friend,' he inquired calmly. 'Do you think you could get over here and lift me?'

Davies calculated the yards also. 'No,' he decided, 'I don't think I could make it. Not that far. But ... now listen Mod, don't despair ... If you crawl over here and I hang on to this drainpipe, then you can hoist yourself up, using me and the drainpipe to hang on to. Once you're on your feet you're generally all right.'

'Lovely idea. Brains, brains,' murmured Mod. He eyed the gap between himself and Davies's feet like a careful coward about to opt for unavoidable heroism. He used his head to count the pavement stones, nodding a greeting at each one. He dared not take as much as a supporting finger away. 'Do you really think I *could* make it, Dangerous?' he whispered fiercely.

'Mod,' said Dangerous, clutching the drainpipe. 'I *know* you can, boy, I know.'

'Faith,' muttered Mod, 'can move mountains. I'm but a mound of flesh. All right, I'll give it a whirl.'

He did not whirl, but moved over the cold stone squares on hands and knees, stumbling twice, even from that lowly posture, before reaching the neighbourhood of Davies's ankles. From there he began to climb, perilously, like a man attempting the Eiger's North Face, hanging on to the pockets, belt and loopholes of Davies's commodious brown overcoat.

'Watch the coat,' warned Davies seriously. 'You'll ruin the bloody thing.' Mod's face drew level with his neck and he knew he was as upright as he would ever be. 'Now grab the drainpipe,' instructed Davies. They hung together like men on a ledge with a thousand-foot drop beyond their toes. Mod's hands touched the rough metal of the downward pipe and grasped it hungrily. It moved under the additional weight (it was already supporting 20 feet of rotten guttering plus Davies) but Mod thought the unsteadiness was within himself.

'Another hand and I'm there, old friend,' he muttered courageously. 'One more swing.' Davies encouraged him to make the attempt. He did so, staggering across the front of Davies and hanging violently onto the pipe with his other hand.

It was a sober drainpipe but old and infirm. Under the force and weight of the four grasping hands it sagged and sighed as it came away from the wall of the public house. Davies and Mod felt it at the same moment and identical cries issued from each of them. They looked up and saw the entire upright pipe and its attached guttering from the roof toppling from above like an avenging cross. It hung wobbling, apparently trying to regain its ancient balance, while their appalled faces looked up. Then, uncompromisingly, it crashed, snaking like a metallic rope right across the road. The old cast-iron made a fine noise as it shattered. Davies and Mod cowered to the pipeless wall. Lights went on in the windows above the shops, sashes were pushed up and, more disturbing, from behind them in the saloon bar they could hear someone fighting to open the chains and locks. Some fool across the street shouted: 'Shrapnel! There's shrapnel on the road. The guns have opened up. The guns!'

With that mysterious power, the drunken's man's adrenalin, that disaster or danger brings to those who were previously incapable. Davies and Mod ran away. They even had the restored wit enough to dodge around the side of the public house and make up a brief alley that joined it to a parallel street. Over the housetops they could hear voices and very soon the yodelling of a police car. 'They've got the boys out of bed,' observed Davies. 'Somebody must have thought it was a smash and grab.'

They began to walk towards Mrs Fulljames's lodging house, bow-legged but now beginning to laugh. They sniggered at first, in the schoolish manner of the inebriate, and then let it go, bellowing, howling into the ear of the urban night.

As they approached 'Bali Hi' their natural caution became restored and they stopped laughing and slowed their pace cautiously. Ahead, in the dark, they heard something and almost at once up the street came the nocturnal wandering horse of the rag-and-bone man. It approached in the welcoming manner of one who is warmed by meeting a fellow creature on a dank night.

'Should be tethered,' said Davies heavily, looking along the black hill of the horse's elongated face. 'Constitutes a danger to traffic.'

'Now, whose door knocker will it be tonight?' inquired Mod secretly. 'The same as before?'

'No. Somebody else,' whispered Davies.

'Dangerous,' grinned Mod, the idea flooding him. 'Why not Mrs Fulljames's?'

Davies smiled a serene smile in the dark. 'We'll have to clear off quickly,' he said. 'But it's a lovely idea, Mod. That woman is cruel. She'd take the last Smartie out of your mouth.'

Mod gave a schoolboyish jerk of his head, as much to the horse as to Davies, the trio mooched along the privet hedges until they reached the door of 'Bali Hi', Furtman Gardens. Then Davies noticed the horse had no halter.

'Bugger it,' he swore. 'We've got to have something to tie it to the knocker.' He looked about him.

'Wait,' cautioned Mod. 'Hold fast a minute. Why just tie him to the door? Why don't we push him inside?'

The great pleased looked that dawned on Davies's face almost shone through the dark. 'What a bloody fine thought,' he whispered. 'We'll shove him in and clear off quick.'

Drunkenly they fumbled until Mod found his key. They tiptoed to the door and the horse, as though eager to enter into the conspiracy, seemed to tiptoe also. The key was revolved and the big Victorian door swung into the entrance hall. Davies gave the horse an accomplice's nudge, and seeming to know what was expected, it tiptoed into the passage. They closed the door after it and escaped, first at a drunken walk, then a trot, and then a wild hooting run. They staggered and ran, overwhelmed with the enormity of what they had perpetrated, until they came to The Moonlight Serenade, an all-night coffee stall hard by the railway station. This was owned by a man called Burney who divided his time between serving coffee there and serving time in Wormwood Scrubs. He and Davies were old friends.

'If necessary,' said Mod cautiously to Davies. 'I expect Mr Burney would provide us with an alibi.'

Davies shook his head, doubt hanging from his face. 'Nobody would believe him,' he decided. 'He's past the credibility stage. He's priced himself out of the alibi business.'

Mod drank his second mug of coffee. 'Mind you,' he said thoughtfully. 'I know where we could get a genuine alibi. Someone anybody would believe. Mr Chrust at the local paper. I think you ought to go there anyway. Remember what I told you. About the report of the murder?'

'He lives above the office,' agreed Davies, still rocking on his feet with the laughing and the drink. 'He won't like being got up. But if we say it's an important inquiry. And there's nobody would doubt his word about us being there. And who is going to check the time by the minute? Yes, let's go and see him.'

'Mod,' said Davies as they thumped along the echoing street. 'I had a good look at the cuttings again, old friend. Read them right through, minutely. Nothing. I couldn't see a single thing. Are you sure you weren't pissed again and read the wrong murder?'

'Listen,' said Mod stopping in mid-stride. He let his foot drop gently to the pavement. He was still drunk and so was Davies, but the helplessness was wearing off. The coffee was still comfortable within them. 'Listen ... and I mean listen. I told you the *files* of the *Citizen*, *not* the cuttings. You'll never make a detective, you know. Not as long as you've got a hole in your arse.'

'That's anatomy,' protested Davies mildly. 'And don't keep insulting my professional ability. Or do you want a fight? Fists?' He doubled his big fists and swayed uncertainly.

'No. Not now. We're nearly there anyway.'

He nodded ahead to the *North-West London Citizen* office, in its converted house in the High Street. It had a bayed shop window full of photographs, pinned grinning civic dignitaries, un-noteworthy amateur opera singers and triumphant school prizewinners. The newspaper's photographer was under a standing instruction to include as many people as possible in every photograph he took, since more people would want to see themselves in the paper, thus sending up or, at least, keeping up, the circulation. The photographer, a man who understood orders – if focuses were occasionally a mystery – once missed a vivid picture of a smash-and-grab raider escaping with his loot. He had failed to press the button because he felt there were not enough people about to make it worthwhile.

'He lives upstairs then,' said Mod, meaning Mr Chrust, the editor and proprietor. 'Let's hope he's not deaf.'

Mr Chrust was not. They had scarcely finished their fourth ring on the front door bell when the windows above them became squares of light. The curtains of both squares were pulled away and both sashes went up. Two middle-aged women, both wearing mob caps, looked out. Even from the ground level Davies could see that each potato face bore a resemblance to the other. 'Excuse me, ladies,' he called up. 'Is Mr Chrust at home?'

'Who wants him?' they inquired together.

'Police,' Mod replied for Davies. Then, not wishing to be accused of impersonating an officer, he pointed at Davies and added: 'That's him.'

Both heads went in as if pulled by the same string and the voices could be heard encouraging Mr Chrust to get from his bed because he was wanted by the police. Mr Chrust apparently took some time to be convinced or to be dressed because the two doughy faces again appeared at the windows and looked down on Davies and Mod for a full two minutes before Mr Chrust appeared. Then, like obedient hand-maidens they vanished, leaving him to conduct the dialogue from the sill.

'Mr Davies, isn't it?' he said peering down on Dangerous. 'It's really a police inquiry then?'

'It is, Mr Chrust,' confirmed Davies, not very firmly for he was beginning to regret the venture. 'Sorry to have disturbed you and ... er, Mrs Chrust.'

'We aren't disturbed, we aren't disturbed,' Mr Chrust replied ambiguously. He was a peanut of a man, with short bristles protruding from his face and otherwise bald head like the airy white fluff of a dandelion clock. 'I'll just be down.'

Through the fanlight of the front door they saw a procession of shadows follow a fitful light down the stair. Then the bulb in the hallway went on and the door was opened. Mr Chrust stood there in a dressing gown across the front of which a Chinese dragon snarled. With him were the two ladies in woolly dressing gowns and mob caps.

'Mrs Chrust passed away last February,' said Mr Chrust hurriedly once they were inside. He seemed to want no misunderstanding. 'These are her sisters. It's a very big flat, up-stairs you know. They look after my wants.'

Davies nodded to the twin moons of Mr Chrust's firmament. It occurred to him that the editor might think that the visit was in connection with immorality charges so he hastened to ask if they could look at the newspaper files for 1951. Mr Chrust beamed with patent relief and the bristles danced blithely on his face.

'If you just show us where they are,' said Davies. 'We'll just take a quick peep and be off. It was most urgent, you understand. Please go back to your bed ... beds.'

'Of course, of course,' said Mr Chrust agreeably. He began to push the nightdressed ladies up the stairs like a lean sheepdog nudging fat ewes towards an upland meadow. He turned after they had waddled away from the landing. 'I don't want to pry, Mr Davies,' he whispered. 'Not into police inquiries. But naturally, we of the press like to know what's going on, under our very noses as it were. Perhaps, when you are free to do so, you will drop a hint of it in my ear.'

'With pleasure, Mr Chrust,' answered Davies. The drink was still loitering around him. 'Now you go off to bed before you get lonely ... well, cold. Goodnight Mr Chrust. We'll close the door when we leave.'

'Please do,' nodded Mr Chrust backing up the stairs. 'The sisters get nervous.'

He went up the staircase and the excited noises of the ladies, which had been filling the upper part of the building like the chattering of fat pigeons in a loft, were stilled. Davies and Mod counted three separate twangings of springs. Mod raised his eyebrows and said: 'I bet he's got a story he wouldn't print in his paper.' Davies hushed him and ran his unsteady finger along the bound years of the newspaper fixed into shelves along the wall of the back office.

It stopped accurately on 1951 and he and Mod pulled the great cardboard slab out between them and eased it on to a table. A new excitement was added to the qualms of the drink. His fingers fumbled and Mod helped him to fold sheaves of pages until they arrived at the date of the week they were seeking.

Carefully Davies turned the front page. Celia Norris's young, faded face, the likeness aged with the paper, looked out of the page. The narrative took up a modest six inches of print under the heading 'Local girl missing'. Davies read it carefully again. There was nothing new he could see.

'It's the same cutting as we have in our files,' he protested to Mod, who remained standing back. 'What's it you can see?'

'It's not the cutting,' insisted Mod still withdrawn behind him. 'It's the *page*. Look at the little morsel in the last column. At the bottom.' Davies did. It said unarrestingly: 'Policeman's Farewell'. Beneath it sat three dull paragraphs describing the retirement of an apparently popular policeman, Sergeant David Morris and a farewell function held for him at the local Sturgeon Rooms.

'All right, so they had a farewell drink for a retiring copper. So what? It often happens.'

'But murders don't – not on the same night,' pointed out Mod hoarsely. 'It was the same night, Dangerous.'

'Yes. Yes, all right then. But . . .'

'There's a picture on page three,' said Mod relentlessly, enjoying himself in the chilly light of the little room.

Davies turned the page and looked at the picture. A group of policemen, pictured at the farewell to Sergeant D. Morris, said the caption. Above the photograph was the heading: 'Cheers, say Policemen' and below it a panel of names of the officers who raised their glasses for the cameraman and for posterity.

'All right,' said Davies. 'But I still don't see . . .'

'Read the names,' said Mod. 'Go on, read them!'

Davies read them. Two names made him swallow so hard he had a fit of coughing. 'PC James Dudley and PC Frederick Fennell,' he said eventually. After a silence, he added: 'And they were supposed to be in the patrol car in the High Street when she vanished.'

'But they weren't, were they,' said Mod.

'I've seen the duty slips and reports they signed,' said Davies. 'And they were drinking with the boys. They lied for a start.'

'And nobody noticed the lie,' said Mod. 'Or nobody cared to notice.'

An apologetic shadow appeared on the stairs. It was Mr Chrust. 'How are you getting on, gentlemen?' he inquired. 'Making some headway? I'm afraid the ladies are so excited they can't get back to sleep.'

'We're just off, thank you Mr Chrust,' said Davies, his thoughts miles, years, away from his voice. 'Just going.'

He and Mod folded the file and heaved it up into its slot on the shelf like a piece of masonry. Mr Chrust walked over and shining his lantern-torch along the bindings pedantically made sure that the years still ran as ordained. 'We sleep above history here, Mr Davies,' he smiled fluffily.

'You certainly do,' agreed Davies his mind still on what he had seen. They had reached the outside door. 'Thank you very much,' he called back. 'Sorry to have disturbed you. Good-night.'

To his astonishment further 'good-nights' came from above and he looked up to see the two plump ladies girlishly framed in the upstairs windows, the sashes thrust up.

Their progress home towards 'Bali Hi', Furtman Gardens, was hung with guilt, slowing their steps and causing them to dawdle at street corners more than was justified by the damp blanket of drink that still loosely enwrapped them. Neither mentioned the horse until they reached the final right-angle, the turn that would take them into Furtman Gardens and a view of whatever there was to be seen. Then Mod leaned back against a privet hedge, causing its dust to fall like pollen, and shook a cowardly head. 'Dangerous,' he said hoarsely. 'I can't go any further. I'm afraid to look.'

Davies tried to hold on to the hedge as one would lean against a wall but his hand kept sticking into the prickly twigs. He found he could stand upright without aid, however, and, pleased by this improvement, he confronted Mod.

'We're going home,' he ordered sternly. 'We're *both* going home. We've got to face this together, Mod. After all we've got an alibi and if I turn up and you don't they'll be sure to think you did it by yourself.'

Mod nodded miserably, acknowledging the logic. 'I wish you wouldn't keep buying me drink, Dangerous,' he mumbled. 'If you didn't buy them I wouldn't be able to drink them. Aw, Christ, come on then. Let's face the foe.'

There was a fire engine, a police car, a horse ambulance and the rag-and-bone man's cart outside the house of Mrs Fulljames. Each was toting a red or blue revolving light, even the rag-and-bone man's cart which had no navigation or warning appliances of its own and had borrowed a spare revolving blue light from the sympathetic attendant of the horse ambulance. From the distant end of the street they could see the crowd gathered and individual shadows moving with the various emergency lights bleeding and bleeping above them. It looked, at that distance, like a modest but busy fairground.

Davies and Mod approached to within a few yards with seemly caution. The horse, looking elated, was being led by its owner to the shafts of the cart. It blinked at the revolving light but otherwise went quietly. The horse ambulance attendant was unemotionally inspecting a kicked door on his vehicle, the front door of 'Bali Hi' was also bereft of its lower panels. Firemen were washing down the path, possibly feeling that since they had been summoned they ought to contribute something. All around were the faces of police and people, trying not to laugh.

The front room bay window on the first floor was open and backed with orange light. Mrs Fulljames, Doris at her side, stood in impressive silhouette as though she were about to jump or make a speech. With unerring aim she spotted the loitering Mod and Davies as soon as they came to the penumbral verge of the incident.

'Did you put that horse in my house?' she bawled hysterically. 'Did you two do it?'

Their faces, innocence and amazement fighting for possession, elevated themselves to the voice. She gave them no time to deny or even reply. 'There's shit everywhere!' she howled. 'Every bloody where.'

Some people in the crowd, neighbours who had to keep the peace with Mrs Fulljames, turned away and hid because they were laughing too much. 'Up the passage, on the stairs, in the front room!' she continued. 'Shit!' The very force of her bellow seemed to draw her forward and people below cried a warning, possibly fearing for themselves as much as her. 'Better get the jumping sheet,' Davies said to an enthralled fireman. 'I think she'll topple over any minute.'

Doris even from the window saw the brief conversation. 'Are you listening to Mrs Fulljames?' she shouted. 'Do you care? That thing has smashed the sideboard in the front room. Antique that was. Antique!'

'Belonged to Mr Fulljames, I bet,' whispered Davies to the speechless fireman.

'That belonged to Mr Fulljames,' screamed Doris obediently. 'The late Mr Fulljames.'

Mrs Fulljames, somewhat ungraciously, pushed Doris violently back into the room and then leaned out menacingly. She looked like Mussolini pressing a point. 'Mr Davies, Mr

Lewis,' she demanded. 'Did you get that horse in here? Did you? I want to know.'

'Mrs Fulljames,' shouted Davies mildly. 'You are making a scene. I have been out on police inquiries of a serious nature and Mr Lewis has been accompanying me.'

His landlady clamped her mouth angrily and then pulled down the window with a sound almost as loud. Davies's fellow policeman, having seen the horse between the shafts and taken its name and that of its owner, now returned. 'This is where you live is it, Dangerous?' inquired a young officer. Davies nodded, still looking up at the finality of the slammed window.

'Seems a nice cosy little place,' murmured the policeman. 'Bit on the quiet side, but cosy.'

'Nothing ever happens,' shrugged Davies. He turned to Mod. 'We'd better go in and see if we've still got beds. Good-night, officer,' he added formally.

'Good-night, Dangerous. I'll be glad when we've finished tonight. We've already had two bloody hooligans pulling down the drainpipe at the pub.'

thirteen

Mrs Edwina Fennell lived in a dying caravan anchored at the centre of a muddy field, ten miles from the streets and the industry her husband had patrolled as a policeman on occasions when he was not in bed with the lady palmist who lived and foresaw the future in the High Street.

'She's over there,' pointed out the farm man from whom Davies had asked directions. He indicated, with a dungy finger, the caravan across the soggy field. 'It'll be a bit damp underfoot, but it's a good job you didn't come in the real winter. Sometimes she gets cut off altogether.'

Davies commenced to sludge across the field. Sometimes the cowpats seemed firmer than the surrounding earth. He

had a quick recollection of walking into the front hall of
'Bali Hi', Furtman Gardens, early on that same morning,
after the horse had been taken away. He winced partly from
the thought and partly at the spasm of a mean wind which
was searching the open land. It was a flat and unpoetic place,
no hills, few trees, just muddy fields holding up a muddy sky.
He was glad of his faithful overcoat, bravely opposing the cut
and buffet of the wind. He looked up and saw he was still
only half-way to Mrs Fennell's caravan, wheelless and listing
listlessly, like some sorry shipwrecked raft.

In such circumstances he was surprised to see an illuminated door chime affixed to the peeling door of the caravan.
He pushed it and released a globular melody not inferior to
that which had heralded his entrance to the council penthouse of Ena Lind. It was necessary to stand in the morass of
the field while he awaited a response, for there was no step.
The caravan had subsided so far into the field, however, that
Edwina Fennell, when she opened the door was on almost
the same level. 'Sorry I was a long time,' she sniffled. 'I get
so fed up with people coming and ringing the bell.'

Bemused, Davies quickly looked around to see if he had
missed a city on his journey. But the field remained dis-
consolate all about. 'Yes,' he replied carefully. 'It's a bit of a
drag to have to keep answering the door. I hope I won't keep
you long. I'm Detective Constable Davies. I'm at your husband's old station.'

'Oh that,' she said, as though it were of only remote
interest. 'Well he's not here. Not any more.'

'I see,' said Davies. She remained resolutely in the small
entrance, thin arms folded over a pallid pinafore. 'I wanted
to have a word with you as well, Mrs Fennell. Do you ...
could I possibly come in? I think I'm sort of sinking here.
The water is getting through into my shoes.'

'Wipe your feet then,' she said dully backing away from
the entrance. He stepped out of the chilly mud, each foot
emitting a reluctant sucking sound as he pulled it clear.
Within the doorway the floor was covered by a piece of
coconut matting. He thought he would destroy it if he wiped
his shoes so, mumbling as one performing a rite, he took

them off and left them in the field, walking into the interior in stockinged feet.

There was little difference in the temperature in the caravan to that of the outside. It was cold and cloying, the fittings damaged and the plastic furniture unkempt. There was an unlit oil lamp and a hand-wound gramophone with a pile of old-fashioned records. They had a damp sheen on them. Mrs Fennell had been occupied in cutting a great careful pile of sandwiches assembled from a sizeable joint of cold beef and three long sliced loaves of bread.

She was a rejected-looking woman in her sixties. Her sunken eyes seemed incapable of rising to look at him. She went behind the barricade of sandwiches and began to butter some bread. 'It gets very muddy out there sometimes,' she said absently. To his surprise she emitted a cackling laugh. 'Sometimes I think I hear the bell and I think it must be one of my million lovers at the door. But when I go they've vanished and I think they must have sunk down in the mud.'

'Yes, it's a trifle damp,' said Davies awkwardly. He wondered if his shoes would still be there when he went out. He nodded towards her sandwiches. 'Looks like a picnic,' he said.

'Foxes,' she replied. 'I cut them up every day for the foxes. They come around after dark and sit and wait. They're so handsome. And it didn't seem right, dignified if you see what I mean, to just chuck bits of food out to them, so I do it properly, in sandwiches and they each have their own plates. You should see them eating. It's a lovely sight when it's a full moon.'

Davies sincerely said he could imagine it was. He half hoped she might offer him a sandwich for himself, but the thought obviously never came to her. 'What did you want then?' she prompted. 'What did you want with Fred Fennell?'

He knew that when a woman called her husband by both Christian and surname he was not in any kind of favour. 'Well, just a few memories of his police days, really,' he said. 'I'm checking on something that happened a long time ago and I thought I might pick his brains.'

'There's not a lot to pick,' she sniffed bluntly. 'He's lost all his brains. He's in the looney house, Mr Davies. The mental hospital. St Austin's at Bedford.'

Davies felt his heart plummet. 'Oh, I'm sorry about that.'

'He's not. Loves it. Every minute. He thinks he's Peter the Great. Well he did last time I went to see him.'

'When was that?' asked Davies.

'Last year,' she cut into the bread fiercely. 'Twelve months ago.'

'Why did you stop?'

'Reasons.' She seemed to be gritting her teeth, trying not to cry. 'I couldn't stand it. All the horrors in there. I couldn't stand hearing him giving orders to the bleeding Russian court and the like. I couldn't face it. I stopped going.'

She stopped cutting the sandwiches. It occurred to Davies that the foxes were in for a feast that night. 'It's horrible in that place,' she said. 'So horrible I can't tell you. You'll see if you go.'

He got up. The smell of the fresh bread and the cold beef was overpowering. 'I'll be off then,' he said. 'What shall I say if he asks when you're going to see him?'

She hesitated, then cleaned the crumbs from the knife with her fingers. 'Tell him ... tell him I'll come after the Revolution,' she said. 'That'll do.'

Immediately he went beyond the gates of St Austin's Hospital, Davies experienced the guilt of the sane going to visit the insane. He drove the Lagonda with consideration through the arched gatehouse and nodded in an agreeably humble way to everyone he saw. At first he was in a wide expanse of playing fields and woodland, but it felt different; it was as if he had entered a strange country. In the distance he could see the bent backs of the buildings among greenery like giants kneeling at a game of dice. He realized that this was a no man's land. There was another, higher wall ahead.

Autumn was thinning the trees and through a belt of white and shaky birches he could see moving coloured figures. Some men with ropes were sawing loudly in an oak tree around which the road curved. They waved to him from the perilous branches and he gladly waved back. As he turned the curve he saw that a football match was being played ahead; a proper match with goalposts and nets, corner flags, and with

148

the players decked in correct shirts, shorts, socks and boots. A referee, in regulation black, danced around controlling the game. The scene pleased Davies immensely. It was Wednesday morning and he was glad to see them playing at that time of the day and the week.

He slowed the car, stopped it almost opposite one of the goals, a few yards from the touchline which, he was again glad to see, was being overseen by a proper linesman in black shirt and shorts holding a bright orange flag. The linesman smiled at Davies and proceeded to pretend he was walking a tightrope along the whitewashed line. Davies laughed heartily at his joke and called: 'Good match?'

'First rate,' responded the linesman soberly, balancing on his imaginary tightrope. His arms went out like stabilizing wings and he prepared to spin slowly and go back the other way. 'Two good teams,' he added before revolving. 'Best teams in the world.'

'Oh,' said Davies uncomfortably.

'Brazil and England,' said the linesman secretly. 'Playing for the World Cup.'

There came a burst of action in front of the adjacent goal. A heavy forward of the yellow team trundled the ball through and, having unceremoniously pushed the advancing goalkeeper away with both hands, scored easily and went dancing joyfully down the pitch to the arms and kisses of his teammates.

Davies shouted from his driving seat. 'Foul! Foul!' The linesman turned with worried, white face. 'You think so?' he inquired.

'He just pushed the goalie out of the way,' Davies pointed out.

A player in the red team standing near the touchline heard him. 'No goal!' he bellowed across the pitch. 'A foul! This man says it was a foul!'

An icy fear caught Davies's heart. The linesman was staring at him drop-mouthed, and across the football pitch twenty-two shouting, arguing, pushing players charged at him with the referee and the other linesmen funeral figures far to the rear.

Kitty, sensing something important was taking place, looked out from below its tarpaulin and, seeing the advancing shirted horde, howled dismally. The sound jerked Davies into fortunate action. 'Must be off!' he shouted handsomely, jabbing the accelerator. 'Play up!'

The Lagonda ran forward quickly. At a safe distance he looked in the mirror and saw them standing in a coloured bunch all shouting at each other. The referee was sitting alone under a tree, one linesman was kicking the ball and the other was still tiptoeing the line.

He found he was trembling. Kitty burrowed below the tarpaulin once more. The road was leading towards a great wooden gate, set in a formidable wall, it curved to an apex like the entrance to a castle or a prison. Set into it was an infant door. Davies stopped the car and walked to it. The sadness of the place was settling upon him. There was a silence too, holding everything, the walls, the peeping roofs, and the grimy sky. Against the inset door was fixed an iron ring-handle, inhospitable to the hand. He turned it and, somewhat to his surprise, it opened without resistance and the little door swung easily in.

Davies was confronted with a framed scene, much as Alice was through her looking glass. Stretching as far as he could see were desolately well-tended lawns and flower beds, set out in squares and oblongs. They appeared perfectly cultured and kept but looked as though no sun ever shone upon them. Set into this there was a solitary human figure, a woman, a bent back and downturned face overlooking some minute job at the corner of the border just beyond the gate. Unhappy, Davies stepped through.

There was no sign or notice of the way he ought to follow. He was within a few feet of the woman, enthralled by a few daisies she had dug from the flower bed with the prongs of a table fork. 'Oh, excuse me, madam,' Davies said.

Her face came around first, old but ageless, bright-eyed. It was followed by the muzzle of a gun, a pistol of nasty aspect, which she held secretly against her blue overall. 'Stick 'em up,' she demanded quietly.

Davies raised his hands above his head. The blood seemed

to run down his arms and into his stomach. He stared at the gun. It looked real. 'I saw you,' she said rising slowly from her knees. 'I detected you coming in.'

'Oh ... oh, yes,' nodded Davies stiffly. He felt, arms up as he was, that his trousers might fall. 'I've come to see the superintendent, Doctor Longton. Do you know ...?'

'Keep 'em up,' she warned grimly. 'And walk.'

He looked wildly about him. There was no other person in the entire garden. It was as though it had all been prepared as a trap for him. She nudged him with the gun and he began to march with his hands held above his ears.

She nudged him through another archway and into a stone corridor, wide, with windows and doors on either side. A man came out of an office with a clipboard in his hand. Davies tried to say something but the man walked by studying the clipboard and taking no heed of the gunwoman or the man she pushed before her. Other people appeared, some in white coats, but his extraordinary progress along the corridor aroused no interest whatever. Some actually wished his captor 'Good morning'. Eventually they turned into a large hall where a physical training class was taking place. An instructor was demonstrating a bend to thirty or so people who watched and then bent with dedication. The woman marched Davies right across the floor at gunpoint and still nobody made a mention of it. Eventually they arrived in front of a short tubby woman with a steady, red face.

'Matron,' said the gunwoman. 'An intruder. He wants Dr Longton.'

The matron hardly glanced at Davies with his hands still hovering in the air. 'He's in his office,' she said. 'Hurry and you'll catch him.'

The muzzle of the gun banged into the small of Davies's back and he was forced to jog across the floor to a further corridor and the entrance to an office. The gunwoman reached around and knocked at the door with the butt of the weapon. A pleasant voice, the voice of someone happy with his work, called out: 'Come in, come in.'

Relief had replaced consternation in Davies by now and he stood sheepishly with his arms still up as his captor ushered him into the room. Doctor Longton smiled understandingly. 'Ah, you came in the back way, I see,' he said. Then to the woman. 'It's all right, Marie. I'll take over. Thank you very much.'

The woman went out without a word. Davies said: 'Can I put my arms down now?' He lowered them. 'That looked like a real gun to me.'

'Oh it was,' the Superintendent said. 'She needs it. We tried giving her a toy but she wouldn't accept it. So we got that one, and she's happy with that. We've taken a few parts out of it, of course, and she has no access to any ammunition. It's her status symbol, if you understand.'

'Yes, I see,' blinked Davies. He introduced himself and they shook hands. 'It was just a bit of a shock, that's all. Unexpected.'

'We expect the unexpected here,' said the doctor as though that was the limit of the discussion. 'You've come to see Mr Fennell?'

'Yes, I went to see his wife . . .'

'It's a pity *she* doesn't come to see him,' said the other man. 'He misses her terribly.'

Davies nodded unhappily, knowing that he was treading where he would prefer not to walk. 'She said she won't come,' he said.

Dr Longton scratched his nose. He was slim and gently bent like a feather. 'A thousand pities,' he said.

'I think she found it too much for her,' said Davies. 'The whole thing.'

'Most people do,' said Dr Longton. 'But not as much as the patients.'

'Yes, I can understand that,' nodded Davies.

'Mr Fennell is not too bad now, though. He has very good days. It seems to be arrested. His delusions of grandeur, being royalty and suchlike, are less pronounced. I think he would like to see you, Mr Davies. And if you get a chance perhaps you could get his wife to come and visit him. It would make his life much brighter.'

Davies nodded uncertainly. 'I'll go and see her again,' he promised. 'I'll see what she says.'

'Good. I've arranged for you to see Mr Fennell away from the ward. If the others saw you talking they would all want to tell you their troubles. They became stored-up, as it were, here. There's a small consulting room where you can talk.' He hesitated. 'Without prying too much into police business,' he ventured. 'Would it be possible for you to tell me something of what this is about? I'm thinking of the patient, you understand.'

Davies nodded. 'Of course. I see that. Actually it's a murder inquiry. It's not quite so dramatic as it sounds because it happened twenty-five years ago. Mr Fennell was a police constable in the area at the time and had some part in the inquiries.'

'You want to see if he remembers,' said the doctor. He seemed to be considering it. 'I'd be grateful if you could tread carefully,' he said. 'Be very careful with him. If he doesn't remember I'd be glad if you'd call it a day and not press him.'

'I will,' promised Davies gently. 'I don't want to mess anything up.'

'Thank you. And don't make it too protracted, if you don't mind. It's a big day for him, you know, having a visitor, and it could be emotionally tiring.' He stopped and thought out the points he had made. 'Right,' he concluded. 'I'll take you along there.'

They went on a short journey as near to a nightmare as Davies had been in waking hours. Each door they reached was double-locked and unlocked, each corridor seemed to go deeper and deeper into the throes of the building. He heard screams and shouts, and faces, faces pallid with amazement appeared at side windows as they walked by. Eventually they reached a door set apart from the others.

'He's in here, waiting,' said Longton quietly. 'Something I forgot to ask, Mr Davies. Does he actually *know* you?'

'No,' replied Davies. 'We've never met. He had left the police before I arrived in the division.'

'I see,' said the doctor. He knocked courteously and a voice inside bade them anxiously, 'Come in.' Even from behind Davies knew that Longton was smiling as he entered.

He could tell by the wrinkles at the nape of his neck. An ashen-faced, ancient, shaking man sat on a wooden chair by a plain table. 'Mr Davies to see you, Mr Fennell,' announced Dr Longton.

Fennell stood irresolutely. His face trembled and, as though it could not hold them, finally cracked into gigantic tears. 'Oh, thank you for coming,' he said to Davies, holding out his hands. 'My old friend, thank you for coming.'

fourteen

Madame Tarantella Phelps-Smith, High Class Gipsy Fortune Teller, was a flitting figure in the town. Over the years less had been seen of her, not merely because she made her outdoor appearances infrequently, but because she seemed to be getting smaller as her life went on. Beryl Adams, as she was before she was touched magically by a Gipsy Soothsayer at a fair on Hackney Marshes, had once lent an exotic touch to the labouring surroundings of the district. She flowed about in robes that moved like a coloured sea. She had rings on her fingers and bells on the long curly toes of her embroidered shoes. Davies had always thought of her as a tall person; even her face seemed to be tall, a high forehead and a deep chin; her eyes were vertically elongated, her eyebrows aloft and arched and her mouth a perpetual upright oval as though she received an amazement every moment of her life.

She used to be seen in various parts of the town dispensing ready magic and telling the futures of the inhabitants who, in that hard and gritty place, always hoped that things might improve. But the years had dimmed her eye and her ambitions and by the time she came to Davies's professional notice she contained her outside forays to dashes to the off-licence and the fish-and-chip shop. By this time her back had bent, her tall arms hung and swung almost to the pavement, and her shoulders were forever hunched.

'It's the years I've spent leaning over this bloody crystal ball,' she complained to Davies. 'It's a risk of the job I suppose. Like miners get that disease, whatever it's called, soothsayers get bent backs and hunched shoulders.'

'You get a lot of business?'

'No, but I have to practise, otherwise you get rusty.'

'Policemen get flat feet,' he sympathized. 'And a pain in the neck. I went to see Fred Fennell yesterday.'

Madame Tarantella seemed unsurprised. 'Fred Fennell,' she mused as though only days had passed since she last read his palm while they lay unclothed in her patchwork bed. 'Dear Fred. How is he? Getting old now, I suppose.'

'He's keeping pace with the rest of us,' agreed Davies. Her room was above a men's plain outfitters, Mr Blake's, who had clothed half the working force of the district, mostly by weekly instalments. As they sat there, Davies could hear the sturdy clothes being moved from their racks which were fixed just below Madame Tarantella's floor. Madame Tarantella herself sat in what she called her driving seat, the little bentwood chair seeming to cling like a child around her skirts. The room was professionally dim with drapes and tassels on the curtains and the signs of the Zodiac on illuminated panels around the wall. On the table with the crystal ball was a used coffee cup, an ashtray full of massacred stubs and a copy of the daily paper open and marked at the racing page.

'You ought to be on a winner every time,' observed Davies, nodding at the newspaper. He was sitting in the client's chair, his overcoat opened because of the closeness of the small room.

'Horses? No damn fear,' she sighed. 'If I could see the winners, I wouldn't be sitting here now, Dangerous. When I try to focus it on Epsom or Sandown Park it turns rogue and gives me one of the back-markers. A gift's a gift but it won't get you rich at fifty-pence a gaze. The only fortune that comes up here is somebody else's.' She looked at him speculatively. 'You wouldn't like to have a consultation while you're here, would you?'

Davies smiled solemnly. 'I've already met two dark

mysterious men,' he said. 'I've still got the scars.'

'You'll meet them again, beware,' she warned abruptly. 'But you will be saved by a beast. Do you have a police dog?'

'Not a *police* dog. I've got Kitty, a damn ratbag of a thing that spends its life sleeping in my car.'

She nodded, 'Ah yes, I've seen the beast. You should give it a wash sometime. Look after it, Dangerous. You will need it.' She seemed tempted to take a quick plunge into the crystal but she resisted. 'And what did Fred Fennell have to say?'

'You ... you knew him pretty well a few years ago? So he told me.'

'Oh come on, Dangerous,' she replied good-humouredly. 'You and me are in the same basic business. Knowing about people. You know he was my lover or you wouldn't be in this room now. But it was donkey's years ago.'

'He's not so bad ... physically. In the circumstances.'

'It's a mental hospital then,' she said quickly. 'I *felt* he was ill, but I didn't get a fix on a mental hospital.'

'Well he is. At Bedford.'

'Oh my. Poor Fred. He was always the big virile policeman, you know. I've seen him standing in this room many a time wearing nothing but his hobnailed boots. A fine sight.'

'I bet,' said Davies. He wanted her to go on.

'What about that wife of his then?' she said. 'Cruel bitch, she was. She had a thing about animals. She'd go out and poison cats and dogs at night. The family had to use force to keep her away from the zoo. Apparently she was in somebody's house once and she tried to strangle their goldfish.'

'That's not easy,' conceded Davies. 'Well she must have reformed because she feeds foxes now – on beef sandwiches. Unless she spreads poison with the butter. I hadn't thought of that.'

'Dreadful woman. Fred used to weep about her. I liked him, Dangerous. But I couldn't see a future for us together.'

'If you couldn't, who could?' acknowledged Davies. 'Do you remember, years ago, the case of Celia Norris. She vanished.'

'Oh her. *That* girl. Yes, I remember, I've still got her bicycle.'

Davies almost fell off the chair. Sweat burst out all over his face. He stared at her. She was idly running her tall fingers over the crystal ball. 'Her bicycle?' he managed to say.

'That's it,' she said practically. 'It's down in my shed some-where. There's a lot of junk in there but I know it's there.'

Davies tried to keep himself calm. 'How ... how did it come to be here?' he asked forcing his voice to be slow. 'How?'

'Fred brought it in,' she said simply. 'There's no harm in telling you now. If he's in the bin they can't touch him and I bet you'd find it hard to arrest me.'

'I won't arrest you,' Davies promised desperately. 'Nobody will, ever. Just tell me.'

'It was the time of that Norris girl thing. The same night as she disappeared. Fred was up here. I remember it very well. He used to pop up for half an hour or sometimes more when he was on duty. He used to be in the little van that went all around the streets, with another policeman, and they used to arrange so that one of them could hop off for a while. They would take turns. The other chap used to go somewhere, I don't know where, and Fred used to come up here. It started off when he came in to have his future foretold – well, that's what he said. It was his excuse for getting to know me. I was young and rather handsome then. And once he'd given me his hand to hold professionally, I found I couldn't let go of it. It happens, Dangerous, even to us who have extra powers.'

Davies nodded solemnly. He wanted to dance around the room with her but he kept his seat in the chair.

'He'd had a few drinks that particular night. Been to some police booze-up, again on the quiet because he was supposed to be on duty. They were devils in those days. I wouldn't have trusted a policeman, believe me, except Fred of course.'

'Terrible lot,' agreed Davies. He did not want to stop her. She was staring at the racing page as if trying to conjure some vision of Mr Fred Fennell from Tipster's Selections from Market Rasen.

'Yes,' she went on eventually. 'That night he'd had a few

and he only came up for a while. Then he went down and not long afterwards he came back with the bike. It's been here ever since. All these years.'

Davies said: 'Why did he bring it here?'

'Well he had just found it. He didn't know whose it was, of course. It was lying by the wall of the cemetery. He'd come across it lying in the grass and he'd brought it here. He was quite clever, Fred, for an ordinary police constable who never got promoted. Or crafty. His idea was to keep it here and then if ever he was found out, you know, if they discovered him here or his wife got suspicious and followed him or had him watched, then he could say he had come after a report of a missing bicycle being found. I would say that I'd found it and hand it over and no one would be any the wiser. It was just a sort of safeguard for him being in here, see.'

'But didn't he realize whose bike it was?'

'No. Of course not. He thought it was just a bike – any bike. Lost or thrown away by somebody who had stolen it. It wasn't until later, when the hue and cry was on, that he realized that it belonged to the girl Norris. And by that time it was too late. He was too scared to take it in.'

Davies hardly trusted his mouth to open. 'Tarantella,' he said pushing his hand across the table and resting it on hers. Her hand felt cold, dead. 'Can I see it? The bike?'

'It's in the shed,' she told him, rising. 'I'll show you. There's years of rubbish down there. It's behind all that.' She led the way from the stuffy room, down a back staircase and into a corrugated iron shed in the miniature yard behind. 'The rest of the building belongs to Mr Blake of the outfitters,' she explained, pulling back a rusted bolt. 'But the shed was in with the flat. It was in the lease.'

It was damp and cold in the yard. Davies tugged his overcoat around him and his hand felt his fiercely beating heart. Growing triumph and fear banged like two clappers in his chest. A stale smell came from the shed. 'I've put a lot of my old things – props and that sort of thing – in here,' she said. 'You know how fashions change even in this game.' She was pushing aside some painted screens. 'And here's my clairvoyant stuff, my trumpet and my smoke machine. I packed that in. Gave me the creeps.' She was clearing a way ahead. Davies took the pieces from her as she handed them back.

'Here it is. I can see it. At the back. Could you get across there, Dangerous?'

'Try and stop me,' he thought. He moved her gently aside and clambered through the lumber. Then he stopped, surrounded by dust and relics, and looked. It was there. Celia's bicycle. He almost choked with excitement. His arms, as they went across to grasp the handlebars, were vibrating. His face was streaming sweat. Then he got it. He touched the cold, dusty metal. He had got it!

Firmly he lifted and pulled the bicycle away from its surroundings. It was pathetically light. He knew it was the right one. He knew that machine as well as its sad owner had known it. He touched the saddle upon which she had ridden those last minutes of her seventeen years. Carefully, despite his urgency, he lifted it clear of the surrounding junk, and eventually rested it on the clear floor. Madame Tarantella looked at it unemotionally. 'Both tyres have gone down,' she said flatly.

Davies did not seem to know what to do next. He began to wipe the dust away from the frame with his fingertips. Then he leaned the tubed metal against his thigh and opened the buckles of the saddle bags.

Like a shock it hit him. Inside, brown and broken and brittle, were the remains of a bunch of flowers.

'They were in there when he brought it,' said Madame Tarantella beyond his shoulder. 'Chrysanthemums and a few irises. They had a card with them, but I threw that away. I think she must have got them from the cemetery.'

'Her mother said she brought her flowers,' murmured Davies. 'I wondered where she picked them.'

'Flowers,' said Mod softly. 'Well, well, fancy them still being there.' He was looking into his glass, both he and Davies keeping their heads down from the suspicion and bale in the face of the landlord. He knew who it was who had demolished his drainpipe.

'She must have gone into the cemetery regularly on her

way home from the youth club,' said Davies. 'To take flowers to her mother. I was wondering where she could have picked the flowers in this neighbourhood.'

'That means she went over the wall or the gates. Being at night,' said Mod.

'She must have.'

'That night without her knickers.'

'Apparently so.'

'Where are we then?'

Davies sighed. 'Yes, where are we! Well, we've got three neo-suspects. None of them fit but they're all vaguely in the running. Just vaguely. Start from the back. Our friend Boot. Now Boot did some naughty things, and to Celia Norris among others. But he says he didn't kill her.'

'That's a fine recommendation,' mumbled Mod, his face semi-submerged in his beer. When he peered over the surface of the drink he looked like an otter swimming half below the top of a pool. 'You'll take his word for it?'

'No. But he told me everything, well, nearly everything, the other night. By the time I'd done with him I had him banging on his mum's door crying to be let in. Not a pretty sight. I don't think it was him, despite all the other bits and pieces, unless he's been craftier than I think he is. But one thing he won't tell. He won't say what he did with her pants. He says he can't remember.'

'And you believe that?' Mod grumbled. 'If you'll swallow that you'll swallow anything.'

'I could swallow another pint,' said Davies absently. Mod braved the landlord's eye and asked for more beer. The landlord filled the glasses with ill-grace and slammed them down in front of them on the bar. 'Drinking I can understand,' he said bitterly. 'Vandalism, I can't.'

Mod and Davies exchanged expressions brimmed with innocent incomprehension. 'Some people never know when they've had enough,' Davies called agreeably at the publican's retreating back. He returned to Mod. 'No, he remembers what he did with them, all right. That will come. He may have gone with her from the youth club – at this distance nobody can remember seeing him or not seeing him that night. It's twenty-five years after all. He could have walked with her as far as the cemetery wall and there the dirty deed was done. I don't know, Mod. But I somehow don't think so. I don't think he did it. But I've still got him on the string. I don't think he's having a very carefree life at the moment.'

The rough woman who sang 'Viva España', her foot still a club of plaster, charged her way like a squat bull through the bar door and made for the juke box. She could have pressed the tab with her eyes closed. Her heavy hips began to jerk even as the first bars of the song shot from the machine. She banged her way down the bar clapping her hands above her head like blocks of wood.

'Then Ramscar,' said Davies determinedly. 'It might *really* have been Ramscar. He could have fixed that alibi, no trouble. And he bobs up all the time, except nobody knows where he is. He knows I'm looking for him. Who but our Cecil would have arranged the dustbin blitz on me? Only Ramscar has that sort of mind or organization.'

Mod was watching the rough woman's performance with calm scorn. 'One day,' he forecast. 'She's going to drop dead right in this bar. And I for one will go and stamp up and down on her prostrate body.' He returned to Davies. 'How about Parsons? Reformed undie-thief? Perhaps it was his Salvation Army mates who shanghaied you.'

'I haven't finished with Parsons, either,' nodded Davies. 'We'll have another chat before long. And we've still got Bill Lind.'

'Ah, the boyfriend. I was wondering when he would come up.'

'Madam,' called Davies to the rough woman. 'If you don't stop carrying on in that manner I will arrest you for being disorderly in a public place.'

'Bollocks,' replied the lady of Spain. 'At least I don't go pulling people's bloody drainpipes off the walls.'

'Bill Lind,' said Davies, returning at once to Mod. 'Well I'm going to wait until Bill Lind comes to me. I'm sure he will.'

'And ...' said the woman now truculent, leaning towards them, all the pride of Andalusia gone. 'Nor do I put a fucking horse in somebody's fucking front passage either. *And* I don't dive in the fucking canal with a fucking dustbin on my fucking head!'

She did not wait for them to react or reply. She stumped towards the door and with a final smashing of her hands above her head and a sluggish whirl of her dirty hung skirt, she went out. They heard her shout 'Bollocks' from the street.

'That,' observed Mod, 'is known as the Iberian clap.' He brought his hands together above his sparse dome.

'And that brings me to Fred Fennell,' went on Davies. 'What about Fred Fennell? A strange tale. And Celia's bike being there. *Did* Fred do her in after creeping, heavy with police party drink, unsatisfied from the arms of Madame Tarantella? He was only a few minutes, remember. He and James Dudley always shared that nice, cosy little duty, cruising around in that van. One would go off and do his thing, then the other. A convenient and simple arrangement, and it passed the lonely hours. That night, as we've seen, they both called into the police farewell party and had a few, despite the fact that they were supposed to be on duty. That's nothing new. Policemen can be very unofficial at times.'

Mod said: 'He could have gone out of the flat and walked up the street, past the cemetery and seen Celia, with no pants, coming over the wall with a bunch of nicked funeral flowers. It all happens then. Afterwards he quietly wheels the bike to Madame Tarantella's place.'

'It doesn't sound bad,' Davies agreed. 'Not bad at all. But it could just as easily have been the other copper, who did it – Dudley. Remember, nobody remembers seeing Celia from the time she left the youth club. People were asked to say if they'd seen a *girl on a bike*. Well, she wasn't on her bike. That was left outside the boneyard. She could have been in the police van with PC Dudley.'

'And what's happened to him?' inquired Mod. He had drained his glass and was moving it around, revolving it, in a fidgety way. Davies steeled himself to look at the landlord and two more pints were grudgingly delivered.

'Dudley, James Dudley, took himself and his family off to

162

Australia. Emigrated twenty years ago. He liked the seaside. They wanted to go to Torquay but they couldn't afford it. He joined the police force in Sydney and worked with the vice squad until eight years ago, when he died when a brothel caught fire.'

'Died on duty, eh?' Mod nodded.

'Off duty,' corrected Davies. 'He'd been suspended on suspicion of accepting bribes.'

'Oh dear,' said Mod as if he knew the man personally.

Davies spread his hands. 'And that's about the lot. I've told you everything now, friend.'

'Celia,' ruminated Mod. 'She appears in *As you Like It* and she's in Spenser's *Faerie Queene* also. Derived from "Caelia", Latin, which means "Heavenly girl". I looked it up.'

'It's grand living in a library,' acknowledged Davies. 'Heavenly girl, eh?'

Mod looked up at the clock. 'Nearly closing time,' he observed. 'We must get back at the proper hour tonight.' He raised his voice so it carried to the landlord. 'Otherwise you get the blame for all manner of incidents and accidents.' Then quietly he said to Davies. 'You know where I think she's buried?'

'Where they're all buried,' sighed Davies.

'In the cemetery,' said Mod.

'That's what I thought,' said Davies.

fifteen

Josie was lying in wait for him outside the saloon bar, insinuated in the doorway like a loitering child. She was wearing an oilskin and a sou-wester against the commonplace evening drizzle.

'Did you guess it was me?' she asked when she and Davies

were walking hunched towards the town. Mod had bidden them good-night and trudged the other way.

'I mistook you for a small lifeboatman,' replied Davies. 'Where are we going?'

'I'm going to show you something,' she said, pushing along in the dark. She seemed very slight at his side. 'I've been looking for you from the window at work but you don't seem to have been around.'

He did not know why he felt so guilty about her. 'I've been kept busy,' he said. 'Inquiries. I'm still on the trail of Mr Ramscar – except there's no trail. I've done the grand tour, strip joints, clip joints, dip joints, places I wouldn't like to tell my mother about I've been to . . .'

'Ramscar's been threatening my mum,' she interrupted bluntly. 'She won't be able to speak to you any more.'

'Ramscar!' He halted like a guardsman in the road. They were just crossing and a bus, like a bright, businesslike dragon, came hissing at them. Josie pulled him across. 'Ramscar?' he said when they got to the pavement not noticing the bus driver shaking his fist. 'Where is he hiding? Do you know?'

'Nobody knows,' she shrugged and continued walking. 'He just sends messages. My old man is petrified. He's scared to go out of the house. They know he talked to you.'

'Tell your mum and dad not to move,' said Davies. He was worried now. 'We ought to get a copper to watch the house.'

'No! That would be worse. They won't move, don't worry. I have to take food into them.'

'Ramscar,' he muttered again. 'I'd really like to know where he is.' Suddenly aware of her smallness and vulnerability he said. 'What about you?'

'Oh me,' she laughed. 'Ramscar don't worry me, Dangerous. I'd just tell him to piss off. Him or any of his mates.' She turned around in the rain, the bright sixpenny face framed in the outsized rim of the oilskin hat, brash, cheeky, confident and without defence. Celia again.

'You lie low,' he said. 'And if you get a whiff of trouble ring me, or anyone at the nick, at once. All right?'

She grinned at him. 'All right, Dangerous,' she said. 'He's

not after me, don't worry. But I'll let you be a big brother if that's what you want.' She took some keys from her raincoat pocket. 'We're going in the salon,' she said seriously, walking on ahead of him. 'There's something I think you ought to see.'

'What is it?'

'Wait for it. It's a hoot,' she said. 'You'll see.' She opened the downstairs door and walked concisely up the narrow stairs to the first floor. She was just ahead of him, the still wet rim of her raincoat almost touching his nose. 'You've been avoiding me,' she grumbled confidently as she went up. 'You've been keeping out of my way. And it's not *just* Ramscar, either.'

He felt hollow and heavy and old. 'I told you I've been busy,' he muttered. 'Anyway you're seventeen, Josie.'

She halted on the stairs one leg just ahead of him and looked back scornfully. 'Seventeen,' she said, 'is not *seven*. At seventeen you can do all sorts of things, you know. Look at Celia.'

'All right, all right,' he said wearily. She had begun to step up the stairs again and, on reaching the landing, switched on the lights and walked into the hairdressing salon. He followed her and looked around. The chairs were lined up like a battery of anti-aircraft guns, each one with its attendant hair-drier like a doused searchlight. 'Take that awful overcoat off,' she said. 'If ever I marry you, Dangerous, that overcoat's going to be the first to go.'

He ignored the remark and sat tiredly in one of the chairs. He read the reversed lettering on the windows facing him. Josie had gone somewhere into the back of the salon. He called out to her. 'Why does she call herself Antoinette of Paris, Switzerland and Hemel Hempstead? How come Paris and Switzerland?'

He could not see her. She was doing something in the shadows behind him. 'It's just a bit of swank,' she called out. 'She went to winter sports in Switzerland once and she didn't like the snow. She kept falling down. So she stayed in the hotel and did people's hair. I don't know what she did in Paris. Did a shampoo and set there once, I expect. Probably for herself.'

'What are you doing back there?' he asked from the chair. He was regarding himself in the ladies' mirror and thinking how pale and bulky he looked. She called back. 'Won't be a minute. Just on the wall in front of you is a switch, Dangerous. When I tell you, you switch it on. Not till I tell you, though.'

'Playing games,' he grumbled.

'How's Kitty?' she called from the shadow.

'Bad chest and bad disposition.'

'How's Mod? I like Mod.'

'You've only just seen Mod . . .'

'Right, Dangerous. Now. The switch!'

He did as she had instructed, leaning out of the chair and putting down the switch. The salon fell into darkness and a moment later a spotlight from the ceiling hit the floor by the entrance, fifteen feet away. He waited.

Josie jumped like a child dancer into the light. He cried out, horrified, when he saw her. She was wearing her murdered sister's clothes. The green gingham dress, the white socks and the brown shoes buckled across the instep. She stood, grinning in the saucer of light. Celia Norris!

'Oh . . . oh, Christ,' he said and tried to back away further into the chair. 'Oh . . . why . . . what did you do that for?'

'I found them,' Josie said triumphantly. 'I found where my mum had hidden them. And I tried them on and they fitted. To the inch, Dangerous!'

She turned daintily in the circle. He still sat dumbstruck at what she had done. 'It's like one of them identi-kit things,' she laughed then paused, leaning forward to peer from the light to the dark at him. 'Are you still watching?'

'Yes I'm still watching,' he said, his mouth like stone. There was a trembling within himself, as if he were a mountain.

'Watch this then,' she laughed. He knew too well what she would do. She twirled like a little dancer and let the short skirt of the dress fly out. 'No pants,' she giggled eerily. 'No pants, either.' He stared desolately at her. She revolved more slowly a second time. The slim legs down to the ankles and the white socks and shoes, and up to the miniature thighs.

166

Daintily she held the skirt and pirouetted once more. The globes of her bottom were small, contoured in the light and shadow. Again she turned. The slightly protruding belly and the darker shadow of hair at the top of her legs.

'Stop it!' he bellowed rising from the chair. He caught his head an idiotic clanging blow on the over-hanging hairdrier. He heard her laugh like an echo and cried again. 'Stop it, Josie. Do you hear me. Stop...'

She did as he asked. She stopped and walked from the light to the dim towards him, on tiptoe. She stood in front of him in the thin dress. He squeezed his eyes together. 'You shouldn't...' he muttered. 'For God's sake...'

'I thought I told you to take your coat off,' she answered practically. She bent over towards him and he could smell the mothballs from the dress. He wanted to touch it, to feel the material, but his hands would not move. She undid the clumsy buttons on his overcoat and divided it open. Then, she climbed on to his lap, in a kneeling position, her thin knees on his trousers, her body like a twig, her arms slim around his thick neck, her face looking intently into his. He could not stop himself then. He allowed his hands to touch her, bringing them around, still encased in the ridiculous tunnels of the overcoat sleeves, and resting his fingers on her hips. The feel of the gingham went through him like a shock. So thin he could feel her hipbones protruding like a cowboy's guns. 'Oh hell...' he said hollowly. 'Oh bloody hell.'

At that she moved her face to his, smooth against tough, and pressed her thin body into his chest. His hands fell down the murderous dress and enveloped the softness of her naked bottom. He held her there while they both trembled. He could feel her young tears running down his face. He pulled her away and looked at her. Her smudged face and the clothes.

Had Celia wept that night long ago?

In the CID room at the police station the detectives were all trying on suits, the proceeds of a thwarted robbery. There was an atmosphere akin to the fitting room of a busy tailor's shop, with comparisons of cloth, style and cut, being bandied about. Davies sat down quietly and wrote a short and almost entirely fanciful report of his efforts to locate Ramscar.

'Pity there wasn't an overcoat among this stuff, Dangerous,' observed one of the young, successful, detectives, smart in a pinstripe. 'Yours is going green with mould.'

'It's comfortable,' shrugged Davies, putting his report in the file for Inspector Yardbird's office. 'I've sort of settled into it now. I don't think I could get used to a new one.' He left them to their fashions and went out and walked towards the cemetery.

It was a good day for visiting the dead. A damaged sky scattered over his immediate area of the world, a sky black but riven with chasms of jagged sunshine, a sky shrieking with dark winds. Wagner might have put it to music.

Davies, however, whistled a simple but jaunty sea-shanty ('Come cheer up my lads, 'tis to glory we steer') as he parked the Lagonda in the half-circle of road at the cemetery gates. The grave keeper came immediately from his small mausoleum-like house at the gate and pointed at the car. Kitty, the unfumigated Kitty, raised itself blandly and blindly in the back seat, looked around and with a surge of disinterest fell down again to customary sloth.

The keeper pointed at once an accusing finger at the car. 'Can't you dump that thing somewhere else?' he demanded. 'It gives this place a bad name. And I can smell that dog, or whatever it is, from here.'

'I suppose I've got used to him,' grimaced Davies mildly. 'I won't take a couple of minutes of your time.' He was tempted to add, 'I just want to inquire about digging up a few graves.' But tact prevented him.

'What is it?' demanded the man. He stood posed between a large laurel and a weeping elm. Davies realized how well trees and shrubs did in this particular plot and felt a distant shudder. The keeper sniffed. 'I hope you don't want to hang around the cemetery all night-again, like last time,' He laughed, almost a snarl. 'Whatever heard of anybody threatening to blow up a place like this!'

'Ah,' said Davies, 'I am glad you mentioned that, friend. I'm afraid that was an administrative error.'

The man got half-way to putting a protective hand on the

nearest bent headstone, but stopped himself. 'What is it you want, this time?' he asked.

'I wondered if I could just have a look at the registers, the Record of Burials, or whatever they're called in the profession,' asked Davies. He smiled grandly as though requesting a list of prizewinners. 'You've got them, I take it?'

'Of course, we've got them,' replied the man. 'Otherwise we wouldn't know *who* was bloody *who*, would we?'

'That's logical,' agreed Davies.

'It's official police business then?'

'Naturally,' lied Davies. 'Would I do this for a pastime?'

The keeper turned and went back to his house, leaving Davies looking around him at the memorial stones, the final imprint of men upon earth. Some of them were quite old and he had to get close to read the inscriptions. Keys sounded behind him making him start. 'It's around the other side,' said the keeper. 'The registry.'

On the short journey to the place where the records were kept he seemed to unbend a little. Perhaps he was one of those persons who cannot bear to walk in silence with anyone, even in a cemetery. 'It's fucking cold this morning,' he said.

Davies remembered him swearing the time before and wondered whether foul language came readily to people who worked among those who cannot listen. It was the man's only comment, however, and he unlocked the registry door with a surly twist of the keys. They walked into a long, icy room lined with racks and heavy ledgers. There was a writing desk with a green baize top, an inkstand and an ominously empty chair. Davies imagined the skeleton figure of Death crouched there at night over his ledgers. He declined the keeper's invitation to sit down.

'Who was it, or when was it?' asked the man.

'Who – I don't know,' said Davies awkwardly. 'But it would be July 1951. About that.'

'About that!' retorted the keeper. 'You don't know *who* it is – and you don't know *where* and you don't know *when*!'

'We're struggling a bit on this one,' admitted Davies. He pulled at his nose thoughtfully. 'Can I ask you – how long before a burial is the grave actually dug?' He wondered why the man showed no arousal of interest in the inquiries.

'Depends,' was the dull answer. 'If we're going to have a rush we might get them done a few days in advance, but normally it's just the day before. It's a business that just ticks over.'

'Well, in that case,' decided Davies. 'Could we check the burials for the 24th, 25th, 26th of July, 1951.'

The man assumed his customary crumpled expression, sighed, but went along the racks until he came to the appropriate book. Davies watched him and, looking along the moribund shelves, fancifully thought that tasteful notices saying 'Thrillers', 'Romances', 'True Life Adventure' might cheer the place. The man came back with a thick ledger. 'Quarter for July to September,' he said thumping the book down. 'I'm glad it wasn't a winter quarter, this is bleeding heavy enough.'

Davies took the occupational grumble with an understanding nod. He sat at the empty chair, now without thinking, and with compressed eagerness began to turn the pages. He reached July 24th, three entries, two on the 25th, three again on the 26th. He borrowed a pencil from the keeper and finding, for once, his notebook wrote down the names.

'Would these graves be all in more or less the same area?' he asked.

The keeper nodded. At last a touch of interest was germinating in his face. 'What's it all for anyway?'

'Just routine inquiries,' replied Davies unconvincingly. 'Which part of the place?'

The keeper checked the book over his shoulders, looking at the serial numbers. 'North-west corner,' he said. 'It's not used now.'

'By the wall?'

'Yes. Well more or less. There's a bit of green this side of the wall, then the path, then this section.'

'Where are all the tools kept?' asked Davies suddenly. 'The spades and such like.'

The man was beginning to look surprised. 'Tools? This is a funny business, isn't it? Tools? Well, they're supposed to be kept in the central store shed, but more often than not they're left out. The blokes you get on this job, they just leave them against the wall or even in the grave. They haven't got a lot of interest or pride in the work and they bugger off as soon as they can, leaving the tools until the next day. Half the gardens around here have been dug with spades nicked from this cemetery.'

'It gets better,' said Davies to himself. He looked at the man. 'So if that area of the cemetery was being worked, as it were, eight burials in three days, then the tools might well be left there.'

'They could have been.'

'Right,' said Davies rising. 'Thanks very much. I'll be off.'

The man was now eager to ask about it, but Davies, wrapping his overcoat like silence about him made only non-committal answers. As they approached the gatehouse again he noticed the yellow splash of an excavator a few hundred yards away across the petrified causeway of headstones.

'What are they doing over there?' he inquired.

'Doing some business with the road,' replied the keeper. 'They've had to move the wall over. And dig up some old graves. I don't hold with that, digging them up.'

'Nasty job,' commented Davies.

'In the olden days,' replied the keeper, apparently glad to dispense some graveyard history, 'they had to get the labourers drunk on whisky before they'd take it on. It was very smelly and so on. But now they've got chemicals and such-like. But I still don't reckon it.'

They had reached the gate now. 'Ever had an exhumation order carried out here?' Davies asked casually.

Shock smothered the keeper's face. 'Oh no,' he said. 'This is a respectable cemetery. Not for donkey's years. Long before my time.'

'Be quite difficult to get *eight* exhumation orders, I imagine,' said Davies, beginning to walk towards the car.

'Eight!' The keeper appeared likely to faint. 'Eight exhumations! Over my dead body!'

'That's what I thought,' said Davies. 'Thanks anyway.'

Without answering the man turned towards his house,

glancing back suspiciously towards the exiting Davies. 'Mad,' he said. 'Absolutely fucking mad.'

Davies got into the Lagonda and thoughtfully started the engine. But he did not put the car into gear. There was something wrong. Slowly he turned and, leaning over, lifted the edge of the tarpaulin and exposed the crouching Kitty underneath. Kitty was gnawing a large bone.

'Listen,' said Davies to Mod. 'If our idea is right, if our murderer caught Celia Norris in the cemetery when she was stealing the flowers, or saw her going over the wall, or coming back, or whatever, did his nasty business, and then buried her in an already dug grave, then we've got to dig up eight coffins.'

'A formidable task,' agreed Mod. They were slouching along to 'Bali Hi', Furtman Gardens, having had to miss their evening drink because Mod had been kept late at the Labour Exchange. An emergency matter had arisen and there was a strong threat that he might be offered a job. He had managed to overcome it, however, before he left for home.

Mod, who never wore an overcoat, never having owned one, was walking comfortably in a sagging purple sports jacket and an open-necked shirt. Davies was curled like a large, walking chrysalis in his brown coat. 'The trouble is,' said Davies. 'No matter how far fetched it seems, the opportunity and the props were all there. That was the part of the cemetery being used at that time, there were several open graves, and the tools were most likely left lying about. He could have raped her, or whatever, killed her and then dug a foot or so deeper into an already dug grave and buried her in there. So that the next day the coffin it was intended for was put in on top of it, and the whole lot buried for good. And the whole thing could have been done in the best possible conditions – at night and in peace and quiet. There's nowhere more private than behind a cemetery wall.'

'Who, for God's sake, is going to let you dig up eight graves?' said Mod.

'Nobody,' admitted Davies. 'I wouldn't even like to inquire.'

Mod glanced at him unhappily. 'And don't think I'm going to help you dig them up on the quiet,' he said. 'Because I'm not. I'm not allowed heavy manual work. I'd have got a job long ago if I was.'

They reached 'Bali Hi', Furtman Gardens. On the coat-rack in the hall was pinned a note, for Davies. It said: 'Mr William Lind wishes to see you at the police station.'

The evenings had become enclosed and dark now and on his walk to the police station Davies passed only five other people, and three of those were walking dogs. He reflected once more how, even in that tightly populated place, the streets were emptied at evenings. In some countries, it would be the time for people to be out promenading, parading themselves, but here it seemed that once the factories had stopped for the day people shot like moles into holes and vanished. Even on a hot summer evening, like the one on which Celia Norris was seen for the last time, there were few people actually out walking. There was the matter of television, of course, but also there were few outdoor places to go. A few small parks and the dead banks of the canal. People did as they did in the winter, they went into the pubs or stayed in their rooms. The only difference was that in the summer they left the windows open.

Venus, the evening whore, waved a customary hand to him from the end of the police station street. She looked lonely, exiled, as only a whore can look. For once the police station interior looked welcoming, its official light optimistic in comparison to the overwhelming weariness of the street. The duty sergeant was leaning over the inquiry counter and, at the safe distance, attempting to comfort an elderly lady who regularly reported being followed by salacious men with long fingers. 'My trouble, officer,' she whinnied, 'is that I look so young *from the back*. They always follow me.'

'She should try walking backwards,' muttered the sergeant when she had gone out complaining and full of anticipation into the awaiting night. 'That would scare them off. Your bloke is in the charge room, Dangerous.'

Davies thanked him and went into the bleak charge room.

William Lind was sitting there, biting his lip. He rose as Davies walked in and knocked his wooden chair over backwards, then jumped violently as it sounded on the floor.

Lind's face looked shocked, as though he had committed a recent malpractice. He fumbled and righted the chair. Davies sat down at the opposite side of the wooden table, his overcoat draped around him like a wigwam. 'Mr Lind,' he said steadily, 'Now what can I do for you?'

'Well Mr Davies, I heard ... I understand from my wife, that is. You're looking into the Celia Norris business.'

Davies glanced over his shoulder to make sure he had shut the door. The Metropolitan Police did not like you doing your own work or your hobby on their premises. The door was closed. A policeman passed by and, out of habit, glanced over the frosted glass horizon into the charge room. But the semi-head floated away and Davies returned to the drawn face of Bill Lind.

'What was it, Mr Lind?' inquired Davies. 'Bill?'

'Just this,' said Lind. He felt into his pocket and produced a plastic bag from which he took Celia Norris's light green knickers. Davies almost fell backwards over the chair.

'They're hers, Celia's,' said Lind. 'They've been kept in mothballs.'

'That's almost the full house,' said Davies aloud but to himself as he reached across to take the small garment. 'It seems like everything has been kept in mothballs.'

'What ... what's that mean?' asked Lind.

'Forget it. How did you come by these?'

'I found them,' said Lind simply. 'Straight up, Mr Davies. In the saddle bag of my bike. The day after she vanished. I opened it up and there they were.'

'How did you know they were hers?' inquired Davies.

'Ah, you can't catch me like that,' said Lind. The denial was made with something near waggish triumph. A finger came up but he stopped short of shaking it. 'I'd seen her in the club, like playing table tennis and netball and that, and all the boys used to have a look. See a flash of the girl's pants. You know, like lads do ...'

174

'Yes, yes, they do,' agreed Davies solemnly. 'But you were her boyfriend, weren't you, Mr Lind! Her regular?'

'Well sort of,' said Lind doubtfully. Davies could visualize him wearing swimming-trunks in the bath. 'But that's not the reason I know they were Celia's. It wasn't like that, see. I was a bit of a little gentleman, you understand, and I liked to be decent about things. I still do. I thought of her in a ... well, pure sort of way.'

'Except when she was playing table tennis or netball. Then you had a look with the other lads?'

Two small red spots, almost like those of a clown, appeared on Lind's white cheeks.

'Now, now, Mr Davies. I didn't come here to have you accusing *me*,' he said primly. 'I came because I wanted to help.'

'It must be a long walk,' commented Davies dryly. 'It's taken you twenty-five years. Why didn't you take this article to the police at the time, Mr Lind? You knew they were looking for her clothes.'

'Not right away, I didn't know. Because it was some time before they started to get really worried about her,' said Lind hurriedly. 'I kept them first of all because I knew they were hers and I just ... wanted them. I wanted to keep them. Can you understand that?'

'Why didn't you go to the police at the time?' insisted Davies heavily. 'You must have known it was the proper thing to do.'

Lind put his face against his fingers. He had strangely effeminate hands for a capstan operator. 'I was scared to. The coppers ... the police came and took statements and I was frightened out of my life. I thought if I'd shown them these they would have jumped to the conclusion that *I* did it. And they could hang you in those days, Mr Davies. I didn't want to hang by mistake. So I didn't tell them ... I'm beginning to wish I hadn't told you now.'

Davies ignored it. 'Where have you kept them?' he said. 'Hidden.'

'In the loft,' said Lind. 'In an old suitcase, with a lot of other stuff.'

'You live in a flat,' said Davies. 'How long have you had a loft?'

'At my mother's place,' said Lind smartly with that little touch of triumph recurring. 'You didn't give me time to tell you, did you. In my mum's loft. That's where they've been. I spend quite a lot of time at my mum's. In fact I may go there for good soon. My wife's getting on my nerves, you see. A couple of weeks ago she was actually *fighting – fighting* with some man on the stairs outside the flat. None of the neighbours think she's any good, Mr Davies.'

Davies tried not to swallow hard but he did. He retreated into the overcoat to hide the lump as it went down. 'How did this garment get in your saddle bag then?' he asked.

'Somebody put them there,' said Lind simply. 'As a joke or something. Before they realized that something had happened to her, I thought she'd done it herself. It was the sort of teasing thing she'd do.'

Davies said, 'She was a bit of a ... *teaser,* wasn't she?'

'*I* would never say that,' sniffed Lind. 'I didn't think like that. And I still don't. I used to think of her very purely. That was the trouble.'

Davies nodded. 'Very gallant I'm sure. Right, it looks as though I'm going to have to get all this down in a statement at some time. Is there anything else, Mr Lind?'

He had asked the question with no hope, but immediately he was overjoyed he had put it. Lind half decided to say something, then thought not, then, looking up to see Davies's eyes jutting out at him, he ventured: 'Yes, there was, sort of.'

'Well, what, sort of?'

'It might be nothing, Mr Davies. But my mum reckons that about ten or twelve years ago she was sitting in one of those shelters in Glazebrook Park, you know the little round shelters, kind of divided into compartments. She was sitting there, having a rest walking back from the shops, when she heard two women talking in the next bit, the other side of the wooden dividing piece.' He glanced up to see if Davies was interested. The policeman's eyes were on him. 'And my mum says she heard one woman saying to the other that her husband had seen Celia walking along the canal towpath with a man. And this bloke had his arm around her. And this woman reckons her husband told the police, when they was asking for information, but she heard nothing more about it. Don't you think that's funny, Mr Davies?'

Davies closed his eyes as if it might stop his heart beating so loudly. 'This woman,' he asked. 'Did your mother know who she was?'

'She saw the two women as they got up and walked away,' said Lind. 'And she knew one of them slightly. But she didn't know which was the one who had said it. The woman she knew was called Mrs Whethers, and she lived somewhere down by the Kensal Green Empire, that was. It was years ago, mind. She might not be there now.'

sixteen

Guiltily Davies filled in his required official report at the police station, borrowing a Yellow Pages Directory for suitable addresses, bookmakers establishments, drinking clubs and the like, where he might have been expected to go in quest of Ramscar. Indeed he had been moved by conscience to pursue some genuine inquiries but these had proved predictably pointless. He believed Ramscar might come to him in the end. In the meantime he found it impossible to think beyond Celia Norris. He filed the report for Yardbird, wondered glumly how long it would be before the inspector began to complain, and then left the station to find Mrs Whethers.

Mrs Whethers was a comfortably heated-looking lady, a flush occupying her face as she hobbled out into the afternoon air on her journey to the Over Sixties' Club in the Kensal Rise Pavilion. A transfixed fox stared glassily from around her neck as if it had jumped there and died. She carried it like a hunter bearing his prey. She had a substantial coat which she had worn for many years but which seemed to have thickened instead of thinned and now had the texture of compressed wood shavings. It banged solidly against her elderly legs as she made her familiar journey down her street.

Davies observed her leave her gate and followed. She reached a bus stop in the main road and stood there substantially. Davies then approached her. 'Mrs Whethers,' he ventured, 'I wonder if I could have a word with you?'

As some people get old their curiosity seeps away and nothing matters. She seemed not very surprised or interested. 'If it's insurance, the Conservatives or Jehovah's Witnesses, I don't want to know,' she said firmly. 'Or soap powders.'

Davies smiled. 'None of them.' he replied. 'Are you going to get a bus from here?'

She sniffed hugely. 'No, I'm waiting to see if Lloyd-George comes along. I haven't got time to talk to you, young man. I'm on my way to my club.'

'Perhaps I could come with you.'

She regarded him with doubt. 'It's over sixties,' she decided. 'But you look a bit threadbare so I expect they'll let you in. Where. for God's sake, did you get that terrible coat?'

'In a sort of auction,' he replied lamely.

'You were done, son,' she told him firmly. 'Diddled. What did you want anyway?'

'I'm a policeman. Plain clothes.'

'Plain clothes is the word,' she agreed surveying the garment again. 'Never saw plainer.'

'Here's the bus,' he said glad to change the course of the talk.

'I don't need the bus,' she said briskly. 'I'm just having a breather. I'm off now. It starts at half past two.'

She hobbled away at a large pace and Davies hurried after her. 'I wanted to ask you something, that's all.'

'I've got nothing to fear from the police,' she said. She was puffing a little. 'And I want to be in time for the dancing lesson.' She stopped and faced him, as though knowing that walking and talking together were too much for her. 'So if you are making police inquiries you'd better come with me and when I get a spare minute I'll see if I can answer them.'

That was definitely that. She slung her bad leg forward and he had to be content to lope along beside her until they arrived. He did not mind very much. He was glad to have found her. He was relieved she was alive.

The Over Sixties' Club was in a corrugated iron church hall, its roof pointed timidly to heaven, its well-used door touched by a simple stone tablet which said 'Mary Ann Smith. Laid by the Grace of God. December 15th, 1919'.

With some doubt Davies followed Mrs Whethers into the hall. It was jolly with old people, limbering up for a dancing lesson about to be expounded by an extensively-built woman in her fifties, wearing a rose in her hair and a long feather boa which curled affectionately about her neck and big, blunt bosom.

'Gather round, gather round,' instructed the lady, flapping her hands at them. 'Today it's the Argentinian Tango.' The old people all breathed. 'Aaah!' The lady's skirt, for the occasion Davies imagined, was cut like that of a girl gaucho. It reached to the middle of her short shins. She had legs like logs.

The old folks, about twenty women and seven smug-looking men, shuffled forward so they could see the demonstration. Their skins were folded and used, their hands shaky, their understanding uncertain, but their eyes were bright. Dancing was a popular afternoon.

'Gaiety, that's what we must have, gaiety,' announced the instructress. 'And élan! That is what the Argentinian Tango is all about. So I want you to abandon yourself to the music and the romance. Mr Bragg, the gramophone if you please.'

Obediently an ancient man broke away from the eager crowd and edged painfully towards the wind-up gramophone. He looked so feathery that Davies felt inclined to help him with the weight of the record. He managed that, but puffed out his cheeks violently as he wound the handle. Into the wintry room, with its exhortation to 'Love Thy God' emblazoned on the far wall, seeped the wheezing sound of South America, played below distant stars many, many years before.

The instructress demonstrated first the basic tango step, the forward glide and the dip of the foot and the body. Davies, standing largely among the small old people, was not difficult to see but she was apparently not surprised at his presence. Now she paused in her Latin progress and asked him to step forward. He felt himself go pale under his coat but the old folks began to shout raucous encouragement and he was pushed forward firmly to the centre of the floor.

'Perhaps it would be better,' suggested the lady, surveying him, 'if you danced without the er ... garment.'

'Yes, yes ... all right,' agreed Davies. He peeled himself out of the coat. The frail Mr Bragg stepped forward to collect it and at once fell to the floor under its weight. Two other men came forward and bore the coat and Mr Bragg, who kept shouting that he was all right, from the arena.

Davies was instructed to enfold the stumpy lady in his arms. She rolled her eyes provocatively. He had to bend into a question mark to embrace her and this impeded his first-ever attempt to dance the Argentinian Tango even more than would have been the case. For a short woman she was very powerful and she dragged him along like a shunting engine with a heavy load. He somehow concluded the sequence with one knee on the ground in an attitude of gallantry.

'You are most clumsy,' she said loudly, rejecting his clutching hands. 'For a young man, most clumsy. What are you doing here anyway?'

'I'm a policeman,' he muttered helplessly. They all heard him and hummed and tutted between themselves about the well-known clumsiness of the police. He vacated the floor with the single applause of Mrs Whethers, who apparently felt some responsibility towards him.

'Most of this lot couldn't do any better,' she confided. 'Silly old sods.'

There was further instruction and then the elderly watchers were told to take their partners for a trial tango. The seven old men were grabbed like prize gigolos and Mrs Whethers claimed Davies and pulled him on to the floor. The dusty rhythm began again and he rambled and stumbled with her, staggering like someone trying to dance in a storm at sea. There was a familiar smell about Mrs Whethers. Mothballs.

There was a good deal of jolly laughing and clapping after

the dance and cheerful cups of tea were passed around. The dance lady put on her coat and went out, her stint done, and Davies found himself sitting on a Sunday School chair almost knee to knee with Mrs Whethers.

'All right, then, what is it?' she said.

She had quite a powerful face for an old lady, not pink and fluffy like some of them, but girded with deep straight lines as though her head were held on with string. The tea they drank was in enormously thick cups. He wondered whether elderly people, gnashing their teeth perhaps or trying to reassure themselves of their strength, bit through more delicate china.

'Celia Norris,' he said. 'Do you remember?'

'I remember,' she said without showing surprise. 'Never been found. Not a sausage.'

'Right,' he confirmed. 'Now I've got the job of digging the whole thing up again, Mrs Whethers.'

'How's that?' she inquired, enjoying her tea with a serene sucking sound. 'It's been a long time.'

'Sometimes these things take a long time,' he said attempting to sound wise. 'Anyway, I've heard whisper that your husband made a statement to the police.'

'My late husband, Bernard,' she agreed. 'Yes, he did. He was willing to swear it on oath too. But he never heard another thing from them, not a word.'

'Raffle.' The disembodied voice came from behind his shoulder. Mrs Whethers began wrestling with a handbag the size of a cat and produced two ten-pence pieces. 'You'd better get some tickets as well,' she advised Davies. 'They don't like it if everybody doesn't put in.' She said it as if they were a foreign tribe indulging in strange insular customs.

Davies burrowed into the pockets of his overcoat. The wasted lady who stood behind him held the book of tickets threateningly like a witchdoctor with an omen. Davies handed her two ten-pence pieces. 'You have to *give* something as well,' Mrs Whethers advised. 'A packet of tea or a tin of beans or some cake mixture.'

'I forgot to bring them,' said Davies. 'I knew there was something . . .'

The ticket lady said: 'Well, you've got to give something. Them's the rules. Right, Mrs Whethers?'

Mrs Whethers nodded grimly. 'If you don't put something in you can't have anything out, even if your ticket wins. Have you got a pound note?'

Davies began reaching into what appeared to be the very fastnesses of his body. 'Yes,' he affirmed. 'Yes, I've got a pound.'

'Good, put that in. It's a good prize. They'll like that.'

Davies gave the hovering lady the note and turned again to Mrs Whethers. To his annoyance she had risen from her seat and was hobbling up and down like a lame sea captain pacing his bridge. 'I've got to do it,' she explained over her shoulder on the outward run. 'It goes dead. My funny leg. I have to get the blood moving again.'

Davies sighed, got up and began walking alongside Mrs Whethers. She pushed him away. 'Sit down,' she said brusquely. 'It will be circulating in a minute. You can wait until then with your questions. And after the raffle.'

Davies sat down impotently. He could sometimes understand how police officers were accused of intimidating witnesses. Mrs Whethers returned to her seat, her perambulations accomplished, and thrust out a sturdy but damaged leg at him. 'Feel that,' she invited. 'Feel the blood moving through it now.'

He obliged patiently. 'Oooooooo, Mrs Whethers! There's a nice young man!' bawled a gummy old hag in the next tribal circle. 'Ask him to give me a rub of mine!'

The old ones swayed with merriment but the raffle mercifully intervened. 'Eyes down, look in,' called a limpid pensioner in a gravy-stained jacket. He called the numbers and the old people pressed forward eagerly to claim the prizes they themselves had provided. 'Ninety-seven, red,' he called and Davies looked down to see he had the number in his hand. 'Go on,' urged Mrs Whethers. 'See what we've won.'

The raffler was holding the pound note which Davies himself had contributed. When he saw Davies coming towards him he quickly switched the prize to a large tin of garden slug pellets. 'You can't have the pound,' said the stained man firmly. 'If you put it in, you can't take it out.' He turned to the ancient tribe. 'It's the rules, innit?' he said. 'It's the rules,' they chorused in return. Davies went back with his slug pellets and sporting applause. 'You should have slipped the ticket to me,' whispered Mrs Whethers. 'You're a bit slow for a copper.'

'That's what they all say,' agreed Davies. He leaned forward. 'Now tell me about what your husband saw.' Around him the groups had dissolved into conversation, the pound having been miraculously won by the raffler himself. Mrs Whethers at last looked businesslike.

'My husband, Mr Whethers,' she said formally, 'was walking home at about ten o'clock on that night, whenever it was. It still wasn't quite dark because it was in the summer. And he said he saw that girl going down the alley towards the canal with a man.'

Davies nodded gladly.

'A man,' she nodded firmly. 'In a dark suit. And not wearing a hat. And he had his arm around the girl's waist. That's what he saw.'

'You say he made a statement to the police to that effect, Mrs Whethers?'

'As soon as all the fuss started and it was in the papers, my Bernard said what he had seen, but he didn't go to the police. He was a great one for minding his own business. He liked to live and let live. But the rumour got around the neighbourhood, like the one about what Mr Harkness saw, and this policeman turned up out of the blue and took a statement. But he said the law would take its course or one of these things policemen say. And that's the last that came of it.'

Davies felt his heart move again. 'Mr Harkness,' he said. 'Who was Mr Harkness?'

'A very old man. We told the police about him too but he was very ill then, and he used to drink, so I don't suppose they took much notice of him. I mean – how long ago was it now?'

'Twenty-five years,' said Davies.

'Well, he would have been seventy-six *then*, old Harkness. So I don't suppose they put much store by him. But he was reckoned to have seen something. But he was ill and old...'

'Did he have family?' asked Davies. 'Around here now?'

'They moved. To Bristol or somewhere. I didn't know any of them very well. I just heard.'

All around them the encampment was breaking up, the elderly tribe gathering its chattels and making for the door. A man approached and asked Davies if he needed the slug pellets and on hearing that he did not, relieved him of them. Davies went towards the door with the hobbling Mrs Whethers.

'Mr Whethers and me,' said Mrs Whethers. 'We always wondered why we never heard any more. Not a dicky bird.'

At three o'clock on almost any afternoon he knew where to find Mod. He went to the public library, warm as a loaf in the middle of the chill November afternoon. Davies had been into the library on other occasions but he had never appreciated how comfortable as well as improving it was. Mod had studied there for years.

The entrance hall served also as a small museum where were displayed various objects of local history. A fragment of mosaic, Roman, an axe-head, which had an air of late Woolworths about it but was sworn to be of the Middle Ages; a spade used by minor royalty to plant a commemorative tree which had died a good many years before its planter; a set of tradesmen's ledgers from the seventeenth century, and a policeman's helmet which Davies noticed was significantly dented.

On the walls was an assortment of iodine-coloured photographs, none of them hanging straight. They were of groups of councillors with mayors in Nelsonian hats and attitudes; the official opening of several buildings including the library itself, celebrations for coronations and jubilees, a scene of wartime bomb damage in the High Street and the local company of the Home Guard crouched at the side of the canal apparently in the strong belief that Hitler would launch his invasion of Britain via that waterway.

There was a potted palm at the library door, the only hint of exotica for miles about. On such a winter's day it was pleasant to brush against it as Davies went into the library. His overcoat immediately caught the assistant's notice and he knew he was under observation as a possible book thief. He saw Mod sitting smug beneath a benevolent reading light over a table at the far end of the Reference Room.

'Lovely,' he sighed approaching Mod. 'What a fine bloody life.'

'Hush,' said Mod with the traditional library caution. 'Would you care to sit down?' Davies sat at the opposite side of the table. It was like visiting some senior businessman in a large office. Mod leaned forward attentively, his elbows on the table, his fingers touching thoughtfully. 'And what can I do for you?' he inquired in a library whisper.

'Christ, you sound like the Chairman of Shell International,' muttered Davies. 'It's a great life, I must say. Sitting here in comfort, drawing the dole, while the likes of me traipse the streets in the rain.'

'I'm studying,' explained Mod simply. 'This world is enriched by study, not by tramping the streets.'

'You could be right. What is it?' he nodded towards the books, their pages open like the palms of many hands on the table.

Mod leaned over conspiratorially. 'There are still courts in this country,' he whispered, 'which can impose the punishment of the stocks or a journey in a cart of dung. Have you ever come across anything so amazing?'

'Frequently,' muttered Davies taking Celia Norris's knickers from his pocket. He took them out of the plastic bag. 'How about these?'

Mod was stunned. 'Good God,' he said. 'You've *found* them!'

Davies sniffed. 'Quite a collection we're getting,' he said. 'We've got her bike and her pants. All we want now is the body and the murderer.'

'Where did you get them?' asked Mod, his voice hushed with wonder and the requirements of the library. 'They sniff of mothballs.'

'The whole case does,' commented Davies. 'Our friend Bill Lind. He decided to come clean after all these long years. He says they were put in the saddle bag of his bicycle and I think he's telling the truth. You can bet your life that they were put there by Dave Boot. Our Bill's had them hidden away all this time in his mummy's loft.'

'Why did he keep them?' asked Mod. 'A sort of relic?'

'He says not.'

'Why do they smell of mothballs, then, Dangerous? He must have meant to preserve them.'

'He says they were in a trunk of old clothes in the loft and the mothballs were among the clothes. You know what people are like around here, not ever throwing anything away.'

'What are you going to do now? Apply for those eight exhumation orders?'

Davies grinned wryly. 'I might as well apply for promotion to detective chief inspector,' he said. 'Anyway, I've changed my mind about that, Mod. I don't think she's in the cemetery.'

'Why not?'

'She was seen walking down the alley by the pawnbroker's – towards the canal – with a man in a dark suit. That night. I've got a witness.'

'Jesus! A witness?'

Davies held out his hands for restraint. 'Well, he *was* a witness. A Mr Bernard Whethers. He's gone where he can't give evidence, unfortunately. He's dead. There was somebody else too. An old man called Harkness, but he's dead too. He was seventy-six then, twenty-five years ago.'

'They're not going to say much now,' agreed Mod morosely.

'Mr Whethers made a statement, his widow says. He didn't volunteer it, but rumours get around and apparently a copper turned up on the strength of these rumours. It doesn't take long for things like that to get to our ears, not when we're searching around. But that statement was never recorded at the police station I know. I made another check and it's not in the file, or ever mentioned.'

Mod looked at him across the books. 'Miasma from the police station again,' he said.

'The man Mr Whethers saw with a girl he thinks was Celia

was wearing a dark suit. So he said. And no hat. It need not rule out a policeman, our friend PC Dudley for example, because it was almost dark and Mr Whethers was some distance away. The uniform would look like a dark suit and he could have been carrying his hat, or even left it in the police van. They teach you at police school, you know, to take your hat off if you want to gain somebody's confidence.'

'Do they now?' said Mod interested. 'The only time I've had dealings with a copper without a hat is when I knocked it off. What good's a statement of a dead witness anyway? Especially when it's not been recorded at the police station.'

He looked up and whispered, 'Watch the knickers.'

Confused, Davies failed to act in time. A stony lady library assistant, journeying past the table, saw the green gingham lying there. Quickly Mod picked up the little garment and pretended to fiercely blow his nose with it. He then folded the books in a muffled way on the table and, stretching himself indulgently, announced that he believed he had worked enough for the day. With casual familiarity he turned out the table lamp and unerringly returned the volumes to their various places on the shelves. Studying him, Davies could not avoid the impression that he would shortly open a cabinet and pour them both a drink from a comprehensive selection of spirits.

Members of the library staff nodded affable good-nights as he and Mod walked towards the door. 'Hadn't you better remind them to lock up?' Davies suggested.

Mod sniffed potently. 'You may well take the piss,' he said quietly. 'But it's my presence here that, to a great extent, justifies the continued operation of the reference section of this municipal library. I am the doyen of the place, you understand. Every now and then a deputation of councillors comes snooping and I have to hurry out and get a few friends in from the streets to sit and peruse the books for a while. That's why I'm appreciated here, Dangerous. There's no waste of the ratepayers' money while Mod Lewis is studying.'

Davies let the perverse logic roll over his shoulder. He pointed to the policeman's helmet in the foyer. 'Did you, by any chance, dent that?' he inquired.

'General Strike,' recited Mod without a second look. 'Attack on police at the Clock Tower. No, I was not present, owing only to the fact that I was yet unborn. Otherwise I would have been there. I like a good attack on the police.'

Davies said: 'Listen, let me talk this whole thing out to you, Mod. Right from the beginning. And let's walk from the Catholic Church to the cemetery, along the High Street, then down to the canal and along the bank. Just to see if it does anything.'

Mod acquiesced thoughtfully. 'Right,' he nodded having apparently made some mental calculation. 'Even walking slowly – and thinking – that ought to see us at The Babe in Arms as they open the gates.'

'We'll keep to that,' promised Davies. They walked. A pinched wintry dark had overcome the town. Window lights and shops lights shone bravely but only a few feet above the ground the pall of late November had laid itself inclemently across the roofs. The first of the home-going cars were on the roads, there were thickening queues at the bus stops. Davies, not for the first time, wondered what economics inspired West Indians and Indians to come and live, and queue for buses, in such a clime. They stood, with the natives, their faces merged in the gloom, not a snake charmer or a calypso singer among them.

Davies turned his huge coat collar up. It was like a giant's arm about his neck. Mod pulled up the stumpy collar of his sports jacket and thrust his hands into his shallow pockets but did not grumble.

Turning from the main road they continued as far as the Catholic Church. It was uncompromisingly shut and dark, as though the faith had gone bankrupt. But there was a modest parcel of light coming from the window of Father Harvey's house and, at first, Davies made towards it, going down the gravel path with Mod hanging behind. Mod did not like the vicinity of religions. It had been Davies's half-intention to talk briefly with the priest before they began their thoughtful journey, but on looking through the window they saw that he was engaged in hammering together some large sections of wood. His hammering was violent but not more so than his expression. His holy robe was hitched around his waist like the skirt of a washerwoman. Davies thought that a tap on the window would probably cause him to hammer his own thumb, so he began to turn again.

Mod, peering around his overcoat, saw the interior industry also. 'What's he making?' he whispered as they went away. 'An Ark? Do you think he knows something we don't know?'

'It's a do-it-yourself confessional box,' Davies said confidently.

'I would have considered that the confessional was one of the things you could *not* do satisfactorily by yourself,' said Mod, pensively. 'Like making love or playing shuttlecock.' He thought again. 'Not that I have a great experience of either.'

Davies pointed to a square roofed shadow beyond the church. 'That's the youth club,' he said. 'It's a new building but it's on the site of the old one. So we can say that Celia Norris began her last bicycle ride from there. Her cycle would have been in the yard and she would have come out through this gate and made off towards the cemetery to get her mum the flowers.'

They began there and followed the trail, humped as a couple of slow bloodhounds. At the cemetery entrance they were inevitably confronted by the graveyard keeper who peered through the gloom and the gates. 'Oh, Christ, it's you again,' he said regarding them as he might have regarded Burke and Hare. 'I hope you haven't got that stinking dog with you.'

Davies immediately worried that they had discovered the missing bone. It was still, violently gnawed, in the back seat of the Lagonda. Every time he had attempted to recapture it Kitty had growled spitefully. 'No, no,' he assured. 'No dog today. Just taking the air. This is Mr Modest Lewis.'

'Funny place to take it,' said the man, ignoring Mod. 'The air around here.'

'Mr Lewis is a famous pathologist,' added Davies trenchantly. The graveyard man was at once impressed. 'Oh, very pleased to meet you,' he said in the manner of one greeting a worker in the same trade. He pushed his hand, white as a bat in the winter darkness, through the bars of the gate. Mod, never unready to assume a part, took it, examined it carefully and let him have it back.

'That's a cold hand,' he said, frowning professionally.

'Is it?' said the man with a hint of worry. 'Is there . . . is there anything I can do for you, Mr Lewis? We don't have that many pathologists visiting us. Anything you'd like to see, perhaps?' He sounded as if he were quite prepared to start digging.

'Nothing, nothing at all,' replied Mod carefully. 'But you just look after your hands. They're very cold.'

'I will, I will,' promised the man apprehensively. 'I'll warm them in front of the fire.' He hurried away with his palms thrust beneath his armpits.

Mod grinned in the dark. 'I enjoyed that,' he said as they continued their trail. 'I've always thought I might like to be a pathologist, you know. No one gets nearer to the human being than the pathologist. Imagine, one day, performing a post-mortem – *and finding a man's trapped soul!* Fluttering away there like a snared butterfly. Now that would be a thing, wouldn't it, Dangerous?'

'If you'd like to start on the ground floor,' observed Davies wryly, 'I can give you a human femur. If I can get it out of Kitty's jaws. He nicked it from the boneyard last time we were here.'

'Dear, dear,' said Mod, shaking his head. 'That dog will get into trouble yet. Just imagine some poor soul limping through eternity without a thighbone.'

They had paused beneath the cemetery wall. Somewhere there PC Frederick Fennell had found the abandoned bicycle. It was a ragged patch of ground, a gathering place for tufted grass and weeds, although sweetened by daisies and dandelions and visited by occasional desperate bees in the summer. The light of the street lamps touched hanging ears of ivy on the brick wall. 'That ivy must have been here then,' said Mod knowledgeably. 'If it could only talk.'

'I'd be glad if some humans would talk, never mind the ivy,' grumbled Davies. He began to walk again in the direction of the main shopping street. The lights were going out all over the World Stores, David Greig's and the Home and Colonial. Men dodged into a small furtive shop for cigarettes and at the corner Job, the newspaper seller, called mournfully, 'Tragedy tonight! Big tragedy!' as he peddled his gloomy wares in the gloom.

As they walked Davies related the events, as he knew them, appertaining as he officially put it to the disappearance and undoubted murder of Celia Norris. Mod walked beside him grunting and listening. They turned eventually down the alley path between the pawnbroker's and the 'Healing Hands Massage Parlour', and plunged into the damp darkness of the canal cut. Davies climbed the bank of the allotments and surveyed the darkened rows of cabbages and sprouts. A platoon of bean poles stood guard in the dark. He got down again and they paced the towpath carefully, Davies still talking, Mod leaning over to look into the oily water as if hoping some clue or inspiration might still be given up from there. They walked the half mile length until they reached the road bridge that transversed the canal. Their journey had been frowned upon by the rears of warehouses and shops and a few terrace houses with their backs to the waterway. Somebody had even parked a little boat by the dead water. There were romantics everywhere.

Back on the road Mod's nose began to twitch towards the distant junction light of The Babe in Arms and they hurried towards the early evening brew. After their customary three pints they repaired to 'Bali Hi', Furtman Gardens where Mrs Fulljames had created tripe and onions for dinner and Mr Smeeton was appropriately disguised in Breton costume. 'French Club tonight,' he mumbled enigmatically. Mr Patel was explaining a metallic bending of a fork to Minnie Banks and Doris who were looking on entranced.

After dinner Davies went to his bedroom. Covering the bedside lamp with a vest (Mrs Fulljames did not approve of lights burning in all parts of the house) he wrote down with great care everything he knew about the case of Celia Norris. Then, on another sheet of paper, borrowed from Minnie and headed 'Kensal Green Primary School', he wrote everything he *thought* he knew, and on a third, the things he *wished* he knew. He folded his work and put it inside a shoe (an odd shoe, the survivor of a battle at an Irish goodwill party) in his wardrobe.

At ten o'clock he thought he would stroll to The Babe in Arms before it closed. It had become misty merging on foggy. He spent only a few minutes in there chiefly because of the woman who sang 'Viva España' and then returned back to Furtman Gardens. Half-way down the foggy street, beneath its only tree, he was violently attacked by three, possibly four men. He was struck on the head and was aware of blows coming from all directions. Even in his pain and confusion he thought he detected the familiar blow of a pick-axe handle. He fell to the pavement and was then gratefully aware of a distant panic among his assailants. At once the blows ceased. He thought they were running away and there was another sound of heavier running, then hot, smelly breathing into his battered face. It needed all his strength to open his eyes once. He found himself looking up into the worried face of the rag-and-bone man's horse.

seventeen

As he hung across a stretcher in the Casualty Department at the hospital Davies opened his eyes and smiled a grating smile at the young doctor nosing over his injuries. 'Could I have my usual room, please?' he asked. He was aware of another figure prostrate on a trolley-stretcher a few feet away. He half-turned and even to his blurred vision the face looked familiar. The man seemed to sense he was looking and scraped his head to the side so that he could face him. It was Josie's father.

'Hello, Mr Norris,' muttered Davies. 'What are you in for?'

'Same as you, you fucking berk,' said Mr Norris unkindly. 'I told you to lay off.'

'Ramscar as well, eh?'

'It wasn't Father Christmas. I told you what would happen. I hope they've duffed you up good.'

The young doctor looked annoyed. 'Will casualties please stop quarrelling among themselves,' he said petulantly. 'It's not a mothers' meeting, you know.' He turned as two orderlies came into the area. 'This one,' he said pointing at Davies. 'Dressings and observation.' Then he nodded at Norris. 'That one, theatre number two. In half an hour.'

Davies's heart fell. He thought at once of Josie. 'Sorry, Mr Norris,' he whispered.

'So am I. Ramscar will nail you, you just bleeding wait. I'm staying inside here for as long as I can. By the time I'm out maybe you and the rest of the berks will have got him. I bloody doubt it, though. I doubt it.'

Davies was beginning to personally doubt it himself. He ached from the waist up, but he knew they had not hurt him as much as before. He decided to buy the rag-and-bone man's horse a complete cabbage once he was released from hospital.

It was his last conscious thought until next day. He awoke in the early afternoon when a pale, round nurse asked him if he would like a bedpan and some custard. He declined the custard.

Mercifully neither Doris nor Mrs Fulljames came to visit him. That would have been beyond his patience. But Mod did, sitting moodily watching his bandaged face with doubt and consternation.

'I suppose,' remarked Mod with Welsh solemnity, 'that a powerful police dragnet is at this very instant closing around the perpetrators of this new outrage against your person.'

Davies grinned and winced. 'I have no doubt that the Metropolitan Police have been moved to vast inactivity,' he said. 'They sent a sergeant over here to get all the thrilling particulars and the cops' doctor came and looked me over. It's been terrific, believe me. My God, by now they'll have enough men in the hunt to throw a cordon around a phone box.'

'A disgraceful situation,' grumbled Mod. 'They seem to have no regard for you at all. Still, I suppose they're so accustomed to seeing you bashed about that the novelty's worn off.'

Josie came to see him too. She sat by the edge of the bed regarding him sorrowfully but saying nothing. He felt like an archer looking through a small slit window, 'You've got a job lot to visit now,' he joked with difficulty. 'How's your old man?'

'In a mess,' she shrugged. 'Worse than you, and that's saying something, that is. Christ, you must have three miles of bandages round your head.'

'Sorry, Josie,' he mumbled. She looked lost. She put her hand on the bedclothes. 'Don't you go blaming yourself, Dangerous,' she replied softly. 'He's been skimming around in that mucky pond for years. First with Ramscar then with others like him. Some time or another he was bound to get done. And you were doing your job as a copper. What else can anyone say?'

'What about your mother?'

'She's got the wind up. It was she who found the old man on the doorstep. He'd gone to the door. I've shoved her off to her sister's in Luton.'

'Is Luton far enough away?' asked Davies. 'From Ramscar?'

'It's got to be. The next nearest relative's in Australia.' She laughed making the joke, but her face was crowded with fear. 'It's got to stop some time,' she said. 'Or else somebody's going to get killed. And it looks like you're favourite, Dangerous.' She suddenly laid her head against the white bedcover, her face small and pinched. He touched her thin shoulder with his fingers and she put her hand up to hold them.

'Do you think it's just Ramscar?' she asked, still with her head on his legs. 'Or is it something to do with that Celia thing? Somebody trying to stop you.'

'It could be both,' he sighed. 'Maybe they're the same thing. Maybe Ramscar did it after all. The more I find out the less I know, Josie. Do you think your father knows where Ramscar is hiding out?'

She laughed wryly. 'If he does there's no bloody way he's going to tell anybody *now*. Not the state he's in. It's a miracle they managed to sew him together again. He's like a patch-work quilt. It's sodded up his looks for good, and he never looked much anyway.' She looked up from her crouching position, slowly, then quickly, as though awakening after a nap. 'Dangerous, have you found out *anything* about Celia? What happened to her.'

He had never told her. He paused a moment now, then he said, 'I've got her bike, Josie, and I've got her pants.'

He thought she was going to fall off the chair. 'You've got what!'

'Her bike and her pants,' repeated Davies carefully.

'Christ! However did you ...?'

'Listen,' he said. He tried to lean forward but it hurt too much. 'Listen, Josie, I've turned up all sorts of things. I'll tell you soon, promise. Not now, because it's too public here, and I feel too rough right now. But I'll tell you before long ex-actly *what* happened to your sister. Perhaps I'll know *who* did it too.'

Josie continued to stare at him in deep disbelief. 'I ... I can't believe it,' she said. 'Honest, I just can't believe it.'

'You didn't think I could do it?'

'No ... no, it's not that. I just didn't think *anybody* could do it. And you've got the bike?'

'Still in working order,' Davies said quietly. 'A bit creaky but nothing more. I've even got the remains of the flowers she was taking home to your mother. She got them from the cemetery, you know.'

She appeared to be unable to digest the information. She slowly got to her feet. 'I've got to go,' she said. 'I've got to think about this.' She looked at him doubtfully. 'You're sure,' she said. 'I mean you're not having me on ...'

'I'm sure,' nodded Davies. 'Very sure. See you, Josie.'

'See you,' she almost stuttered. She moved forward quickly and kissed him on the piece of cheek that was showing. As she moved away she produced a small smile. 'You're brighter than I reckoned,' she said.

'Thanks,' he replied. 'Sometimes I surprise myself.'

She went without looking back. He realized that his head was throbbing from the encounter. He slept briefly and then lay, in the night dimness of the ward, thinking about Celia Norris and her bicycle journey to eternity twenty-five years before. He followed every turn of the pedals by those brown shoes. From the youth club to the cemetery. He saw her brazenly climb the wall, knickerless, and steal the flowers from a grave. He knew she would be capable of that. He could see Josie doing it. And then what? Waiting outside the wall, or just approaching it as she climbed over again in the gloom, was the mooching police van. At its wheel, a policeman who had been drinking at the social function shortly before; alone in the van while his colleague spent time with his fortune-telling lover.

What did he do, that policeman? Did he get out of the car and stand waiting under the wall while she climbed over? Did he see then that this seventeen-year-old girl was wearing nothing below her gingham dress? Was he stern with her and did he take her into the police van, not seeing her bicycle left in the dandelions and weeds? Did they drive slowly up the High Street that humid summer night? And while they drove did that inebriated policeman suggest to that young girl that they went down by the canal bank together? Did he cajole or threaten her?

Davies saw them walking in the dusk, the policeman without a hat, as Mr Whethers had seen. Down to the foot of the valley and by the bank. And then it happened. That policeman raped Celia Norris and murdered her. And disposed of her body. But not her clothes. Disposed of her body ... but not her clothes...

Suddenly Dangerous Davies shot up in bed so fast that his head sang with pain. He clasped it with a cry that was almost exultation. A man across the ward called out eerily: 'Are you all right? Shall I get the nurse?'

'No, no,' warned Davies hoarsely. 'Nothing, thank you.'

The last thing he wanted was the nurse. He looked at his watch. It was only ten o'clock. They closed down early in hospitals. He slid clumsily out of bed, stood up and put his pillow beneath the sheet. His head banged in protest as though somebody were trying to get out through the bandages. There was an ante-room just outside the ward and last time that was where they had kept his clothes. He went painfully but hopefully across the polished floor of the ward, his head feeling like a turnip. But his hope was realized. His suit and his overcoat were keeping each other forlorn company on a single iron hanger. His shoes were in a locker beneath, but he could not find his socks, his underwear or his shirt. He took the clothes and the shoes and went into the toilet. He put them on over his pyjamas, and pulling the faithful overcoat up around his plastered ears he crept heavily towards the corridor. There was no one there. The night nurse was in a side room and the doorway to the outside was only a few yards down the passage. He gained it in three strides and let himself out into the chill air.

He was a mile and a half from the single room of Andrew Parsons of the Salvation Army, which is where he wanted to be. Not even the most optimistic of taxis ever patrolled that threadbare area and he was thinking he might have to walk or to steal a bicycle when he saw a bus illuminating the distance. The bus stop was just outside the hospital. No one at the gatehouse took any heed of him and he timed his walk so that he gained the pavement just before the bus. Gratefully he boarded it, miraculously found some coins in his overcoat pocket, and sat on the cross-seat feeling relieved and elated. He thought he knew where Celia Norris was.

At the next stop a couple, arms entwined, boarded the bus and sat opposite him. Their interest in each other was gradually transferred to him. At first they studied his heavily embalmed head, intently as though following every whorl and curve. Then the girl's gaze dropped to his ankles. Awkwardly he followed her eyes down and saw that his pyjama legs were protruding below the turn-ups of his trousers and that immediately below that incongruity he was showing segments of bare feet.

He smiled feebly across at them. 'Night shift,' he said as though confident that that would explain everything.

They nodded dumbly but continued to stare until he left the bus in the High Street. When he last saw them, as the vehicle made off into the latening evening, they were with their faces pushed to the window, together with that of the conductor, to whom they had obviously reported the phenomenon. Davies waved to them as he crossed the road.

He kept into the best shadows of the terrace houses until he came to the front door of Andrew Parsons's lodgings. He knocked with misgiving which was justified by the beginnings of a scream which came from the flowered-overalled woman who answered. He tried to smile through the bandages which made matters worse, but fortunately he arrived at an explanation before she arrived at a screech. 'Mr Parsons, please,' he pleaded. 'Salvation Army. It's an emergency.'

To his relief and her credit, she subsided. 'It looks like an emergency too,' she commented. 'I'll call him. He's up there with his cronies. Blaring away.' She advanced to the bottom of the stairs and bellowed 'Mr Parsons!' up into the gloom. She called twice more and eventually a phase of light showed that a door had been opened. 'Mr Parsons, there's somebody for you. Says it's an emergency.'

'Emergency?' Davies heard Parsons return. 'Who is it?'

'Don't ask me,' she bawled back. 'Looks like the Invisible Man.' She turned to Davies. 'Go on up,' she said. 'I can't stand here shouting my head off.'

Davies thanked her and advanced up the stairs. When he had gained the first landing, Parsons, on the third, called doubtfully again. 'Who is it?'

Davies chanted:

'I am the ghost of General Booth,
I've come to make you tell the truth.'

He was pleased with his extemporaneous effort. He heard Parsons give a quick sob in the gloom and he knew he had been recognized. Parsons almost tumbled down the stairs to meet him. 'Mr Davies...' he said. Then, seeing Davies's state, 'Oh my goodness ... what happened?'

'I tripped over my collection,' said Davies in the dark. 'I want to have a chat, Andy. I've come specially to see you. Can I come up?'

'Oh, for God's sake,' pleaded Parsons. 'Not now. Not in the room. We've got bandsmen practising.'

As though to corroborate the statement a subdued trump issued through the open door above. Then a piping whistle noise. 'All right,' whispered Davies. 'Tell me something, exactly and no bloody lies mate, and you can go back and get on with Crimond, otherwise we go up and talk about it there.'

Parsons's head had dropped. He was muttering, perhaps praying. 'What? What is it then?' he asked.

'Right,' Davies moved closer to him on the landing. 'Where did you *really* find those clothes? *Not* in the public bog. Come on, tell me – they were *not* in there, were they?'

'No,' nodded Parsons. 'Dear God, I knew it would all come out one day. I'm trying to live it down ... The Army ...'

'Where?' asked Davies stonily.

'No, not the convenience. I took them to the convenience when I tried to put them back, after I'd realized that they were that girl's things. But I lied about finding them there. I was just all confused and upset, Mr Davies.'

'Where?' repeated Davies grimly. His heart jerked when Parsons said. 'By the canal. They were just lying there. I nicked them. But when I heard about the girl I panicked and took them to the convenience. That's when they copped me. I couldn't tell them the truth about where I got them. I was already on probation, and they knew I collected things from lines and that. They tried to get me for that girl, Mr Davies and I didn't do it. I stuck to my story, every detail. And they couldn't break me.' A small triumph had entered his voice. Davies leaned out in the half-dark and caught him by the collar. Parsons stifled a squeak. 'They could ... you know ... hang you in those days,' he stammered.

'That's what they all say,' said Davies, remembering Lind. 'Now *exactly* where, Mr Parsons? To the inch.'

Parsons's face was shining with sweat in the dark. 'Yes, yes,' he nodded. 'Exactly. Just at the bottom of the alley, Where the old wartime blockhouse used to be. Just there. I was walking down the alley, towards the canal and I saw them. I was tempted by Satan and I picked them up. God how many times I've regretted that weakness.'

Davies could feel himself smiling painfully within the helmet of his dressings. 'Lovely,' he breathed. 'Lovely. At the bottom of the alley, right. At the foot of those gardens, allotments.'

'It was there,' nodded Parsons. 'By the allotments.'

'Right,' said Davies. 'You can go back to your oompah-pah, now. Have a good blow. But don't piss off to any band festivals or anything. I want to know where I can find you.'

'That's all, then?'

'Yes, that's all. Why, was there anything else?'

'No. Oh no. I'll be going back.'

Davies said: 'All right. Play a tune for me.'

Parsons ran gratefully up the grimy stairs. To satisfy his friends in his room he called over the banisters. 'Good-night Mr Davies. And God bless. I'll pray for you in your trouble.'

It was eleven-thirty when Davies roused Mr Chrust and his two sisters-in-law from their beds above the newspaper office. The same lights and the same entranced faces materialized. They shuffled about and opened the door for him, a strong family politeness apparently preventing them asking how he came to be swathed in ghostly bandages. He did not keep them long from their rest. It was merely a matter of checking the recent issues of the *Citizen* for the report of the prosecution of the vegetable garden thief. Davies noted his name. George Tilth, 47, Harrow Gardens. He thanked Mr Chrust and said a muffled good-night to the ladies of the place. Then he went to see Mr Tilth.

He was relieved to perceive that it was not yet bedtime in the Tilth household. There were lights downstairs in the modest terraced house and Mr Tilth answered his knock fully clothed and appropriately cradling a squat potted plant.

'I don't suppose you remember me?' began Davies.

'I can't see you for a start,' replied Mr Tilth reasonably. 'Not through all that first-aid stuff. Who are you anyway?'

'Police,' said Davies. 'Detective Constable Davies.'

The man went white as lime. 'I've done nothing, officer,' he protested. He glanced down at the pot-plant as a woman might look at her nursing baby. 'This is mine. I grew it all by myself.'

'All right, all right,' calmed Davies. 'I haven't come about anything like that. You're the man who knows all about gardens and I want some information.'

'Information? Horticultural information?'

'Yes, you could say that. Can I come in for a moment?'

Mr Tilth nodded. 'Yes, all right,' he agreed. 'I've got nothing to conceal, Mr Davies. But perhaps you wouldn't mind just waiting here for a moment.'

Davies loitered while from the front room of the house came the sounds of furtive but urgent movements. He was tempted to step in but he knew he could not spoil it now for anything. Eventually Mr Tilth returned, a guilty flush replacing the former pallid countenance. 'Yes, it's all right now. To come in. Just wanted to get the place tidy for you. You don't expect visitors at this time of night, do you? Not generally.'

'Not generally,' acknowledged Davies. He walked in. Even through his mask of dressings he could smell a greenhouse damp. He went into the front room where a table was covered with newspaper, flower pots, plants and scattered compost.

'Taking cuttings,' explained Mr Tilth, 'Messy job.'

Davies glanced around as he was guided towards a chair at the table. A large clothes-horse hung with towels had been awkwardly placed in the corner of the room, strategically, but not so strategically that it completely concealed the fronds of a palm tree coyly curling over its edge. Davies sat down. 'Mr Tilth,' he said firmly. 'This visit is unconnected with any dealings you may have had with the police previously. I want to assure you of that.' He hesitated then rephrased it. 'No, that's not strictly true. It *is* to do with that.' He watched the consternation cram into the man's face. 'But not in the way you think. I want your help.'

'Well, what is it, Mr Davies?' asked Mr Tilth, still not convinced.

'Your allotment. The one by the canal.'

'As was,' said Mr Tilth. 'It's not mine any more. Like I said in court, the Council took it away from me. After all those years of work.'

'Yes, it's the years I'm interested in. Your ownership went back to 1951, didn't it? Before that even.'

'Back to the nineteen forties,' asserted the man, a glimmer of pride rising in his eyes. 'In the dark days of nineteen-forty, when Britain stood alone. And it was my old father's before that. Like I told them in court, it's been our 'eritage, that allotment.'

'You remember when the wartime blockhouse that was built along the bottom, by the canal.'

'Blimey, I'll say. We had our nursery bed there and they came and built that bloody thing. I had a real row with the Home Guard captain or whatever he was. Told him, I did, that I was doing more for the war-effort than him and his tin bleeding soldiers. And he tried to tell me that it was there to *defend* my sprouts and my spuds from the Germans. Load of horseshit.'

Davies let him finish. 'When was it knocked down?' he asked.

'Oh, a couple of years after the war,' considered the man. 'About forty-seven, forty-eight, I'd say.'

Davies felt his hopes sigh as they deflated. 'Not later. Not nineteen-fifty-one?'

'No. Definitely not. My dad died in forty-nine and it was gone then. I remember I was annoyed when they knocked it down in the end because it was useful for keeping tools and that. But it was gone in forty-nine because I remember putting the garden shed what we built and the cold frames we had. I remember putting them on the base of the thing, the concrete foundation.'

'Oh, what a pity,' muttered Davies.

The man regarded him, for the first time, with some measure of curiosity. He sniffed thoughtfully. 'And that was in forty-nine,' he repeated. 'Definitely.'

Davies rose wearily. His face was beginning to ache. The soreness below the bandages was making him shudder. 'Right then,' he said. 'It was just an idea I had, that's all.'

'It must have been an important idea, Mr Davies, for you to come around here in that state.' He glanced apprehensively towards the corner where the palm, like a disobedient child, was poking its head around the clothes horse meant to be concealing it. 'It wasn't for nothing else, then, was it?'

'No, no,' Davies assured him. 'Nothing else.' He went to the front door. He wondered why the man had not asked him to go into the kitchen since the front room had proved such an embarrassment. Perhaps the kitchen would have been even more so.

At the front door they lingered for a moment. The night air felt cold coming in through the triangular eye, nose and mouth gap of the dressing. 'That bit of the allotment was never any good for growing things,' said the man reflectively. 'It wasn't just the concrete floor. We might have got that up, I suppose. But underneath there, there was another room, see...'

The poor man thought Davies had attacked him. He jumped clear from the ground as he was caught by the detective's hands. 'A room? Underneath?' demanded Davies hoarsely. 'A room?'

'Let me go!' pleaded Mr Tilth. Davies dropped him. From his enclosed face his eyes shone. The garden man trembled. 'Yes, that's right, a room underneath. It was a sort of command post, I suppose, for the Home Guard. Like an air-raid shelter would be. There was a trap-door, a sort of metal cover, like a manhole.'

'And when they knocked the blockhouse down, they left the other bit under the ground? So it's still there? And there's a trap-door?'

'Still there,' confirmed the man more steadily. His anxiety was now becoming overtaken by curiosity. 'Why?'

'Come on,' said Davies taking his hand like a child. 'We're going down there.'

'What, now?' The man backed away. 'At this hour of night?'

'There's no better time,' insisted Davies. 'Come on. Now.'

'I'll ... I'll get my coat and tell the missus,' said Mr Tilth. He backed away still staring at the glowing Davies. A female voice called down the stairs. 'I'm getting my coat,' the man called up. 'I'm going out.'

'Are they taking you in?' inquired the woman, as though it was thoroughly expected.

'Shut up, for God's sake,' Mr Tilth called back. 'I'm going to help the detective.'

'That's what they always say,' returned the woman stoically. She came down two stairs from the top and Davies could see her thin shins trapped in large furry slippers. 'Helping the police with their inquiries,' she taunted. 'That's what they say.'

'Mr Tilth is not being arrested for anything,' Davies called up to her. 'He has some valuable information for the police, that's all. We won't be long.'

As they went out into the street she creaked open an upstairs window and leaned out. 'It's a bleeding trick, mate,' she called to her husband. 'Don't you admit nothing.'

'Go to bed, for Christ's sake,' ordered the gardener.

'All right,' she returned angrily. 'But don't expect me to wait for you to come out of prison this time. Don't say I didn't warn you.'

'Silly mare,' commented Mr Tilth. They said nothing more.

It was about ten minutes' walk and they went silently through the hollow streets. Davies was conscious of a shiver in his stomach. He increased their pace. They crossed the main road and then went down along the bank of the canal. It was a dark night and they could not see the water, only sense it and hear its fidgeting. The lamp at the bridge stood in the distance like a mariners' lighthouse; under it there was a reflected yellow sheen on the dull water and its illumination touched the boundary hedge of the allotments.

'I'm glad I'm with you,' said Mr Tilth. 'The magistrate told me that the next time I came here I'd get three months minimum.' He looked at Davies and even in the dark Davies could discern the question all over his face. 'It *is* all right, isn't it?'

'Don't worry,' Davies said ambiguously. 'We won't be here long.'

'I wish I knew what we're going to do.'

'Well, we've not come after turnips or sprouts,' said Davies. 'Not this time.'

The man obligingly showed him the easiest place to climb over the hedge and then followed him into the garden. It was an inhospitable patch, draped with cold darkness, damp rising to the knee. In a strange manner the crammed town seemed to have vanished. They might have been standing in a bog. Davies's attention went straight to the end of the plot.

'He's got his greenhouse on it,' sniffed Mr Tilth. 'Rickety old thing.'

Davies walked slowly along the garden path. The greenhouse stood like a beached ship, a faint light coming through its ribs. The ground around was muddy, but Mr Tilth scratched the surface expertly with his shoe and Davies touched the concrete underneath.

'Where was the entrance, the trap-door?' he whispered.

'About here,' said Mr Tilth. 'He's got the greenhouse over the top of it.' He took a pace forward and opened the wheezy door of the wooden-framed building. Davies saw the whole structure wobble at the touch.

'Bloody awful old thing, this,' the other man complained. 'Rotten. The wooden ones always fall to bits in the end.'

'Is it inside, the trapdoor?' asked Davies anxiously. He shone the torch to get his answer. It illuminated a small glade of pots and plants.

'A mess, just like I thought,' grumbled Mr Tilth. 'Look at that Fatsia. Mr Davies. Ever seen such a disgrace?' He pulled at a large leaf like a hand and it obediently came adrift from its stalk. He looked to the floor. 'It's all wooden boards,' he said. 'I thought he might have concreted it over again, but he wouldn't bother. Not him.'

'Good for him,' remarked Davies. 'Where's the trap door then? Where is it?'

'Let's see. It would just about be at the far end, as I remember.' He bent with the torch. 'He's got a whole lot of Pelegorams overwintering just there.' He sniffed. 'This lot won't see the spring, anyway.' He began to shift the pots without care, tossing them to both sides. There followed some seed boxes and then a brief struggle with some rotten planks which formed the floor. The debris began to pile up on the side. Eventually Mr Tilth straightened up. 'There it is,' he said simply.

Davies almost fell forward, stumbling in his bulky coat over the short planks, seed boxes and plastic flower plots. Mr Tilth was shining the torch downward. It illuminated a rusty metal cover, a yard square, fitted deep into the ground. Davies felt a frightening expectation. 'We'll need a shovel and a pick,' he whispered. 'Can you find them?'

'I might have to break the toolshed lock,' said Mr Tilth with patent hope.

'Do it, then.'

'Right. Won't be a minute. The shed's rotten as well. This bloke's got no idea. No idea at all.'

He went out leaving Davies crouched in almost a prayer-like attitude in front of the rusty metal square. He leaned forward, tapped it with his fist and backed minutely away as though expecting an answer.

A busy splintering of wood came from the darkness outside and then a grunt of accomplishment. Mr Tilth loomed behind him with a spade and a pickaxe. 'You'd better let me do it,' the gardener suggested. 'I know the best way. And with your face all like that . . .'

Davies did not ponder the logic of the statement. He stood back and let the man go to work with a nocturnal profession-alism. In that confined place it was like digging in a coal mine. Small cargoes of stony earth came back as Mr Tilth cleaned the fringe of the metal plate. Eventually he stopped and remarked quietly over his shoulder, 'There's a sort of metal ring at one end. If we can hook the toe of the pickaxe into it we might be able to see if it's going to shift.'

Eagerly Davies passed the pickaxe to him. He was feeling sweaty now, with the inherent warmth of the greenhouse, his heavy clothes, his bandages and his mounting excitement. Mr Tilth took the tool and manoeuvred while Davies shone the torch between his legs, the only convenient aperture. The point of the implement eventually engaged the ring and Davies heard it creak as the ring moved on its hinge. 'Right, let's give it a try,' suggested Mr Tilth. 'Let me have a go first.' His small muscular body bent in the dimness but there was no answering scrape from the horizontal trap. He tried again, fiercely, but then gave it up. 'Good and fixed,' he panted. 'Been fixed for too long.'

'Let's both have a go,' suggested Davies. With difficulty he found space beside Mr Tilth, pushing plants and pots roughly aside to make room. There were two benches now confining them, one on each side. Mr Tilth straightened up and with dark enjoyment tipped one of them on its side sending a further avalanche of nurtured greenery to the floor. Davies took the cue and capsized the other. 'Serve the bugger right,' muttered the deposed gardener happily.

They now had room to both hold the pick. The area of the trap had been cleared but it seemed to have rusted into the very earth. The point of the pick was still engaged in the corroded ring. 'Right,' said Davies. 'Let's try it.'

They both bore down on the handle, seeking to lever the plate from its setting. Nothing happened. They eased off and rested, panting, then tried again. This time they felt it move. 'Steady a minute,' said Davies. They relaxed. 'Next time it'll come.'

It did. They felt it shudder and then begin to move upwards towards them. Davies knew he was shaking with anticipation. 'Keep it up,' he snorted. 'Another good one.'

Then the handle came out of the pickaxe. They were heaving at their utmost when it happened and the release sent them violently staggering back. The considerable weight of Davies, followed by Mr Tilth, collided with the flimsy end wall of the greenhouse behind them. The rotting wood bulged, buckled and collapsed, splintered and split all about them, the panes of glass sliding like a glacier over a precipice. With a sigh the rest of the aged greenhouse followed the collapse, sagging forward and easing itself gratefully to the ground. It fell with no great sound as though it had been awaiting the moment for years. It stretched itself out, some of the glass breaking, but most of the panes simply slithering away. Davies and Mr Tilth found themselves lying under a blanket of wreckage.

'Oh dear,' said Mr Tilth inadequately. 'That's fucking done it.'

Davies dragged himself clear and he and the gardener got to their feet beside what now appeared to be the debris of some disastrous Zeppelin.

'Come on,' said Davies limping around to the rear of the wreckage. Mr Tilth, who was patiently enjoying himself on what he saw as some sort of licensed destruction, wiped the wood-dust from his eyes and followed. 'Ah, that's good,' said Davies. Mr Tilth followed his downward look. The wall's falling the opposite way had almost cleared the metal plate. It required only a few random pushes with their shoes to clear away some stray wood and glass and there it was as exposed as before. 'Can you get the pick,' said Davies almost absently.

'The pick's no bloody good,' answered Mr Tilth. 'The man can't even look after his tools. Anyway we've loosened it up, what we want now is some wire. There's some hanging outside his shed. Hang on, Mr Davies. Just hang on.'

He returned quickly with the wire, it was stout and tough. They hooked and bent it around the upturned ring and then moving to the side, clear of the debris, they heaved on it like a tug-of-war team. They felt the metal shift, scrape, then shift again. Another effort, another taking of the strain, and they heard the whole plate come away. Just ahead of them, in the dark, was a hole.

'Now what?' asked Mr Tilth.

He looked through the night in surprise. Davies was merely standing there, stiff, as though unable to make the final move. 'Now what, indeed,' he said and his voice trembled over the few words. They had put the torch on the ground and now he reached for it and went deliberately towards the square aperture they had opened in the earth. Mr Tilth stood back, wondering, in the manner of someone watching a secret ritual they do not comprehend. Davies reached the hole and stood looking down, still not shining the torch into the opening. Then he did.

It shone immediately on the bones. A pathetic, lonely pile of cold, damp bones. Davies kneeled and looked closer. The torch wavered in his hands. He felt a huge engulfing sadness rising in his throat. Tears flooded his eyes. 'Oh, Celia,' he muttered. 'What a rotten trick.'

eighteen

In the morning the ward sister stopped by his bed and said: 'Ah, there, now you look a whole lot better for a good night's sleep.'

Since he had not returned to his bed before three o'clock he raised his eyebrows as far as he was able. She could only see the triangle of his face between eyes and point of chin, a small area from which to judge that someone was looking better, so he concluded that it was just hospital small talk. Nevertheless after two hours a doctor examined him and said he could go home but had to return every day to the out-patients' department. He went gladly.

Mod was at his desk in the library, like an archbishop wallowing in his books. As Davies walked into the foyer, and paused to smile gratefully at the Home Guard photograph on the wall, he could see a girl from the staff taking Mod a cup of coffee at the distant end of the reference room.

He walked in, evoking disapproving looks from staff and customers, people in bandages apparently being unwelcome. Mod saw him coming and smiled felicitations.

'All better, then, son?' he whispered drinking the coffee above the pages of the open volume before him. 'Glad to see you out.'

Davies sat down and stared from the aperture in his bandages. 'I've found her,' he said simply. 'I've found the body.'

Mod jerked a wave of coffee over the side of the cup and on to the printed page. His sharp and guilty look was followed by a swift sweep of his sleeve to wipe it away. 'Where?' he asked.

Davies told him where and how it had taken place. 'I remembered that Home Guard photo out in the lobby there,' he said. 'It's got a picture of the blockhouse that used to be along by the canal. It's been knocked down, but it had a basement room, a kind of concrete operations room. That's where he put her. Down there.'

Mod's library whisper whistled across the table. 'What did you do?'

'I left her there,' Davies said simply. 'I pulled the cover back and left her there. I've told the gardening bloke, Mr Tilth, that if he says a word to anyone I'll investigate the theft of a palm tree, which he's got standing in his living room at the moment. That scared him. He won't tell.'

'You won't do anything? Not report it?'

Davies shook his head, still a painful achievement. 'I'm going to risk it, Mod,' he said. 'I've got *her* but I haven't got *him* yet.'

'It looks more and more like our policeman friend,' muttered Mod. 'Police Constable Dudley. And he's dead. So you'll never get him.' He touched the coffee-damp pages of his book then closed it. 'Nobody will open that again for a few years anyway,' he shrugged. 'By that time it won't matter, will it.'

'Sounds like a summing up of our case,' said Davies. 'I don't know what to do next, Mod.'

'You would have thought that places like that underground room would have been searched when they were looking for the girl,' said Mod thoughtfully. 'You know, police with tracker dogs, like you see on the television.'

Davies said: 'Well, to start with nobody took her disappearance all that seriously for about a month. I mean she was seventeen, it wasn't a little kid vanishing, and she'd gone off before, remember. There was a search but we'll never know how thorough it was. Perhaps PC Dudley got that area allocated to himself during the search. That wouldn't be all that difficult. Remember a *policeman* actually went to see Mr Whethers, but nothing was ever done, as far as we know, about that statement, or about following up whatever the other old chap, Mr Harkness saw, or thought he saw. Was that policeman PC Dudley as well? Remember Mr Whethers never actually reported what he saw. The policeman *came of his own accord* after hearing the stories going around the district.'

'Perhaps *nobody* at the police station wanted that evidence to come out,' sniffed Mod.

Davies looked at him steadily. 'Yes,' he said slowly. 'I hadn't thought of that. I suppose that's possible.'

'On the evidence,' added Mod. 'Half the force were pissed out of their minds that night. One, who should have been on duty, was screwing a fortune teller, and another, who was also on duty, was committing rape and murder. Join London's police for a worthwhile career.'

Davies scowled at him. 'All right, all right. It's all "mights and maybes" though, isn't it.' He paused, then inquired. 'I don't suppose you've got your dole money yet, have you?'

'Social Security,' corrected Mod. 'No. I get paid tomorrow.'

'I thought so. I was toying with the idea of you buying me a drink.'

'I'll accompany you,' said Mod closing the books with finality. 'And, if you'll honour me with a loan, I'll buy the drinks, repaying the debt tomorrow.' He looked doubtfully at Davies's head. 'I can't see you getting a pint glass in that little window in the bandages,' he said.

'I'll have to drink shorts,' replied Davies. He waited while Mod replaced his books on the various shelves. 'Amazing, you know,' said Mod as they made for the door. 'The period from 3000 BC to 500 BC, two thousand five hundred years, in Britain was a time of almost uninterrupted peace and progress.'

'I'm pleased to hear it,' replied Davies soberly.

'Due to the fact that nobody really *wanted* anything,' said Mod. 'There were only a few tribes, and lots of land for their needs and plenty of room for invaders. It has also been said that the people turned from worshipping the Gods of War, which had always attracted the menfolk, to worshipping the Gods of Fertility and the like, which were kind of Women's Lib Gods.'

'I bet the police force was crooked,' suggested Davies. He tapped the Home Guard picture affectionately as they reached the foyer. Mod nodded at it sagely. 'What are you going to do next?'

'Well, one thing I want to do and that is tell Josie nearly everything.'

'Nearly? You won't tell her you've found the body?'

'No. I won't tell her that.'

They walked along the shut and shadowed street. It was eleven-thirty and urban cats were beginning to sound and wander. Once more everybody for miles about seemed to have gone home and locked their doors against the night. The crowds were in their beds. They had abandoned the town to the dark.

Josie's footfalls progressed deftly along the pavements while Davies's large feet made only a muffled scraping in the gutter. He chose to walk there so as to bring their heights somewhere into proximity although, even with the adjustment he still looked down at her.

His overcoat hung largely about him while she was small and neatly wrapped as a package. They walked without touching or speaking. He had not told her that he had found her sister's body.

Close to her house was one of the district's innumerable alleys, afterthoughts, shortcuts, planning compromises, sprouting through the lines of streets. As they went past she caught his large hand and encouraged him into its darkness. He stood there, awkward as ever, she with her back to somebody's fence, he facing her but only touching her by placing his hands lightly about her waist. She regarded him morosely in the gloom.

'Oh, Dangerous,' she said. 'You'll never make a teenager.'

'I can't remember being much of a teenager even when I was one,' he confessed wryly. 'And now I'm a bit far gone for necking against fences.'

'God,' she sighed. 'You stand there like a dummy from Burton's window. Have a go at kissing me. Go on.'

He eased forward from the waist and her face rose to kiss

him. They had taken some more of his bandages off that day so that his face was now exposed although he still looked oddly like a man peering through a window. With the kiss she pushed her slight body closer to him, unbuttoning the overcoat briskly as she did so. He folded it protectively about her. They had spent half an hour that evening going over his notes written on the paper appropriated from Minnie Banks, the school teacher.

'I'm glad you've told me everything,' she said. 'About Celia.' Then she repeated: 'That's if it is everything.'

'There are further inquiries,' he said looking down at the crown of her dark hair.

'Further inquiries,' she mocked gently. 'You can't help sounding like a copper, can you?' Then she said: 'You remember that day by the Welsh Harp you told me that Percival was your proper name. Well it's not, is it.'

'I lied,' he said. 'It's Peregrine.'

'Bugger off,' she sighed.

There was a long enclosed silence from within the coat. Then she said: 'Dangerous, I've got something to tell you.'

He laughed gently and patted her on top of her head. 'What is it?' he asked.

'I've found something out.'

'What?'

'My father *does* know where Ramscar is.'

He eased her away and looked down at the defined, pale face. 'Where is he? he asked.

'I said *he* knows, *I* don't,' she replied. 'I wasn't going to tell you. You've had enough beatings-up as it is. But I've begun thinking you ought to know.'

'What's he told you?'

'I didn't tell you before, but he had a heart attack yesterday. In the hospital. Brought on by being duffed up. It wasn't much as heart attacks go, but it's scared the living daylights out of him. He thinks he'll die if he has another one. I went to see him and tonight he was in a terrible state. He's got all confessional. He started doing the "my dearest daughter" act,' she laughed caustically. 'After all these bloody years.' She glanced up at his chin. He was still waiting. 'Ramscar's up to something very big, according to the old man. And very soon.'

'What sort of thing?'

'I don't know. Even the old man doesn't. But I reckon he's got a good idea where Ramscar is hanging out. That's why he feels safer in hospital.'

'He's probably right,' nodded Davies. He looked at her steadily. 'Will you find out for me?'

She did not reply at once, but remained hidden inside his coat. 'I'll think about it,' she told eventually. 'But I'm not making any promises.'

'If we know where he is we can wind up the whole business,' said Davies. 'Get him.'

'Will you put your hands inside my dress for a minute, Dangerous?' she asked. 'If I undo the buttons.'

Bemused at her habitual change of direction he did not say anything. But she undid the buttons on the front of her dress, carefully, and took his hands and pushed them inside against some material covering her small breasts. He could feel the brief point of each nipple. He bent forward and kissed her on the face. 'What's this thing you've got underneath?' he asked.

'A vest,' she responded simply. 'My mum makes me wear a vest this weather. Even now she's up at Luton I still wear it. A promise is a promise. She knitted it herself. Yards of it. It goes down for miles, Dangerous. Here, go on, give it a pull.'

Smiling, he did as she instructed. Using both hands he began to tug at the vest and it came up, and continued coming up, from somewhere in her nether regions. Josie giggled. 'I told you. There's yards of it. It's like a bale of bloody cloth.'

Eventually the garment was assembled above her waist, making her dress bulge spectacularly. She laughed quietly and gave a mischievous wriggle. It fell down, dropping beyond her skirt and hanging to her knees. Davies clasped her to him. 'Do you want to come in the house?' she asked. 'It's empty.'

'I thought you were staying with some other family,' he said anxiously. 'I hope you're not in the house by yourself.'

'I'm not,' she assured him. 'I'm living with the Fieldings two doors up. But I've still got our key.'

'It's time you got some sleep,' he said gently. He put his arms protectively about her. 'When it's all done,' he said. 'All finished. Then I'm going to take some leave.'

'And you'll take me too?'

'If you'll come. When I was a boy I was sent up to Stoke-on-Trent once. I've always thought of going back.'

'It sounds dreamy,' she said. 'I've still got a week of my holiday to come. Stoke-on-Trent!'

'You'd better go,' he said. They kissed seriously and he helped her to tuck the extraordinary vest away. Then they walked along the street to the house where she was staying. He said good-night and she went into the house. He had walked a few yards down the street when the door opened behind him and Josie came out again to the pavement. 'Dangerous,' she called. There was something different in her voice. 'The hospital phoned. He's had another heart attack. I've got to go.'

He waited until two o'clock in the painfully familiar surroundings of the hospital. It was cold and desolate in the waiting room. When she came out he saw that she had dried tears smudged about her eyes.

'He snuffed it,' she said. 'Six minutes past one.'

He had often wondered at the curiosity of people recording the exact weight of a baby at birth and the precise time of death. Why not the time of birth and the weight at death? 'I'm sorry, Josie,' he said, drawing her kindly to him.

'He thought I was Celia,' she shrugged.

He telephoned for a taxi and they sat in the waiting room until it arrived. They said very little either there or on the journey to the house of her friends. As she got out of the taxi and the front door of the house opened, she kissed him dumbly on the cheek. 'Ramscar's at a place called Bracken Farm,' she said. 'Uxbridge way.'

It was ten miles away, part of the dead land between the town and the eventual country, a place of pig farms, scrap yards, small untidy fields and struggling hedgerows. Davies collected the Lagonda and drove out there through the cold, early hours. Kitty moaned grotesquely for the first part of the journey, taking unhappily to being disturbed, but then settled to a bronchial sleep under the tarpaulin once more. Davies did not tell anyone he was going. It hardly occurred to him. He had his own score to settle.

He had telephoned the Uxbridge fire brigade to find out the farm's location. He did not want to ask the police. It was at the end of a rutted lane off the main Oxford road. He drove down it carefully, headlights out, threading the Lagonda between piles of rubbish, wrecked vehicles and other peripheral trash. There was a gipsy encampment one field away and his approach set some dogs baying. He cursed them. He could see lights ahead, a high illuminated window, which he thought might be a watching point. He pulled the car close into a farm gate and went studiously forward on foot.

Everything about him smelled damp. Mud eased from beneath his feet with stifled sighs. There were two big cars standing in the yard of the farm. The house looked substantial but unkempt even at night. Apart from the light in the high upper window there were two lit but red-curtained windows on the ground floor. He moved, large but silent, into the yard. He touched the bonnet of the nearest car. It was warm. So was the next one. He intended to try and get to the window, but he guessed there would be someone left outside to keep guard. He saw the man come around the corner of the house while he was shadowed by the cars. The man was lighting a cigarette and grumbling to himself. Davies got on his hands and knees and shuffled to the door of what looked to be an outside lavatory. It was a coalhouse. His eyes were accustomed now to the dark. There was a scattering of coal on the floor and a coal shovel by the wall.

Davies could hear the man moving about outside. Then he walked right past the open door of the outhouse. Davies picked up the shovel. It was the normal household implement, fashioned from one piece of metal, the handle formed by turning the metal into a short tube. Pointing the tube forward, Davies left his concealment. The man was standing only four yards away smoking and looking out to the anonymity of the ragged night. Davies approached and pushed the circular end of the shovel into the pit of the watcher's back.

The man went stiff, but he could feel the round impression well enough. 'Drop your shooter on the ground,' said Davies. 'Behind you.' With a shrug the man reached in his pocket and dropped his gun on Davies's toe. Davies picked it up.

'Right, we're going to walk towards the house.'

The man spoke. 'The whole lot's in there,' he said quietly as if trying to convey a favour. 'If there's any shooting, mate, I don't want to be in it. I don't reckon this fucking thing at all.'

'How many?' asked Davies.

'Seven,' said the man.

'I've got the place surrounded by hundreds,' Davies told him. 'Just walk. Now.'

They progressed gingerly along the narrow path of the farm's front garden, like partners on a high wire. Fifteen feet from the door was an empty dustbin. Davies noted it grimly. Then he whispered for his captive to stop. 'I'm going to make things difficult for you, son,' he said quietly. 'But, get this, if you try anything, or make a row, I'll shoot you. Got that?'

'Got it,' nodded the man. Davies bent and sweetly put the dustbin over the man's head and shoulders. The man shivered and staggered for a moment, but recovered and stood there like some strange midnight robot. Davies jogged him forward with the coal shovel. He had the gun but he used the shovel in case the man should know the gun was not loaded. They went to the door.

It was a big Georgian door and Davies saw with satisfaction that his dustbinned prisoner would be able to get in. There was a low brass doorknob. He turned it and the door swung in. He pushed the man forward into the room. 'My old man's a dustman,' he announced walking in behind him. 'Anyone move and they're a goner.'

A group of men were sitting around a table eating fish and chips. All the faces came up and around to him. He recognized Ramscar at once, 'I've come for you, Ramscar,' he said.

'Fuck it,' said Ramscar taking a chip from his mouth.

A small, tanned man, sitting at the near side of the table suddenly jumped up and, with a wild cry, ran towards Davies. Davies banged him on his approaching head with the coal shovel, but the diversion had been enough. In a moment they had rushed him. They came like a rugby scrum flying across the room. They hit him from all directions at once and he felt himself reeling. There were shots and he felt his legs burning. Then lights. But somehow more logical than the usual exploding lights in his head. Someone shouted: 'Piss off, there's coppers outside.'

Before he tumbled to what he now recognized as unconsciousness Davies looked up to see the face of a strange police inspector. 'Just right,' Davies managed to smile. 'Everything okay?'

'Great,' grunted the inspector. 'Except the bloke you crowned with the shovel is a bloody American ambassador.'

The desk sergeant was looking through the crime book for the local reporter when Davies propelled his wheeled chair through the police station door. The lady cleaner and Venus, who was just on her way to her evening patrol, had helped him up the outside steps.

'Interesting one here,' said the sergeant. 'Theft of rare minute palms from Kew Gardens. General to all stations, this...' He saw Davies and came round the counter to shake his hand. 'So glad you're all right, Dangerous. The old man's upstairs. I'll help you with the lift.'

The sergeant and the reporter got him into the lift. He knocked on Inspector Yardbird's door with his toe and after the customary pause Yardbird called him to go in.

His wheeled chair rolled through the office door. They had re-bandaged his head and set his right leg and left ankle in plaster. There was not much they could do about the bruising on his ribs except let it heal. The nurses had given him a joke season-ticket to the hospital.

Yardbird looked up from behind his desk. 'Ah, jolly good. I think we did jolly well, Davies,' he said.

Davies moved his head gingerly. 'Yes, sir, I think we did.'

'We ... ee ... ll, we got Ramscar, which was the whole

object of my plan from the very beginning, as you will appreciate, Davies. And that's a feather in the cap of the division. On the other hand to hit a United States diplomat on the head with a coal shovel was pretty unfortunate.'

'I'm sorry,' shrugged Davies. Every movement seemed to hurt. 'I didn't know who he was. I thought he was one of the gang. Nobody told me.'

'We *couldn't* tell every Tom, Dick and Harry, Davies,' yawned Yardbird. 'It would have been gossiped all around the place. We knew that Ramscar was lying low because he was involved in something big, much bigger than anything he had done before. We knew he had become involved with what we call "Overseas Interests" you understand.'

'Yes. I understand,' said Davies.

'And these Interests had decided to kidnap this American wallah on his way to the Airport. Which they did, of course, but fortunately we nailed them.'

'Oh yes, we nailed them,' replied Davies.

'Quite a feather in the cap of the division, as I mentioned.'

'Yes sir, you said.'

'Once I'd got you to actually concentrate on the proper job in hand, it worked like a charm, didn't it? We got Ramscar.' For the first time Yardbird got from behind his desk. He kicked the wheel of the invalid chair as though to make sure it was safe. 'Well,' he said. 'As I've said before this is all good experience for you.'

'Great experience,' agreed Davies.

'How long will it be?' He pushed his expression in the general direction of Davies's injuries. 'Couple of weeks?'

'Two months, they say,' said Davies. 'And a bit of convalescence just to get the feel of my legs again. I may go to Stoke-on-Trent.'

'You'll like that,' muttered Yardbird absently. 'In the meantime perhaps you'd like to give your thoughts to the business of who stole that brass bedstead from your lodgings. And the antique hall stand. That landlady of yours, what's her name, Mrs Brownjohn?'

'Mrs Fulljames,' said Davies.

'Yes, her. Stupid old cow. Button-holed me at the Chamber

of Commerce Dinner the other evening and demanded that something be done about it. It does look a bit bad, I suppose actually having a CID man in the house and having unsolved crime hanging about. Have you given it any consideration at all?'

'I've thought of very little else,' replied Davies. It did not appear to penetrate. Yardbird appeared submerged in worries.

'And there was another thing, while you're here. That idiotic dog of yours. It bit three policemen during the raid on the farm.'

Davies nodded. 'I know. It doesn't like coppers. It's had a go at me before now.'

'Well you must control it, you know. If not, have it put down. Might be the best way in the end. Get you into no end of bother.'

Davies said: 'Right, I'll see he behaves. And I'll think about the brass bedstead. Can I go now, sir? My arms get tired.'

'Yes, yes. Off you go. I'm busy as hell. And ... Davies...'

'Sir?'

'Keep out of aggravation, eh?'

As he went through the corridor Davies could clearly hear Yardbird laughing at his own joke.

Father Harvey trundled Davies in his wheeled chair alongside the canal. Davies was glad of the privacy because their progress through the High Street had been approaching the triumphal. People he did not recognize, but who clearly knew him intimately, approached to inquire about his injuries and to shake his hand. Mr Chrust appeared at the door of the newspaper office and had shown him a copy of the *Citizen* embellished by Davies's chair-borne photograph, while from the upper windows the sisters-in-law waved in bright sympathy. Madame Tarantella Phelps-Smith hooted greetings from her door and shouted clairvoyant encouragement: 'You'll be better soon. Your lucky colour is blue! Blue!' Even his wife Doris, shopping with Mrs Fulljames, had come out of the bakers and given him a jam doughnut. 'It's getting

220

like the Entry of the Queen of Sheba,' commented Father Harvey.

Josie joined them at the canal bridge and helped to get the wheeled chair down the inclined path to the canal bank. She walked with them hungrily nuzzling a lunchbag.

'I hear through my excellent intelligence services that a police award is to be made to you,' mentioned the priest. 'So your wounds will not have been entirely in vain.'

'Listen, Yardbird wouldn't recommend anyone for a sick pass let alone an award,' observed Davies. It was a nice day for that town at that time of year. Ducks followed the fitful sunshine on the straight water. Josie emptied the crumbs from her lunchbag into the canal. The ducks clamoured as though it were already spring.

'Somebody over the top of Yardbird has put you up,' said Father Harvey. 'I get to know these things. The confessional is not merely for the telling of sins, you know, Dangerous. It is useful for handy tit-bits of information.'

'How's the confessional box anyway?' inquired Davies over his shoulder.

'The new one is fine. Never heard better confessions. But the one I built myself was more frail than the parishioners, I'm afraid. Mrs Bryant, who becomes a trifle histrionic during the unburdening of her soul, put her elbow through one of the panels. So I rang the bishop and kicked up bloody hell and they've sent a new portable effort, in plastic you'll know, pending the arrival of a proper replacement. It was there, in that plastic shell, that I heard the whisper of your impending award.'

'Award?' Davies grinned. '*I'm* the mug who did it all wrong. If Josie hadn't telephoned the police to say I was on my way to Bracken Farm I'd still be there now. Buried under the cowshed.'

His voice slowed as they approached the footbridge, the three of them, the priest, the policeman and the poppet, and fifteen yards away, beyond the allotment hedge, Celia Norris was buried. He glanced at Josie. She was devouring a yoghurt from a small tub. 'I thought you'd have the sense to go with other coppers,' she said. A strawberry blob squatted on her chin, like Celia again. She wiped it away. 'I thought even *you* would have the bleeding gumption to do that, Dangerous. But then, when I got in the house, I thought probably you *wouldn't* have the bleeding gumption. So I rang nine-nine-nine.'

Although they talked, Davies's awareness of their location and his sadness because of it, seeped to the others. They turned at the bridge and, now silent, went back the way they came. The ducks, spotting their return, queued up hopefully. A water rat dropped without fuss into the brown depths. 'Dangerous,' said Josie suddenly. 'How old is Doris?'

'Doris? God knows. Thirty or thereabouts.'

'And Mod?'

'Mod's in his forties. I think.'

'You think. Do you know the age of *anyone* in that house of yours?'

'No ... no, I don't think I actually do.'

'Father Harvey,' she pursued. 'How old do you think I am?'

'Ah, it's a game,' decided the priest. 'Well, let me see. Oh, you're a young girl. What, nineteen, twenty or so.'

'It's funny,' she said thoughtfully. 'When my father died the other week, I didn't know how old he was. And I'm not sure about my mother. I'm seventeen.'

Davies was eyeing her. 'What are you getting at, Josie?'

She laughed. 'Blimey, you look like Chief Ironside in that chair, Dangerous. On the television.'

He did not pursue it then. The priest got the invalid chair up to the road and then left them. Josie was to push it along the street to the library for the afternoon and Mod was to propel it to The Babe in Arms at the opening time and then to 'Bali Hi', Furtman Gardens. The sunshine persisted uncannily. Around the power station cooling towers played small cherubs of steam. 'What was all that about people's ages?' he asked.

Josie waved to a friend in the street. Then she began speaking as she pushed. 'It was just you said a funny thing, Dangerous. Before all the farm business, when you told me all about Celia. Or you *reckoned* you'd told me all. You

222

remember when we went all through your notes? All on that school notepaper.'

'Yes, of course. What did I say?'

'About that old Mrs Whethers. You'd written down everything you remember her saying, right?'

'Right.'

'The old man. Mr Harkness. How old did she say he was when it all happened with Celia?'

'Seventy-six,' he said. 'And that was twenty-five years ago.'

'But according to her, she hardly *knew* him. She'd just heard that he'd seen something that night and she knew he'd been ill. *But to know that he was seventy-six, twenty-five years ago is very odd*. Not seventy-five, nor anything else. Exactly *seventy-six*.' She had halted the chair in the middle of the shopping street now and Davies was painfully half-turned around to her. She went around to the front of the chair and knelt, pretending to rearrange the rug around his legs.

'What did she say, exactly, this Mrs Whethers?' asked Josie. 'Have you got those notes?'

Davies hurriedly thrust his hand into the deep inside pocket of the overcoat. 'My favourite reading,' he said. He began to turn over the crammed, scrawled pages of school paper. 'Here, it's here,' he said. 'Mrs Whethers. Ah, yes. She asked me how long ago the Celia business was and I said twenty-five years and she said . . .'

'Mr Harkness was seventy-six,' Josie concluded. 'She knew his *exact* age, but she didn't know how long ago the murder was. What a funny thing.'

'She calculated it by deducting the twenty-five years. She was in no doubt, either. Seventy-six.'

'All I'm saying,' said Josie. She had gone behind and began to push the chair again. 'Is that it's strange she knew his right age, but she didn't know him well. We've just tested you and Father Harvey out. People hardly ever know other people's ages. Sometimes not even their own family and friends.'

'So,' he said. 'There got to be something special about Mr Harkness, so that she is quite sure of his age.'

She nodded. 'You've tumbled. I reckon he's still alive, Dangerous. And he's a hundred and one.'

nineteen

Mod pushed him all the way from the library to the Kensal Green Old Folks' Club. It was the hardest afternoon's work he had done for twenty years.

The ancients were doing a *paso doble*, stamping worn feet and cracking rheumy hands over their heads, led by the fat and fiery dancing teacher. Mod was astounded at the activity. 'I wondered why none of them ever gets to the library,' he said.

They all stopped sympathetically when they saw him in the chair. 'Oh dear,' said the dance teacher. 'Whatever have you been up to?'

'Practising,' said Davies.

'I knew you'd do yourself an injury,' she replied confidently. 'Altogether too unsupple. No rhythm.' She returned to the elderly class. 'Right, old people,' she called. 'Finish for today. Let's all have one good clap and leave it there.'

They banged their hands together and those that had not already stiffened up during the pause stamped their feet a few token times, then spread out about the hall for teatime. Mrs Whethers, clucking sympathy, brought a free cup of tea for Davies but Mod had to pay for his own. They sat down in a triangle.

'Mrs Whethers,' said Davies. 'I'm sorry to bother you again but I wanted to ask you one more thing.'

'Fire away,' she said jovially. 'I didn't do it.'

'Indeed not. But, Mrs Whethers, is there any chance that Mr Harkness is still alive?'

She looked at him in astonishment. '*Of course* he's still alive!' she exclaimed. 'I took it for granted you knew that. He's a hundred and one. It was in the local paper back in the summer. He lives in Bristol with his daughter or somebody but she sent the bit of news to the *Citizen*.'

'He was seventy-six twenty-five years ago,' nodded Davies. 'That's how you knew his exact age. Because of his being a hundred and one.'

She smiled in an old way. 'I always was good at sums,' she said.

'And I thought we were talking about somebody who was dead,' he sighed. 'I must go and see him.'

'You'd better get those wheels turning, then,' she laughed. 'At a hundred and one you don't know where you'll be from one day to another. How about buying a ticket for the raffle?'

St Fridewide's Church had a van, fitted with seats for use on parish-outings and it was in this, with Father Harvey driving, that Davies journeyed to see Mr Harkness at Bristol. Fortunately the centenarian lived in a ground-floor flat and with Mod, who had never been to Bristol but had eruditely lectured on the place throughout the journey, pushing, the invalid chair was manoeuvred through the small entrance hall and into the old man's sitting room.

'He's still getting dressed,' his elderly daughter said. 'He takes his time at his age, you understand, but he won't let me help him. He says I'm too old to dress myself.' She was a grey tub of a lady. Davies wondered what her father would look like.

It was a pleasing apartment, its expansive front window framing the choppy water of the Bristol docks, with the enclosing land easing itself up from the shore on all sides. They could see the hull of Brunel's fine old ship The *Great Britain* lying in her special berth.

'That ship and my father are both over a century old,' she said. 'They sort of keep each other company.'

She asked them if they would like coffee. Father Harvey had parked the van and gone to visit a retired priest, a drinking companion of former days.

'Mr Harkness will be very glad to see you,' smiled his daughter. 'He was very excited when I told him you had telephoned. He loves to talk over old times. I told him you were a policeman and he seemed more taken with the idea than ever. This is quite a big day for him. He'll probably wear his red velvet jacket.' She went and listened at the door and then returned. 'Normally that's for birthdays only, his velvet jacket, although I don't suppose, at a hundred and one, he can hope to get a great deal more wear out of it now.' They were aware of a movement in the passage outside the room. 'Ah, I think he's arrived,' said the lady. She turned warningly. 'One thing I must tell you. Mr Harkness is deaf.'

Through the door shuffled the centenarian, almost pixie-like in his smallness, a jovial pointed face, bright china eyes, and pink-cheeked. A little dewdrop dangled like a decoration from the tip of his nose. He wiped it away with the sleeve of his red velvet jacket. 'Hello, hello,' he greeted them. 'I'm Charlie Harkness. I'm a hundred and one years old.'

His very presence made them glad. Davies smiled, so did Mod. The daughter looked pleased.

'Sit down, sit down,' called the old man blithely. 'I'm a bit on the short side. They won't have to dig out much earth for me.' He cackled at his joke. They sat down grinning. He said he would like his morning milk with a few drops in it.

'I'm supposed to be deaf,' he confided when the lady had gone from the room. 'But I'm not as deaf as I make out. I only pretend to her because otherwise she rambles on all day, and I don't want to listen. You know how women get when they're knocking on in years. But if you get close enough to my left ear I'll be able to hear you fair enough. And I've got all my nuts and bolts too. So I'll know what you're talking about.' Davies had a mental picture of him in the witness box.

Mod was looking at one of a series of sere military pictures on the wall. 'You fought in Zululand, then, Mr Harkness?' he remarked.

'Zululand? Oh, yes I was there. Fighting. Not that it did much good. They're all in Bristol now, you know. Last summer I went out for a bit of a stroll and there's blackies all over the place! I thought to myself at the time, last time I saw a Fuzzy-wuzzy as close as that he was stuck on the end of my lance.'

His daughter brought in a tray with the cups of coffee and the beaker of milk. Mr Harkness sniffed the milk to make sure she'd splashed the scotch in it. 'I heard what you said,' she reproved. 'About blackies. You can be sent to prison for saying things like that these days. And Mr Davies is a policeman.'

'Blow it,' returned the old man. 'There's not a prison could hold me.' He stopped and considered Davies. 'Oh yes, you're from the force. I'd forgot that. What are you after, young man?'

Davies felt relieved that he had been saved the approach. 'It's something that happened a few years ago,' he said moving close to the ancient ear. 'And I wondered if you would remember something about it. Back in London. Do you remember a girl called Celia Norris...?'

The name did not register. Davies could see that. 'Oh I've known a few girls in my time...' began the old man with customary joviality.

'She disappeared,' continued Davies. 'In fact it seems she was murdered.' He saw the alarm jump into the woman's face and she began to move forward protectively. But Mr Harkness pushed her away excitedly. 'Ah that. Oh, I remember that, all right. The night I fell in the canal.'

'What can you remember about it?' called Davies, relief warming him. 'Tell us everything you can remember.'

'Oh, I remember, I remember,' said Mr Harkness making a little song of it. 'I used to drink a little drop in those days. Well, I was a youngster then, in my seventies, I suppose. But that night just about put the end to my drinking, my big drinking anyway. Because I fell in the bleeding canal and I went home in wet things and I got bronchitis and pneumonia and all the rest of it. They thought I was going to collect my cards, I can tell you.'

'That was when I took him firmly in hand,' interrupted his daughter. 'I nursed him better and I kept him away from the bottle. My husband had just passed away and Mr Harkness was all I had. I've kept him well. Well enough to see a hundred and one.'

'For Christ's sake, don't go on so, Dulcie,' said Mr Harkness, irritated. 'They've come to hear *me* not you. Why don't you take the cups out?'

'No,' she replied firmly. 'I'd like to hear what this is about. It all sounds a bit unpleasant to me.'

Davies nodded to her. She sat down and folded her hands in her rounded lap. Mr Harkness ignored her. 'Yes, I remember it.'

'Mr Harkness,' said Davies creeping close to the fragile ear. 'What exactly did you *see* that night? Did you see a girl?'

'I'd been to the Labour Club,' recalled the old man, determined to tell it his way. He closed his eyes reflectively. 'We used to have some very good times there at the Labour Club. You could get pissed there for a couple of bob in those days. Easy.' Dulcie drew in a deep breath but Davies's hand asked that she should not interrupt. The breath softened to a sigh.

'And that night I was drunk as a monkey. Hot summer that was and I'd taken on a load of ale, I can tell you. That's why I tumbled in the canal. Blind drunk. Blotto. I used to go home along the canal bank, like it was a short cut for me, and I was leaning over, I remember, trying to see myself in the water. Just where that lamp is on the bridge. Or was, I don't know whether it's there now.' He stopped. He seemed breathless. Davies turned to his daughter. 'Is he all right?' he whispered. 'I don't want to distress him.'

'Are you still listening?' demanded the old man. 'I'm just getting to the interesting part.'

'Still listening,' nodded Davies.

'Well listen, then,' said Mr Harkness. 'Next time you come I might be dead and gone so I won't be able to tell you a sausage, will I?'

'Please go on.'

'Where was I? In the water? No, looking down at it. Anyway in a trice I was *in* the bloody water. I just fell in. That sobered me up a bit. I can still feel the cold now. It stinks too, that canal. Everybody's shit goes in there. Dead cats and everything.'

Davies nodded agreement.

'And it was while I was in the water, hanging on to the bank actually, that I saw them.'

'Them? Who?'

'The policeman and the girl,' said Mr Harkness patiently. 'On the bank. I was in the dark, hanging on to the bank and they was on the path at the side. At first I thought I was in luck there being a copper handy. I mean, generally you can never find one when you want one. But there he was and there was me in the canal. But I was just about to holler and I saw he was kissing the girl. I thought, oi oi! There's little of what you fancy going on here. So I stayed with my head out of the water and they were on the bank. At first I thought they was cuddling, but I couldn't be sure about that. Because he sort of pulled her away towards the alley that goes up to the pawnshop.'

'Towards where the old Home Guard blockhouse used to be?'

'That's it. That's just it. I forgot that was there. I think they'd knocked it down by then, but it used to be just there.'

'And you're sure you saw all that?'

'Sure? Of course I'm sure. I wouldn't be telling you would I? I thought somebody would come around to see me from the police station because I told Dulcie here what I'd seen. After all the fuss about the girl, I mean.'

'I thought he was rambling,' said his daughter. 'He was ever so ill. Bronchial pneumonia. He wasn't far from dead. It was a year before he was really right. That's when we moved out here to Bristol. I'm glad we did. Bristol air's kept him alive.'

'How dark was it?' asked Davies. Mod was sitting staring at the photographs of the Zulu wars. He got up to inspect one closely as though he did not want to listen to what was not his business.

'Not very dark,' said Mr Harkness thoughtfully. 'Except under the bleeding water. That was smelly and dark. But it was summer, like I said, and it was quite light really. And there was the light from that lamp on the bridge.'

'So you're sure in your own mind,' ventured Davies, 'that it was a policeman and a girl. Not just a courting couple?'

Mr Harkness smiled felicitously. 'Oh, it was a copper all right. I'd been in court for drunk and incapable so many times that I knew a copper when I saw one. I even saw *who* it was.'

He paused. Davies, tight as a drum inside, stared unbelievingly. Mod was standing and staring too. With my luck, thought Davies in deadpan panic, Mr Harkness will now drop dead.

'Well,' said Mr Harkness, more alive than any of them. 'Do you want me to say who it was?'

'Er ... yes, please,' nodded Davies with stiff calmness. 'That would be most helpful.'

'Well I knew him because he'd run me in so many times,' said the old man. 'Some of the young coppers were all right, but he was a miserable bugger. Yardbird, his name was. Police Constable Yardbird.'

All the way home in the back of the church conveyance Mod had to keep hold of the wheeled chair to prevent it careering carelessly about when Father Harvey took a bend, accelerated or applied the brakes, all three of which he was inclined to do with some violence and a degree of after-thought. On the outward journey to Bristol an abrupt halt at some traffic lights had resulted in Davies being propelled fiercely from one end of the vehicle to the other. After that Mod held tight to the chair.

'Yardbird,' Davies kept saying. 'Yardbird. Christ, whatever are we going to do now? He might just as well have said it was the Prime Minister or the Archbishop of Canterbury.'

'Your duty is clear,' Mod said ponderously. 'You must walk into his office and formally charge him with murder.'

Davies grimaced at him. 'Apart from not being able to stand up, let alone walk, at the moment, I doubt if I'd ever be able to say the words. Not to *him*.' He tried in a quivering voice: 'Inspector Yardbird, I charge you that on the night of July 23rd, 1951, at Canal Towpath, London NW10 you did murder Celia Norris...' He shook his head miserably. 'He'd have *me* in the bloody cells before I could finish it off.' Mod rocked the invalid chair minutely to and fro like a nurse with a worrying child. 'Mr Harkness would make a grand witness,' he said without conviction.

'If he lives that long,' grumbled Davies. '*If* he can hear, *if* they've got an oxygen machine handy. Christ, Mod, he's a hundred and one and the betting is about the same odds. A couple of nifty adjournments by the defence, a sharp draught coming through the court-room door, and our witness is no witness because he's dead.'

Mod nodded his sympathy. He stood and opened the small aperture to the driver's cabin. Father Harvey was singing a Gregorian Chant, a difficult task while driving at speed along the motorway. Mod closed the panel without saying anything.

'I've got a body, exhibits including the girl's bicycle, a witness and an accused, and I still don't know why the hell I became a detective in the first place,' said Davies miserably.

'It's something I've often asked myself,' agreed Mod uncharitably. 'Can I make a suggestion?'

'You want me to forget the whole thing?'

'No indeed not. Not now. You're nearly there, boy. But think, is there anybody, anybody you've already talked to or anybody you think you should have talked to, who might just give it that extra couple of yards it needs? Anybody?'

Davies remained gloomy. The rest of the journey was made in general silence with Father Harvey's muted praises, punctuated by curses directed at other drivers, filtering through to them. Mod took out an antique copy of *Clarendon's Rebellion*, Volume Three and read it assiduously. Davies thought but nothing happened.

When they reached 'Bali Hi', Furtman Gardens, Mod wheeled Davies into the downstairs front room which Mrs Fulljames, with some grudging generosity, had put at his disposal for the time of his incapability, and at only a small extra cost. On the mantelshelf was a letter. It was from Frederick Fennell in the St Austin's Mental Hospital, Bedford. It said simply: 'Come and see me again for interesting news.' Beneath his signature was the drawing of a girl's bicycle.

Fortunately it was the off-season for outings from St Fridewide's and Father Harvey was able to bring the church vehicle around the following day so that Davies could be transported to see Fred Fennell. 'I'll see you get repaid one day,' Davies promised the priest. 'If all this becomes official police business.'

Father Harvey, who had shown remarkable incuriosity for a priest, nodded generously as he and Mod guided the invalid chair into the open rear of the vehicle. 'I'd quite like to have one of those blue flashing lights on the roof,' grunted the priest as he heaved the heavy load up an improvised ramp. 'And maybe a police siren. Oh yes, I'd certainly like that.'

As they drove towards Bedford, Mod again rocked the chair moodily. 'What d'you hope to get from this?' he sighed. 'Another witness? Your case gets better and better, Dangerous. One witness over a hundred and likely to pop off during his evidence, and another who's convinced he's Peter the Great.'

'It's not much of a line-up,' acknowledged Davies. 'But there's got to be something. Something somewhere.'

Father Harvey helped them to disembark then obligingly went off to see the hospital chaplain whom he knew from an occasion when they had taken part in a religious brains trust in Wandsworth Prison. There was no question of the wheeled chair going through the main door, so Mod, on Davies's guidance, took it through the rear garden gates. The solitary lady was still prodding at her private weeds with a table fork. Davies had warned Mod of what might occur so they were not surprised to be marched to the Superintendent's office at gunpoint. Davies raised both hands, but Mod only one since the captor acknowledged that he needed the other to push the chair. Davies gave her a disarming smile as she delivered them to the main office and the Superintendent took them to see Frederick Fennell sitting calmly in the room where Davies had first met him.

'Oh God help us, you're in a state,' said Fennell when he saw Davies. 'I was told you'd been in a dispute.'

'Described to a nicety,' acknowledged Davies. 'This is Modest Lewis, my assistant on this case. How did you hear about me?'

'Tarantella, Madame Phelps-Smith, came to see me,' said Fennell. He talked quietly and rationally. His face was no longer haunted. He smiled at the memory of her visit. 'She said that she had shown you the bicycle. So I thought I ought to tell you the rest.'

Davies fidgeted forward in his chair. 'Yes, Fred,' he said steadily. 'That would be very useful.'

'My wife's been to see me too,' continued Fennell. 'She came because you went back to her and asked her. I'm very grateful to you. That's why I want to tell you.' He paused and smiled, almost secretly. 'Funny thing, I've been stuck in thus nuthouse all this time and nobody's bothered and all at once they both came to see me.' He sighed. 'I've had to tell Tarantella that it's all over between us, of course. I think I'll be on my way out of here before too long and then my good wife and I will start somewhere again. She brought me some nice cold beef sandwiches last time.'

'In that case you're definitely back in favour,' said Davies firmly. 'What else did you want to tell us?'

'Oh yes. You don't want to listen to all my personal gossip. When you came here last I wasn't sure what you were after. You didn't tell me in so many words. But Tarantella filled it all in. Anyway, if it's any use to you, I've got something. By the way, did you like Edwina's little place in the country?'

Davies remembered the swamped caravan. 'Oh yes,' he murmured. 'Very rural.'

'I want to sell it. Get right away from here. Down to Cornwall, somewhere fresh.' He caught Davies's glance. 'Yes, well that's me, again, isn't it. Sorry, but so many things have happened. I feel like I'm alive again.'

'You're looking a great deal better,' said Davies truthfully.

'And thanks to you. It was like the sun coming up ... Anyway, listen. I've got something for you. Edwina brought it in to me. I told her where to find it in my old police relics. Here – it's for you, Mr Davies.'

He held out a registered envelope. Puzzled, Davies took it. Mod was watching over his shoulder. 'Registered,' said Fennell. 'See, it's registered London, NW10, 20th August 1951. And it's never been opened.'

'What's in it?' asked Davies.

'A statement by PC Dudley,' said Fennell undramatically and simply. 'He was a careful bloke, Dudley, and he wanted to be sure to cover himself. He wrote this when they started treating the Norris girl business as murder. He wrote it all down and then sent it to himself by registered post. If it remained unopened that would be proof that it was written at the time the registered post label was dated. Got me?'

'Yes. But we can't know what's in it without opening it

ourselves. And that would destroy its value as evidence.'

'Right. But he made a copy. I've got that too. It was sealed up with sealing wax and I've opened it. They came from Australia, after Dudley died in that fire. A solicitor in Melbourne sent them to me. He said Dudley had lodged them with him with instructions that they were to be forwarded to me in the event of his death. He was in all sorts of trouble, you know. Maybe he planned to commit suicide. But anyway that fire settled it for him. And these arrived in the post.'

Fennell smiled wryly. 'It was about the time when I went off my head.' He glanced in a suddenly embarrassed manner as if he thought that Mod might not realize why he was in the building. 'The envelope got stuck away with my other things and, to tell the truth I forgot all about them. I had enough trouble remembering who I was!' He laughed. 'You won't believe this but I actually thought I was Peter the Great. And he's been dead years!'

Davies glanced at him with alarm. But it was a joke. Fennell grinned knowingly at that. 'Here's the second envelope.' He handed a foolscap envelope blotched with sealing wax to them. Davies took it. He was surprised to find himself so calm.

'It's about that night,' said Fennell thoughtfully. 'The night the girl disappeared. We'd been to the party for Davie Morris who was leaving the force and had had quite a few drinks, even though we were on duty. You could get away with, well, sort of unofficial things. Anyway we, that's Dudley and myself, we were supposed to be on duty in the little van. I sneaked in to see Tarantella and when I went out again I walked up the street towards the cemetery because that's where I thought Dudley would be waiting. We used to meet up there. One of us would park the van by the cemetery gates and let the other go off for an hour. On this night the van wasn't there, but there was this bike lying by the wall. I'd had it in the back of my mind for a long time to kind of have a bit of evidence standing by, you know, to produce if anybody wanted to know what I was doing in Tarantella's place. And my wife was getting suspicious. I would say that Tarantella

234

had found it and I'd gone there in response to her call. The bike was some *solid* evidence, if you know what I mean. It all seems so bloody paltry now ... and so far away.'

'What happened to Dudley that night, do you think?' Davies did not want him to slip away now.

'Don't worry,' nodded Fennell. 'I'm coming to that. I suppose we were just young coppers and up to all sorts of roguery. And we were allowed to get away with it. Anyway, this bike. I took it into Tarantella's place and then I went back to find Dudley in the van. It was parked in the main road by the alley leading to the canal. By the pawnbroker's. Dudley was in the front but was still feeling terrible. He never could take his drink. In fact, you'll see in the statement, he'd only just got there. He felt so bad that he'd been lying down in his girlfriend's flat. There's more about that in the statement. Anyway I told him to clear off early and I did the rest of the stint myself. I signed in for him when I got back to the station. There was never any difficulty about that either. It was easy.'

'So Dudley was in the car when you got there?' said Davies. In imagination he could see Mr Harkness cheerfully spilling false evidence in every sentence. He sighed wearily.

'Yes, he was sat there. I remember how bad he looked. Silly bugger had been drinking rum. But ... but something else had happened. Something ... he's put in the statement. You've got to read that for yourself. Even though we used to share that duty nearly all the time, and we'd fixed it to fiddle time off, we were never very pally. We never really trusted each other.'

'But it was to *you* that he arranged to have these envelopes sent.'

'Because I was *there* that night. That's the reason. In a way I was *in it* with him. Whatever it was. Read it. Go on, read it.'

Fennell leaned forward, eagerness overcoming his carefully arranged calm. He watched Davies open the thin envelope. Davies read aloud.

'At the top it says: "This is a true copy of my statement of 20th August 1951, sealed in a registered envelope also in possession of Maxley Davidson of Flinders Street, Melbourne. The statement is as follows:

' "On the night of July 23rd 1951, I was on duty with PC Frederick Fennell, patrolling the area of the High Street, London NW10. There was a police social function at the nearby 'Sturgeon Rooms', a farewell party for a colleague, David Morris, who was leaving the force. During the course of our patrol in the police van PC Fennell and I called into this function and had some drinks. I drank rum which always has a bad effect on me and I felt ill. PC Fennell left before me and, as he often did, went to visit a woman friend. We arranged to meet at the gates of the cemetery an hour later. Sometimes one of us would take unofficial time off and sometimes the other would do the same. The one who remained with the van would be at the cemetery entrance at a prearranged time. We had done this for more than a year and nothing had gone wrong with the arrangement.

' "But on this night, I felt so bad after drinking the rum that I did not think I could drive the van to the rendezvous. It was then that PC Vernon Yardbird offered to take over the duty for me. He had been drinking with the rest but he seemed to be all right. I let him take over and I went to the flat of a friend in the district and had a cup of coffee and a lie down. After about an hour I felt better and I walked to the cemetery gates intending to meet PC Yardbird with the van. It was not there and I walked along the High Street until I finally spotted it near the pawnbroker's shop. There was no one in it. I could see someone moving down the alleyway leading to the canal. Someone was in the verge by the allotments.

' "I called and eventually PC Yardbird came up the alley. He looked very strange, white-faced, sweating and there was blood on his cheek as though he had been scratched, and he told me he was going home because he thought he had drunk too much. I thanked him for doing me the favour and I got into the driving seat of the van. On the floor by the passenger seat I found a lipstick. I put this in my pocket but later I threw it away in case my wife found it. It is not until now – a month later – when the case of Celia Norris's disappearance has come into prominence, that I have begun to think that the lipstick and the state PC Yardbird was in that night might have had any bearing on the case. The lipstick was a type sold in Woolworth's and was of the same type that Celia Norris was said to have had. This statement is true." '

Davies looked up at the others. 'He's signed it. James Henry Dudley, PC. August, 1951.' He held the registered envelope in his hands, as though weighing it. 'And that is a duplicate of the statement contained in this package.' His natural pessimism asserted itself. 'I hope.'

twenty

It was difficult to hold a cosy gathering at the police station. Nevertheless the cleaning lady had dusted the charge room for once and had put a bunch of dried flowers on the table which, remembering Celia's flowers, Davies thought was accidentally appropriate.

Detective Sergeant Green of the Special Branch helped Mod to get Davies's wheeled chair up the front steps to the station. He had come out purposely and leaned close to Davies's ear when they had reached the top step. 'What have you been doing to Yardbird?' he inquired quietly. 'He's bloody livid. He's supposed to make this presentation to you this morning but something's happened. I think he'd rather strangle you.'

'Oh dear,' said Davies mildly. 'I think I must have embarrassed him.'

'Christ, you've done more than embarrassed him. Apparently went berserk in his office half an hour ago and he said he wasn't going to make the presentation. But my boss, Bob Carter, has insisted that he does it. And Yardbird won't say why he's blowing his top.'

'I see,' said Davies. 'I think I know why he's so upset, Mr Green.'

'What is it?'

'I'll tell you soon. Would you do me a favour?'

'What?'

'After our little ceremony is over – as soon as I give you the eye – would you take your boss, Detective Superintendent Carter, into the CID room. I'll come in very shortly after with Inspector Yardbird. I have something I would like to say to him in your presence.'

Green nodded silently. He was a man well accustomed to the odd twists of life. He let Mod push the wheeled chair towards the charge room when the duty sergeant, the shiny Ben, appeared like a substantial shadow and pulled him aside.

'Very quickly,' whispered Ben. 'I don't know what you've been up to, Dangerous, but the old man is fucking furious. It happened first thing this morning, as soon as Yardbird came in. I gather there's been a complaint against you from somebody called Boot. Says you've been terrorizing him, beating him up, he says. Anyway he's been telling tales on you. Then old Yardbird comes down to the CID room and gets the key to your locker, which he empties all over the floor. And he went out frothing at the bloody mouth with a photograph of some young girl. I didn't see this, but PC Westerman was in there with a nosebleed. He said it was a photo of a girl.' Ben looked at Davies curiously. 'You haven't been dabbling in indecent pictures, have you, Dangerous?'

Davies smiled. 'Sort of,' he said.

Ben stared at him but said nothing more. He helped Mod to wheel the chair into the charge room which was full of people drinking Cyprus sherry. As he came in they all clapped and he gave a short, embarrassed wave. Then through the door came Detective Superintendent Carter and Detective Sergeant Green of the Special Branch and, stiff-faced, Inspector Yardbird.

Davies sat in his chair, feeling its wheels vibrating from his own trembling. Mod stood one side of him and Josie on the other. To his amazement Doris and Mrs Fulljames then arrived both extravagantly kissing him before retiring to a short distance, looking smug and apparently not noticing Josie or her proximity to Davies.

He knew that Mrs Fulljames was pleased because the rag-

and-bone man had that day restored the brass bedstead to 'Bali Hi', Furtman Gardens. Davies had seen the piece in the yard when he had gone to give the horse a cabbage for saving his life. He purchased it, at a special police discount, the man alleging that he bought it from an honest-looking Persian who was in a hurry.

It was Detective Superintendent Carter who made the speech. Inspector Yardbird stood behind like a wax figure.

'This is in the nature of a very private function,' Carter said. 'The implications in the matter which was concluded at Bracken Farm, Uxbridge, are still going on. Mr Ramscar and others are still to go for trial, as you know. But I felt, and I know others did, that in some personal and private way we should make some presentation to Detective Constable Davies, known to you all as Dangerous Davies. Official recognition of his performance may well follow. That's not for me to say. But this is our own private show. As we can all see he has been severely injured in this affair, although I am glad to hear that he will soon be walking again. I hope that this small presentation from his colleagues will make up for some of it. I will ask his own station inspector, Inspector Yardbird, who himself has known the unique difficulties of a policeman's life in this particular district, for a good many years, to make the presentation.'

Yardbird, staring at Davies, stepped forward. Davies wheeled the chair across the floor. His hands trembled on the rim of the wheels. The Inspector, shaking more than Davies, presented a silver marmalade pot, plate and spoon. He said no word. Davies thanked them all from his wheeled chair, shook hands with Carter and then held his hand out to Yardbird. Yardbird pushed out a freezing hand. Davies held it strongly.

All around there was more applause and the Cyprus sherry began to flow. Davies was in his chair next to the stiff legs of Yardbird. As Yardbird was about to move away, Davies reached up and tentatively tugged the edge of his tunic. Yardbird looked down into a big stony smile.

'Sir,' Davies said diffidently. 'Do you think I might have a few words with you? In private?'

Leslie Thomas
The Virgin Soldiers 70p

The virgin soldiers did not ask to be conscripted, they did not ask to
fight. On the brink of war they all wanted to make one frantic
attempt at living before dying ...

Onward Virgin Soldiers 75p

Bursting with life and bawdy humour, National Serviceman Brigg is
now a regular army sergeant defending the Empire in the beds and
bars of Hong Kong.

Stand up Virgin Soldiers 75p

On the eve of their return to Blighty, Brigg and the other boozy,
browned-off reluctant heroes of National Service, are sentenced
to a further six months in Panglin Barracks, Singapore ...

Tropic of Ruislip 90p

'A romp among the adulteries, daydreams and nasty woodsheds of
an executive housing estate ... there are Peeping Toms, clandestine
couplings, miscegenation on the wrong side of the tracks, the
spilling of gin and home truths on the G/Plan furniture and the
steady susurrus of doffed knickers' THE GUARDIAN

You can buy these and other Pan books from booksellers and
newsagents; or direct from the following address:
Pan Books, Sales Office, Cavaye Place, London SW10 9PG
Send purchase price plus 20p for the first book and 10p for
each additional book, to allow for postage and packing
Prices quoted are applicable in the UK

While every effort is made to keep prices low, it is sometimes
necessary to increase prices at short notice. Pan Books reserve
the right to show on covers and charge new retail prices which
may differ from those advertised in the text or elsewhere